THE
INFINITE

THE
INFINITE

Lori M. Lee

SKYSCAPE

SKYSCAPE

Published by Skyscape, New York
www.apub.com

Amazon, the Amazon logo, and Skyscape are trademarks
of Amazon.com, Inc., or its affiliates.

Hardcover ISBN-13: 9781477828267
Hardcover ISBN-10: 1477828265
Paperback ISBN-13: 9781477828250
Paperback ISBN-10: 1477828257

Library of Congress Control Number: 2014918596

Book design by Tony Sahara
Map by Megan McNinch

Printed in the United States of America

For Cha

THE
INFINITE

CHAPTER 1

I LIVED IN THE HOME OF THE MAN I'D KILLED. THE THOUGHT
didn't occur to me until two months after his death, when the
nightmares began. Maybe because the palace had been an opu-
lent and spacious distraction, its white halls and crimson banners a convincing veneer. Maybe because Kahl Ninu hadn't been
a man at all.

Or maybe because a part of me, a part I didn't want to
acknowledge, was just as cold as the Infinite.

The idea worried me sometimes, but the nightmares were
quick to chase away the notion. Besides, if it was true, seeing
Avan every day would hurt less.

The pain never kept me away, though.

"Where are you going today?"

The mirror on the wall showed my brother, Reev, standing behind me, his arms crossed as he tried and failed to keep from scowling. To anyone else, he would have looked adequately imposing, but I only smiled. We weren't in the Labyrinth anymore, and his ongoing struggle to accept that I no longer needed his restrictions amused me.

Instead of answering, I picked up the comb on my dressing table. I ran the fine metal teeth through my hair, taking my time to untangle the knots in the long black strands. The comb had been a gift from Avan. Its curved spine fit comfortably into the groove of my palm, and it shone a lustrous blue. Using it always made me think about how little the old Avan would have valued a pretty comb.

This was all so wrong. In the last few months, I had grown used to living in the palace, but it was that comfort that made me uneasy.

The room I'd been given—I had begun to think of it as *my* room—was twice the size of the freight container I'd shared with Reev in the Labyrinth, not even counting the attached washroom. Colorful, tightly woven tapestries hung from white stone walls. A fire roared in the hearth, kept burning by a servant who came and went only when I wasn't here, because I'd refused to be attended by the palace servants. Thick rugs warmed the floor. A massive bed sat imperiously on a raised platform at one end of the room. Wooden columns braced the bed at each corner, dressed in a canopy of gauzy white drapes and heavier red ones.

For the first week, I'd slept in the armchair because the bed seemed so excessive. The ache that had formed in my back, however, had forced me to relocate.

Staying here was only meant to be temporary, but our place in the Labyrinth had been taken by new tenants. Returning to the Labyrinth wouldn't have been my first choice anyway, and the North District carried too many memories.

I wondered if Reev felt the same or if being in the White Court was worse for him, having been a sentinel.

"Kai," Reev said impatiently.

I set down the comb and swung around on the stool to face him. "I haven't decided yet."

He uncrossed his arms and rolled his shoulders. They looked tense beneath his black tunic. "Has he . . . remembered anything?"

My amusement over Reev's hovering fizzled. I stood, shifting away as I reached for the gown lying over the back of the armchair. My hand rested over the dark-green cloth.

"No," I said.

As silence settled between us, my gaze traced the silvery damask that covered the armchair. I lifted the gown, folding the material over my arm, and turned to look at him again.

His shoulder was leaning against the door frame, and he regarded me with a tilt of his head. I had no idea what he was thinking.

"Do you think he ever will?" Reev asked.

My fingers tightened around the dress. "I don't know. But I can't give up."

Reev's lips compressed into an unhappy line. He looked like he wanted to argue, but his mouth remained closed. A muscle flexed in his jaw.

Why could he fuss about my comings and goings and yet refuse to say the things that actually mattered? Why did he insist on being so careful with me? A fissure had formed between us since that day in Kalla's tower, when I'd killed Ninu and severed his control over Reev and the other sentinels. Despite my efforts, I couldn't figure out how to repair our relationship.

Reev had allowed me to question him about how he'd found me on that riverbank all those years ago, but he still refused to speak of his past, before my father, Kronos, freed him the first time. It wasn't that he needed to confide these things to me. I understood his desire to let the past lie. But he still seemed to carry guilt for keeping his secrets. And for what had happened to Avan.

The growing fracture between us wasn't only Reev's doing. Although I'd told him that I didn't blame him for his actions, I hadn't been completely honest, and I felt he knew that. The resentment jabbed at me like a pebble in my heel that I couldn't dislodge.

It was stupid of me. Reev had been as helpless against Ninu's power as Avan, but my emotions cared very little for logic and truth.

I held up the gown. "I should change."

Reev nodded. Before he turned away, he said, "Be careful out there. There's been trouble with some of the sentinels."

I hadn't heard of any trouble, but that didn't mean much considering I hadn't heard anything from anyone. Even though I'd killed Ninu, I apparently wasn't significant enough to be kept informed.

Still, it was hard to be upset when being left alone was what I'd wanted.

Once the door shut behind Reev, I grabbed the hem of my tunic and dragged it over my head. I pulled on a loose, cream-colored undershirt first. The green gown was made from a stiff brocade with swirling designs hand-stitched in pale-gold thread. I thrust my arms through the sleeves and tightened the lacing down the front. It probably would have been easier to dress with assistance, but the idea of *needing* to be helped into my clothes felt ridiculous.

With the gown cinched closed, the material fit snugly through my torso and waist, and then flared out at my hips. The front skirt fell in elegant pleats to mid-thigh, but the back gathered into a bustled half skirt that dusted my calves. It came with pants that were tailored to fit like a second skin. The palace steward, Master Hathney, had commissioned one of the White Court's most admired dressmakers to construct a few gowns for me.

The clothes were another thing I didn't want to get used to, but Master Hathney had been appalled to see me walking around in an old tunic Reev had sewn for me. And if I was completely honest with myself, I sort of enjoyed the gowns. They made me feel girly in a way I'd never been able to, or even cared to, before. I didn't see the harm in liking them.

I pulled on my ankle-high boots and faced the mirror. I barely recognized the girl looking back at me. The gown was like a costume, transforming me into someone else. I squinted, trying to find the girl I knew underneath. My hair now fell past my shoulder blades and was in need of a trim. I was still too pale, but my cheeks had something of a warm tint to them, and my thin frame had lost its starved look.

I smoothed my palms down the front of my gown, my fingers tense against my stomach as if I could press away the anxiety there. Even though I met with Avan almost daily, my heart continued to herald the moment by pounding against my rib cage. I couldn't stifle the hope that maybe, today, he would remember.

As I left my room, I tucked my hands into the pockets that I'd requested be sewn into the skirt. The gown should have *some* practical function. Reev's door was a couple of rooms down. It was shut, so I hurried past in case he decided to question me again.

I passed a maid dusting off a painting. There were a lot of servants in a palace with very few actual inhabitants. Most of the Kahl's ministers lived in expansive suites throughout the White Court, probably with their own armies of servants. I'd discovered the sentinels lived in barracks behind the palace. They had their own kitchen and staff, armory, and training yard. The barracks were constructed from the same white stone as the palace and with the same level of architectural detail.

I didn't know why Ninu would bother with such lavish lodgings, seeing as I doubted his efforts had been fully appreciated by his mind-controlled soldiers. Maybe he'd just wanted the buildings to match.

The sound of my footsteps echoed up through the high ceilings as I turned down a long, airy hallway. This was one of my favorite places in the palace.

Skillfully sculpted stone columns flanked the Hall of Memories. Each column depicted something different: fur-covered hunters on horseback; herds of angel stags, their massive horns curling above their heads like halos; orchards of fruit trees; packs of large shaggy beasts with two tails; even the Outlands with its sparse landscape, spotted with gargoyles.

On and on it went, history chiseled into the foundations of the palace. I'd spent whole days picking out the delicately carved pictures, running my fingers along the grooves. I wondered if Ninu had commissioned these during his time as Kahl or if the images of long-changed landscapes and extinct creatures had been here from before Rebirth, inspiring Ninu to continue them.

Beyond the Hall of Memories was a spiral staircase and then another series of corridors with plain walls, except for the occasional painting or tapestry. I passed through the throne room, heading for the broad door that led outside. The home of the Kahl was surprisingly unguarded. There were no Watchmen on the palace grounds. The Watchmen operated under the regulations of the Minister of Law, whose authority didn't extend to palace security. That was the sentinels' domain, and Ninu alone had overseen them.

Sentinels who'd chosen to remain, this time in paid service, were posted outside and at the gates. Without Ninu's brand of order, though, security had fallen somewhat lax.

I had to push open the heavy wood-and-metal door with both hands. Light filtered through. I averted my face from the rush of air that swept inside.

"You're late."

My stomach gave a familiar flip. Avan stood on the flagstones, a smile tilting his lips. His dark hair was combed neatly back, the steel bar in his eyebrow had been long removed, and he was dressed in the finery of his new station. His eyes, which had once been brown, now glinted like sunlight behind thinning clouds. This wasn't the boy from the Alley. Unlike my dress, his appearance wasn't a costume.

And yet, the sight of him standing there—tall, confident, and devastatingly beautiful—kindled a warmth in my stomach and an ache in my chest. When I was with him, pain and longing were my constant companions.

He reached for me. I took his hand, my fingers brushing over the calluses on his palm. Did he ever look in the mirror—at the tattoo and the scars and the calluses, grave markers of his past— and wonder, *Who are you?*

"Shouldn't keeping track of the time be a skill of yours?" he asked as he tucked my hand into the crook of his arm. We made our way down the path toward the curling iron gates that led out into the bustling streets of the White Court.

"You'd think," I mumbled, dipping my head so that my hair shielded my eyes.

Before all of this, I used to enjoy studying the way the threads of time connected everything. There had been wonder in pressing my hand against the continuous flow and watching the world catch and slow around me. Meeting the Infinite had changed everything, and I would sooner give up my powers than join them.

The thing is, I may have gotten my wish. I hadn't touched the threads since Ninu died. In the months afterward, I'd ignored the shimmery fibers, denying their existence—until one day, they began to fade and disappear.

I could no longer see, much less manipulate, the threads of time.

CHAPTER 2

NO ONE KNEW. FOR NOW, I WANTED TO KEEP IT THAT WAY.

However long I had left before Kronos returned, demanding things of me, seemed to matter less now that I'd lost the abilities inherited from him. I'd tried to picture the threads in my mind, tried imagining my fingers tangling in the current, but they wouldn't appear to me.

Maybe this meant I was stuck being human. All I knew was that I no longer felt like I was walking around with a ticking clock over my head. What could Kronos do with an heir who had no power?

Avan stroked his thumb over the back of my hand as his fingers rested atop my knuckles. The physical contact, the ease with which he initiated it, was new. When he'd been human, even once we grew more comfortable with each other, he'd always shown restraint in the way he touched me, as if he wasn't entirely convinced the touch was welcome. This new Avan had no such reservations.

Those turbulent years of his past, the dark episodes with his father—the boy who'd hidden behind so many faces that I'd never quite known which was real—all of that had died with him.

But traces remained. Sometimes, he would say something or he would look at me a certain way or his mouth would twist into a crooked smile, and I could see him there—*my* Avan— just beneath the surface, battling to break through. Every time, it was like the air was ripped from my lungs, like I was the one drowning.

But this was only my imagination. My Avan wasn't slowly suffocating behind those lucent eyes. He was gone.

As one of the Infinite—immortal beings very much like gods—he was the physical embodiment of Conquest, chosen as a replacement for Ninu. To me . . . I didn't know what he was yet. But I was trying to find out.

A Gray in the form of a horse waited on the cobblestone road past the gates. The numerous metal sheets that made up its body shone even beneath the pall of yellow clouds. It had been recently washed and polished. Behind the grills in its chest, the Gray's energy stone glowed a healthy red. A thick seam scarred its neck where the metal had been welded back together. I had been unexpectedly overwhelmed when Mason had arrived from Etu Gahl with Avan's Gray. This Gray had carried me and Avan a long way.

"You look beautiful," he said with an appreciative nod at my gown.

I tried not to tug self-consciously at the fabric. "Thanks. It's . . ." I fingered the tight lacing over my ribs. "Different."

"Different can be good," Avan said.

I tilted my head to look up at him. My gaze followed the jagged black ink of his tattoo, peeking out from behind his high collar.

I knew the tattoo continued down his shoulder and upper arm in the shape of a gnarled tree with twining roots. Across his chest, the branches stretched out, bare except for three bright-green leaves. Those leaves had meant something to him once. Did he care to know what?

Different could be good, but I didn't know yet if it was better.

"Did Reev make you late?" he asked lightly.

"He wanted to know where we were going."

Avan released me so he could grip the Gray's saddle and pull himself up. As soon as I was settled behind him, my hands rested against his hips like they'd never left. It seemed wrong to feel this way about him, but I couldn't control the way my face grew warm and my pulse quickened. We'd spent hours in this position, on this same Gray. I knew every curve and plane of Avan's back.

Annoyed, I shoved the memories away. It was pointless to sit here reminiscing about something he couldn't even remember.

"Where *are* we going?" he asked, glancing over his shoulder at me.

"I haven't decided yet," I said. "Let's just . . . ride."

He faced forward, his fingers fiddling with the controls on the Gray's neck. "You got it."

I wanted to rest my cheek against his back, but I didn't. We had yet to establish anything between us other than that he wanted to share my company, and I didn't have the heart or will-power to refuse him.

Our Gray carried us over the cobblestones, slipping easily into traffic, which was light at this time of morning. I watched the buildings pass: tall structures of stone and glass broken up by smaller, squat businesses with cheerful red bricks and brightly painted signs. People were out, strolling down the sidewalks in their neat gray tunics with embroidered sleeves or colorful gowns with cinched corsets, lacy collars, asymmetrical neck-lines, and dramatic bustles. It was a different sight from what I'd been used to in the North District.

I hadn't done much exploring yet, but I'd followed the wall as it wrapped around the westernmost section of the White Court. The ground beneath my feet had been loose and grainy, like sand. I'd even found the remnants of wooden posts and planks, evidence of a dock that had been long buried. It was strange to think that, once, the walls of the city hadn't existed; instead the city had opened to a vast sea speckled with fishing boats.

The Watchmen had found me a short time later and ordered me away from the wall. The White Court wasn't as expansive as the North District, but there was still a lot to see yet, and I wanted to see some of it at least with Reev.

Even though I'd been content making do in the Labyrinth, I was glad that Reev didn't have to worry anymore about supporting us. Now, he was free to do whatever he wanted with his days instead of working long hours at the Raging Bull.

I took a deep, cleansing breath. Even the air smelled better in the White Court. It didn't have that sour tang from garbage tossed into the gutters or the bitter mustiness of the river.

But I missed the river. Not its stench nor the rickety bridge that lost another few planks every year, and definitely not the pleasure houses like the Raging Bull lined up behind the docks. I missed the walks that Reev and I used to take along the bank, and how he'd taught me to skip stones and where to step so my feet wouldn't sink into the thick mud.

A scout—a sleek, single-rider Gray in the form of a large cat—sped past, its sentinel rider guiding it around traffic. The scout turned onto the main road and bounded through the gates of the twenty-foot walls that separated the White Court from the North District.

"Where do you think they go?" I asked, watching until the scout disappeared from view.

Avan gave a slight shake of his head. "I've never thought to ask Kalla."

"What has she been doing lately?" I asked. Kalla had been known as Death among those who lived in the North District because she'd been Kahl Ninu's executioner. After I'd learned about the Infinite, I discovered she was, in fact, *Death*. It was with her scythe, disguised as a common knife, that I'd been able to kill Ninu.

I hadn't seen her in weeks. Not that I minded, but it made me suspicious when the Infinite were so silent.

"Breaking in the new Kahl. Apparently, it's a rather involved job," he said wryly. "She's trying to win over the ministers. It'll be easier to work with the existing officials rather than having to appoint entirely new ones. I think they're cooperating."

"At last," I muttered, and Avan made a sound of agreement.

When Kalla had announced Kahl Ninu's successor, the ministers had been vehemently opposed. Taking their cue from the sentinels, who had scattered in the wake of Ninu's death, the ministers had insisted that a Kahl who could not even command the loyalty of her personal guard had no right to rule anyone. They hadn't known that the sentinels' "loyalty" to Ninu had been due to their collars and that his death had meant their freedom.

Many sentinels had since returned of their own volition. After a brief attempt to hire the sentinels for themselves—an endeavor Kalla had swiftly ended—the ministers seemed to have at last realized that their own livelihoods, and political ranks, were at stake.

There was some irony in the fact that, in spite of how everything else had changed, Avan was still my best source of information.

As Avan switched to talking about a street smithy he'd met, my gaze kept returning to the open gates leading into the North

District. Avan guided the Gray to the left toward Penny's Bakery, my favorite shop in the White Court.

I gripped his forearm. "Let's go into the North District."

Avan hesitated, his arm tensing beneath my touch. But a moment later, he swung the Gray around and we turned onto the main road.

"I thought you didn't like it there," he said.

"I never said that." I just didn't like the constant reminder of Avan's absence. Which was illogical because every moment I spent with him reminded me.

This would be the second time I'd ventured into the North District since we returned to Ninurta. The first time was when I discovered the Labyrinth's leaders had cleaned out the freight container I'd shared with Reev and given it to new tenants. I hadn't yet the courage to visit Avan's parents. When he'd left with me to find Reev, he hadn't said good-bye to them. They didn't know where he'd gone or why he hadn't come back—why he might never come back. I owed them an explanation. But I couldn't face them yet.

Our Gray alone wouldn't draw much attention, but our clothing would. Now I wished I'd dressed more plainly. People from the White Court didn't stroll around the Alley, and when they did, it was usually with curiosity and disdain. I felt a pang of self-disgust that I would be seen in this light by the Alley folks. Maybe we should go back and change.

But Avan was already slowing our mount as we approached the Watchman on duty. Avan let him know in brisk, authoritative words that we would be making a trip through the North District. The Watchman, the same one who used to wave me through the gate when I'd worked as a carrier for the District Mail Center, nodded agreeably. He seemed like a decent guy, but his eagerness to please Avan was due to the color and style of Avan's tunic.

The tunic was dark red, and tailored perfectly to fit Avan's broad shoulders. It fell to below his hips, and was belted with a braided length of leather. The sleeves and hem were trimmed in a distinct gold pattern that echoed the Ninurtan emblem—the sword and the scythe—which only a few were allowed to wear. Paired with black pants and leather boots, the whole uniform was as clear an indication as any that Avan was a member of the Kahl's private council.

The Watchman bowed first to Avan and then to me, giving me a polite but impersonal smile. He didn't recognize me. Not that I expected him to. The last time he'd seen me, I was just another mail carrier from the Alley, weary and underfed.

Avan nudged our Gray forward and we passed into the North District. As Avan guided our mount, I surveyed the familiar weathered streets. The storefronts with their ripped awnings and peeling paint hadn't changed. Nor had the plain brown buildings with the occasional broken window. Despite the conditions, and the way the people on the sidewalks cast us distrustful and even hateful glares, a wave of nostalgia washed over me.

"Kai." Avan's head turned enough so I could see his profile. "Where to?"

"Let's go this way," I said, pointing at the corner ahead, which led into a much smaller street.

The muscles in Avan's back had tensed the moment we'd entered the North District, and he had yet to relax. His unease made me want to laugh, but not because it was funny. Okay, it was a little funny, but not entirely. My Avan had been so good at pretending to be okay, even when the situation called for panic. Sometimes it was refreshing that this Avan was so open.

"Do you remember any of this?" I asked.

As far as I knew, this was his first visit to the North District since Kalla had brought him back from death, and I could see his answer in the way he stared a little too long at his surroundings. His gaze followed a jagged pothole in the street to a web of cracks that fractured the sidewalk. The ruptured stones were left from Rebirth, when the frenzy of a magical and technological war had shaken the world, leveling mountains, scorching the oceans, and cracking open the earth.

His brows pinched as he tilted his head back to study the lines of laundry strung above. His hesitant observations were strange to watch. He'd once known these crooked buildings and dark nooks as well as I did. Probably better.

"No," he said softly, but there was a note of uncertainty that lit the barest ember of hope in me.

"What *do* you remember?" I'd been hesitant to ask this question, not wanting the specifics of how lonely he must feel. I didn't need to imagine what it must be like, to know nothing of yourself other than what you could touch and see and feel in that exact moment.

The curiosity and the stirring of hope had won out, though, and I awaited his response.

He took his time replying. "I remember too much and too little. There are memories from the Conquest before me and the one before him—images of things I've had to look up in the history texts in order to understand, as well as moments with a strong emotional connection. It's all jumbled," he murmured, "like pieces from separate puzzles tossed together, and no way of ever forming a complete picture."

I soothed my thumb against the back of his arm, offering my wordless support. Given his circumstances, it was a wonder he'd been able to sort himself out at all.

"What about *your* life before? Not as Conquest, but as . . . Avan?"

He took even longer to answer. "It's hard to describe," he said finally. "It's like . . . looking at storm clouds and knowing what's to come—the cold shock of the first few raindrops striking skin, the crack of thunder and the way it can shake the ground beneath your feet when it's right on top of you—but not being able to recall where the knowledge comes from." He glanced back at me. "Or how, even before Kalla introduced us, I could have described to you the exact color of your eyes."

My thumb continued to rub circles on his arm as I mulled over his words. In truth, he seemed to have a better foundation on which to stand than I had when I was eight. I gestured for him to lead us into another left turn and then pointed to the intersection ahead.

"Pull up here," I said.

Avan guided our Gray closer to the gutter. He stopped us at the corner. On the sidewalk, a dented lamppost was plastered with a poster too faded to be legible. Avan looked back at me, one eyebrow raised in question.

Across the street at the opposite corner sat a shop. It had flaking green paint and the name *Drivas* painted above the window front. The shop looked much the same as Avan had left it, except the window had been broken and was now clumsily boarded over. If I closed my eyes, I could imagine Avan sitting on the sidewalk in a gray tunic with a cup of water in hand.

A pair of boys on the sidewalk slowed as they passed us, and I gave them a hard glare. We were too conspicuous, standing here like a beacon to street gangs and thieves. Avan and I wouldn't be easy targets, even without my powers, but we looked like we might be.

Avan's gaze had fastened to the shop sign across the street. I could see only his profile, but he was frowning, as if trying to remember.

"Drivas," he said quietly to himself. "My last name."

Please. Please remember.

"Avan?" a voice said.

Cold dread spilled down my spine. For a fleeting second, I toyed with the idea of ignoring him and telling Avan to get us back on the road.

But I couldn't. So I turned, knowing whom I'd find.

CHAPTER 3

"WHAT IS THIS?" MR. DRIVAS GESTURED BROADLY AT AVAN'S refined clothing and hair. All I got was a dismissive glance. "Where have you been?"

The half-eaten apple in his hand slipped from his slack fingers, and it rolled off the curb into the gutter. He didn't notice. He had the same olive skin tone as Avan, but it was quickly darkening with anger.

Drek. I'd been expecting Avan's father to be either tending to the shop or laid out in his bed upstairs, drunk as usual. The last thing I'd wanted was to force a confrontation for which neither of them was ready.

"You disappeared without a word," Mr. Drivas said, his voice rising. The people on the street who hadn't already been gawking at us were definitely staring now. "Your mom thought you were dead!"

"My mom?" Avan murmured, looking back to the shop.

I realized I was digging my hands into his hips and forced my fingers to relax. Avan was tense, but he didn't seem afraid, only wary. This Avan had no reason to fear his dad.

"Nothing to say for yourself?" Mr. Drivas's mouth twisted into an ugly sneer. He might have been a handsome man if not for how the years of drinking had ruined him. His attention rested on me now, and the look there made me want to climb off the Gray and reacquaint my boot with his crotch. "I see how it is," he said to Avan. "Finally whored your way up to someone with money."

Avan made no response, but I drew a small, stunned gasp. Fury flushed my cheeks. In an instant, I was standing on the ground, shouting into Mr. Drivas's face. "You're a despicable person. How can you say such terrible things to your son?"

Mr. Drivas gave me a once-over before taking a threatening step forward. I let him, staring him down. He didn't intimidate me. One swift rise of my knee and he'd be curled up on the sidewalk. It wouldn't be the first time.

"Go on then, protect your *pet*," he spat with a disgusted glance at Avan. "Who the drek are you anyw—" He cut himself off, his eyes narrowing at me. "*You.*"

The way he said it—so much venom packed into a single word. I flinched.

Behind me, I could hear Avan dismount. "Kai, what—"

"I should have known it was you," Mr. Drivas said. He shoved his finger at me, jabbing it into the skin beneath my collarbone. He was so close I could smell his sour breath against my face. "Always coming around, distracting Avan from his duties, acting like you're so much better." His gaze darted back to Avan, and his scowl deepened, as if Avan's lack of fear infuriated him. "I should have put you in your place a long time ag—"

He was suddenly torn from me. I blinked, rocking back on my heels. Avan had grabbed him by the front of his tunic.

"If you ever threaten her again, I'll rip out your tongue and make you wear it around your neck," Avan said. Every word penetrated the air with the blistering power that he had, until now, kept leashed. The gold of his eyes smoldered as if a furnace burned inside him.

"Avan," I said as Mr. Drivas shrank in Avan's grip. Fear pulled the lines of his face taut. I pressed a hand against Avan's shoulder. "Stop."

He released his dad, who stumbled away, ashen.

"Who are you?" Mr. Drivas asked, regarding Avan with eyes so wide that I almost expected them to fall out.

I grabbed Avan's arm and tugged him back to the Gray. "We should leave."

Fortunately, Avan didn't argue. We were back on the main road within minutes.

"I'm sorry," I said, rubbing an ache in my temple. "I'm an idiot. I shouldn't have taken you there. I thought it might jog a memory or something."

He shrugged, but the motion looked forced. "I'm assuming that was my father."

"I wasn't expecting him to be outside."

Avan didn't respond. I left him to his thoughts as we neared the gate to the White Court. At either side of the road, people had stopped on the sidewalk. The murmur of their raised voices finally reached my ears now that I was paying attention. What were they all looking at?

I peered around Avan's shoulder. Up ahead, black smoke billowed from Death's tower.

CHAPTER 4

BY THE TIME WE GOT BACK TO THE WHITE COURT, IT WAS NEARLY impossible to wade through the crowd pressed up against the tall iron fence that enclosed the palace grounds. Avan maneuvered our Gray between the others gathered outside the entrance. Watchmen saw us coming and wedged the gate open wide enough to let us pass.

Avan directed the Gray off the path, cutting across the lawn. Other government buildings blocked the view around the base of Kalla's tower, but dark plumes were still rising into the sky.

"Where are the sentinels?" I asked, glancing back at the Watchmen who'd shut and barricaded the gate against the surge of gawkers. Sentinels should have been guarding the palace grounds, not Watchmen.

"Engaged," Avan said.

I turned forward again to see what he meant. Kalla's tower had come into view. The glass doors were thrown open, belching smoke as a frantic red glow danced inside. Hollows and sentinels collided in the chaos. Hollows were former sentinels who were now loyal to Ninu's brother Irra. I cringed as a hollow smashed his fist into a sentinel's nose with a meaty crunch. What was going on?

Amid the fighting and the smoke, I picked out a bright spot of sandy hair.

"Mason." Mason was a hollow I'd met during my search for Reev a few months ago. He'd since become one of my dearest friends.

He was fighting off a much larger sentinel. I turned, about to swing my leg over the back of the Gray, but Avan stopped me with a hand on my thigh. My breath hitched. I brushed away his touch, irritated with my body's response.

"He'll be fine," Avan said. Our Gray shot forward, weaving through the fighting bodies and straight into the choking heat spilling out the doors.

I tucked my head into Avan's back, coughing as smoke assailed my nostrils and singed my throat. The lobby was ablaze. I covered my mouth and nose with the sleeve of my gown and slid from the saddle to crouch closer to the ground. Avan pushed ahead on the Gray, and I squinted through the haze to see what was happening.

Up ahead, an archway led into a staircase that spiraled up through the full height of the tower. A group of sentinels was gathered before the archway. Avan pulled his mount short of them, its metal hooves skidding against the gleaming tiles. Irra stood a few steps above the landing. I could feel his looming presence like a cold vacuum, siphoning the heat that suffused the lobby.

Behind him, a considerable portion of the staircase had rotted away. Only blackened dust and pocked, shriveled stone remained. Irra's handiwork. As the physical embodiment of Famine, he possessed a withering touch.

Irra was not one to demonstrate his power needlessly. For a moment, fear slid beneath my ribs.

The sentinels shifted restlessly on their feet, probably working up the courage to attack him. I counted ourselves lucky that Kalla had seized every sentinel's torch blade months ago. They had only their fists against Irra's terrifying power. It wouldn't be much of a fight, even with their enhanced physical abilities. They had to know that.

Avan's voice rang out: "*Stop.*"

His command reverberated through the room, riding the billows of smoke out into the street. Avan's magic swooped down on me, gouging hooks into my skin. I gritted my teeth and pushed away the oppressive force. His voice echoed around me in hypnotic whispers, but I shook it off.

The sentinels had gone still. A moment later, their stiff bodies seemed to thaw as their heads swiveled left and right, their unfocused eyes following something I couldn't see. Confusion clouded their faces.

I pushed to my feet and shouted through the shield of my sleeve, "What are you doing to them?"

Avan wasn't listening.

"Collect the rebels," Irra ordered. He didn't have Avan's invasive power, but I still felt his voice echo inside me, opening up an emptiness in my chest that made me want to curl into myself.

A rush of activity sped past me as Irra's hollows dashed in to round up the sentinels. The sentinels' confusion had given way to blank acceptance. They appeared unaware of what was happening. Their glazed expressions looked far too much like when their collars had been active.

For sentinel and hollow alike, the collars were a permanent reminder of Ninu's touch. He had seared the magic into the backs of their necks, allowing him to control them. The only reason they'd survived being branded with a collar was because they were all *mahjo*, human descendants of the Infinite. Before the Mahjo War, before the Infinite had stripped them of their magic, *mahjo* had been worshipped for their abilities.

I coughed harshly, my lungs burning, but I pushed forward. "Avan, stop it," I rasped, grabbing his arm. "Stop it!"

His eyes rested on me, blazing with unnatural light. "They must be controlled," he said, his voice soft but piercing.

"*No one* should be controlled."

More hollows had filed in, carrying buckets of water and hoses to put out the fire, which appeared to have been contained to the lobby. The added steam made it impossible to breathe.

Coughs racked my chest. I left Avan behind, making my way out into the fresh air.

Once outside, I bent over, bracing my palms against my knees as another round of coughing rattled me. Pain jabbed my lungs.

"Ow," I muttered.

A quick look around revealed that the hollows had corralled the rebel sentinels and bound their arms. I was surprised to see less than a dozen sentinels. In the tumult of smoke and fighting, they had seemed countless.

Where was Reev? He must have seen the smoke. Mason sat farther down the path on a boulder, glowering at the proceedings. He looked unharmed.

The *clop* of metal hooves sounded from the building. I straightened as Avan rode his Gray into my path.

"Irra has asked for you," he said.

I turned away without acknowledging him, heading toward the doors. But I wasn't going back inside, so if Irra wanted to talk, we could do it out here. Avan dropped from his Gray.

His fingers brushed my hand, but I twisted away. "The hollows could have handled them," I snapped. "You didn't need to do that."

"You would have rather risked their lives when I could easily spare them all?"

"Look at them!" I gestured wildly at the glassy-eyed sentinels not ten feet away. "How can you justify this? How is this any different than what Ninu did to them? To Reev?"

He said nothing, but I could see that he wouldn't relent. I made a sound of disgust and strode away.

Irra had emerged from the building. Tall, gaunt, and dressed in a tattered black robe, he looked part shadow and smoke himself, as if he had materialized from the dark plumes. Maybe he had. His magic could enfold all of Etu Gahl in shawls of mist, concealing the fortress from detection. I would put nothing past him. When he caught my eye, he nodded to his left before heading around the side of the building. I ran to catch up with him.

"Where are we going?" I asked.

"To see Kalla."

"But the stairs—"

"You didn't think that was the only way up, did you?"

I guess I had. We went in through a locked entrance in the back. Inside was a simple foyer with a door in the opposite wall. Irra slid open the door to reveal a tiny room, empty except for a metal lever sticking out from the floor. He stepped inside and then motioned for me to follow.

"What is this?" I warily joined him. The room was barely five feet wide.

"A pulley system," Irra said, shutting the door. He grabbed the lever and swung it forward.

The room shuddered. My stomach lurched, and I slapped my palm against the wall to stabilize my legs. From somewhere far above us, the clank and clangor of gears and cables and who knew what else vibrated beneath my palm and through my feet.

"Are we . . . moving?" My fingers clenched against the wall, trying to find something to grip.

"The technology was lost after Rebirth, but Kalla's penchant for tall buildings forced her to revive it."

I swallowed down my nervousness and then winced at my painfully dry throat. I swallowed again, gingerly this time. "You should install this in Etu Gahl."

"The gargoyles prefer the stairs."

I couldn't tell if he was joking. The room shuddered again, and I flattened myself against the wall, glaring at Irra's nonchalance.

"It's quite safe," Irra said mildly. The top of his wild black-and-gray hair dusted the ceiling, but he had yet to lose his balance as the room jostled upward.

I'd have to take his word for it. But I didn't move from my spot against the wall. "Why were the sentinels attacking the tower?"

"Why do you think?"

I rolled my eyes. Why did the Infinite always have to skirt around a straight answer? "To get to Kalla."

"Yes." He didn't elaborate.

"Again—why?" And what did Kalla and Irra want with me now?

"Because they don't like us."

I stared at the frayed sleeve of his robe. He fit into the beauty and opulence of the White Court about as well as I did. Even though he'd been here as long as I had, I'd never seen him wear anything but his usual threadbare black, still hanging too loosely from his unnervingly thin shoulders. The fire hadn't caused more damage to him or his robe than what was already there.

Before meeting Irra, I'd known him only as the Black Rider—an old name originating from a time when people still worshipped the Infinite. Back then, the statues erected in his image had portrayed a rider cloaked in black. These days, his appearance was far less intimidating. At least until you looked into his eyes. Then there was no mistaking his power.

I surveyed the state of my own clothes. The brocade gown was ruined. Smoke had blackened the green, and there were holes in the sleeve and front skirt where the heat and stray embers had singed the fabric.

"Then they're going to be really mad when they wake up from whatever Avan did to them."

"I imagine so," he said. He rummaged in the deep pockets of his robe before withdrawing a couple of cream-colored bread bites. He popped both into his mouth.

I was glad Irra hadn't changed. My anger with him for deceiving me in Etu Gahl had faded somewhat, although I knew now not to trust everything he said.

"What *did* Avan do?" I asked.

Irra took his time chewing his bread bites before answering. "The Infinite Conquest will always have certain unique abilities. But when the position must be passed to a successor, those abilities may alter somewhat. Avan's particular power is not one I've seen before with Conquest."

"Okay," I said slowly. Avan's power *had* felt different from Ninu's. It had been a much stronger presence. "So he can control people more easily?"

"In a way. Ninu could manipulate emotion and thought, but Avan seems able to transform his will into actual sensory images."

"He can create illusions." That would explain the glazed looks and the confusion.

I let that knowledge settle inside me, where it grew and twisted into something too overwhelming and horrible to consider.

Then I closed my eyes and sealed away the fear.

CHAPTER 5

KALLA WORE A FAMILIAR FACE. WITH THE ABILITY TO ALTER HER physical appearance—except the color of her skin, eyes, and hair—she rarely met me with the same features. But today, she looked as she had the first day we'd met. At the time, I'd thought she was an Alley kid.

Instead of the stained and ragged tunic she'd worn then, satin robes draped her porcelain shoulders and framed her corseted gown. Her lips were still that slick shade of blood red, and her eyes were the color of polished metal. Her powder white hair with its single black streak had been styled into the same Mohawk she'd worn that day months ago in the garbage-strewn alley. The Mohawk was an unusual combination with the elegance of her gown, but the severe hair did very little to distract from her unnatural beauty.

She stood by the windows that stretched from floor to ceiling. Smoke from far below obscured parts of the city, but not enough to ruin the view. This was the highest point in all of Ninurta, and I could see clear to the rusty boxes of the Labyrinth and beyond.

For as brief a time as I'd spent here, this tower held a lot of unpleasant memories. All of which tried to surge forward the moment my boot touched the mosaic tiles.

A settee and two armchairs were placed around a low table at the center of the expansive room. In one of the armchairs was Miraya, the sentinel that Kalla had chosen as our next Kahl. Miraya sat hunched over, her forearms resting on her thighs and her hands lacing and unlacing in agitation. Her head jerked up at our arrival.

"It's been taken care of," Irra said, sinking onto the settee and arranging his robes over his long legs and sharp knees. He moved fluidly, without any of the awkwardness you might expect from such a skinny man.

Miraya rubbed her palms rapidly over her thighs. "I should have been down there."

"A Kahl does not engage in trivial disputes," Kalla said casually.

My brows rose. "Trivial disputes? They were trying to burn down a government building."

"No," Kalla said, "they were trying, rather clumsily, to force me down from this tower." Through her reflection in the window, I saw her red lips curve.

I could imagine how that would have ended. Fighting Death would result in only one possible outcome.

"Because they don't like you," I said, repeating Irra's words with a sigh of exasperation. "Can you be more specific?"

"The rebels want to eject us from the city, and assert their own control," she said.

My gaze shifted from Kalla to Irra before settling on Miraya.

"Well," I said tentatively, "we've got Miraya. All she needs is a proper coronation, and she'll officially be Kahl. If we can persuade the sentinels to unite under her rule, then everyone would get what they want." When only silence followed my statement, I added, "Right?"

"They killed two of my hollows," Irra said.

Anger underscored his voice, quivering in the air around him. I felt it in my gut like a pain clawing outward. It lasted only half a second, but I clutched at my stomach and barely kept from gasping. The way Miraya tensed meant she'd felt it, too. I'd hate to know what would happen if the Infinite ever truly lost control of their emotions. Or at least, whatever emotions they were capable of feeling.

"They cannot be allowed a hand in the governing of the city," Kalla said, turning away from the window to face us. "Such bitter vengeance would do no good for Ninurta."

She seemed to be ignoring the role that she and the Infinite had played in inciting the sentinels' anger. "They spent years of their lives as mindless soldiers under Ninu, with you as his second in command. They have good reason to hate you," I pointed out.

"Yes," Kalla said simply, "but they have also refused to follow Miraya."

Miraya straightened and tugged at her tunic as if it didn't quite fit right, even though it must have been tailored for her. A couple of months ago, she had been just another sentinel trying to make sense of her newfound freedom. Then, Kalla had plucked her out of the ranks and convinced her to take the title of Kahl.

What little I knew about Miraya, I'd learned from Avan. Ninu put a collar on her when she was sixteen. Most sentinels gradually lost their sense of self while under Ninu's control, but Miraya had somehow retained her self-awareness even through repeated attempts to cleanse her mind. Kalla had watched her for years. How this contributed to whatever qualifications Kalla must have been looking for was a mystery to me, but Miraya seemed cautious of the political power given her, which I thought was an intelligent reaction.

Now, instead of sturdy leather armor, she wore a silver tunic with billowy sleeves and a flowing train that trailed behind her when she walked. Impractical for a soldier, but fitting for a Kahl. Although Miraya still appeared unaccustomed to the new clothes, she wore them well. The silver contrasted beautifully with her dark skin. When she grew more comfortable in her position, I hoped she would also wear its power well.

"They won't have someone the Infinite picked sitting on the throne." Miraya raked her fingers through her short black hair. "They think I'm a puppet. And they want all the ministers replaced as well. They won't take any chances that one of them might have been originally planted by Ninu or Kalla."

"They've selected their own leader," Irra said. "Someone with the rebels' loyalty. Or so I've heard. I've been trying to gauge their plans for weeks, but nothing hinted at an attack."

"Talk to them," I said. Had they even considered actually hearing these sentinels out? "Tell them they're wrong about Miraya."

"We're beyond talking," Kalla said.

I crumpled my ruined gown in my hands. "Why am I here? What did you want me for?"

"Miraya is the one who requested you," she said. Her slender fingers played with the glass beading that crawled in icy swirls across her corseted waist.

Miraya stood and clasped her hands behind her back. "I wanted to ask if you would consider becoming my adviser."

It took a moment for her meaning to sink in. Kalla had always been the Kahl's adviser, a position higher than any of the ministers. "Adviser?" I repeated. "Why would you want *me*?"

"You defeated Kahl Ninu. You freed the sentinels. They owe you a great debt. And the hollows respect you as well. But more than that, you went to great lengths to rescue your brother. I can't imagine anyone more suited to advise me in leading the city."

My face grew hot. I tried not to fidget. She made me sound like a hero, but I wasn't. I didn't kill Ninu to save Ninurta or any of the other sentinels. I'd done it only for Reev and Avan. I hadn't even planned to stick around after he was gone. I'd wanted to take Reev back to Etu Gahl or somewhere else and leave Ninurta to its fate, whatever that might be.

That was no longer an option now that Avan was Infinite. Leaving meant giving up on him.

"I can't," I said. Maybe it was selfish of me, but I had enough worries without adding the whole of Ninurta to them. "Besides, I don't know how much time I have left."

"Should you consent to becoming Miraya's adviser, I will see to it that Kronos extends his absence," Kalla said.

I looked at her warily. "Why would you do that for me?"

She lowered her snowy lashes. "Is it so wrong of me to wish that my brother remain a while longer? When you succeed him as the Keeper of Time, Kronos will fade into the River."

The River—the current through which all of time flowed, and the place to which Ninu had wanted access in order to alter his past. Kalla's words surprised me, but they also made sense. She and Irra had both said the number of Infinite was fixed. Once I took my father's place, he would be gone.

Of course, no one knew yet that I couldn't see the threads anymore.

"Is this not what you wanted?" Kalla asked. Although she spoke quietly, her voice always commanded attention. "To remain here with the humans?"

It was, but not burdened by what Miraya was asking of me. "I'll think about it," I said. "I can't give you an answer right now."

"Certainly," Miraya said, nodding. "Take as much time as you need."

Irra flicked lint from his sleeve and said, "Sooner rather than later."

CHAPTER 6

BACK IN THE LOBBY, THE FIRE APPEARED TO HAVE BEEN PUT OUT, although smoke still trailed out the glass doors in gray wisps. The rebel sentinels were gone, presumably herded away to cells until Miraya—and Kalla—decided what would be done with them.

Most of the hollows had cleared out as well, although a few lingered, deep in discussion with sentinels who hadn't been involved with the attack. The sentinels were easy to pick out among the hollows because they wore the black leather tunics of their rank.

I hoped this incident wouldn't cause a rift between them. So many of the hollows had been happy to return home.

Farther up the path, Avan was lounging on the same boulder that Mason had been sitting on earlier. My steps slowed and I debated taking another route. But that would be too much trouble, so I picked up my pace, determined to ignore him.

He called out as he stood. A moment later, he fell into step beside me. "Kai—"

"I don't want to talk to you right now, especially if you're going to try to justify what you did."

Avan drew a slow breath. I sneaked a glance at him. He looked contemplative.

"I'm sorry I upset you," he said.

"I don't need an apology." How could I make him see that what he'd done was wrong? That the old Avan would never have allowed himself to use such a power?

We had reached the front steps of the palace, and he followed me inside. Since I wasn't about to let him walk me all the way to my room, I stopped alongside a white pillar at the back of the throne room.

"What *do* you need?" he asked evenly.

Probably some water. My throat was killing me. But that wasn't what Avan meant, so I said, "Promise me that you won't do it again."

The corners of his lips tightened. Then something flashed across his face—frustration or pain. "You have to understand, it's not always a choice."

"What do you mean?"

"There's . . ." He frowned as he searched for the right words. He rubbed his neck, his fingers passing over his tattoo. "There's a darkness inside me. Like an ink spot, and the more I rub at it, the larger the stain becomes."

His admission was discomfiting. I couldn't hold on to my anger, so I let it go. I reached out, my fingers tracing his tattoo. His gaze flicked to mine.

"Does it scare you?" I asked—because that unknowable part of him scared me. How would he change if he gave in to that darkness?

His face softened at my touch. "Not usually." His hand came up to toy with a dark strand of hair falling over my shoulder. "But it can surprise me sometimes. I don't think it's something I can wipe away. It feels fixed, like my powers. Or like this consuming need to protect you. I'm not even sure what I'm supposed to be protecting you from."

He touched his forehead to mine. I closed my eyes and breathed in, trying to catch a hint of his scent. All I could smell was ash. He had a gray stain along his jaw, and the vibrant red of his tunic had gone dusky from the smoke, but he appeared as unaffected by the fire as Irra.

I licked my dry lips. "When you saw me for the first time in Kalla's tower, you said you wanted to remember. Is that still true?"

He pulled back to look at me. For a long moment, he was silent. He seemed to be studying my face. Maybe he was trying to remember. Or maybe he was deciding whether I was worth remembering.

"I do," he said with little conviction.

My heart gave a miserable twist that I desperately hoped didn't show on my face. I didn't want him to see how much his answer meant to me.

"I wish I could pick and choose which memories to recover," he said. "But the bright spots in your past don't happen without the dark ones, and it would be impossible to remember one thing without the other."

"It would make things a lot less complicated, though," I mumbled.

His dimple appeared as a sad smile flickered across his lips. "It would. It's just that I wonder whether some things are better left unremembered."

After what had just happened with his dad, I couldn't argue.

Except for his eyes, everything about Avan's face, sharp and beautiful, was the same. He seemed so much like my Avan that my heart ached with missing him.

Before I could think better of it, I lifted up on my toes and kissed him.

Memories crashed down on me, sweeping me under. We'd kissed only twice before now, but each one had been seared into my mind and my heart.

He whispered my name in surprise as his hands found the small of my back. Too many emotions clamored inside me, pressing behind my eyelids even as I kissed him harder. His palms slid over my hips, down the sides of my thighs. His mouth was hot, desperate, as if he was searching for something that only I could give. He gripped the backs of my thighs, jerking me closer. I gasped into his mouth. My head spun. My fingers clutched at his hair.

Wasn't I supposed to be angry with him about something? I couldn't string my thoughts together long enough to remember.

There was a loud cough behind me.

Avan and I sprang apart. My heart, which had been racing a moment ago, nearly stopped at the knowledge of who stood behind us. I slowly spun to face my brother.

Reev looked murderous, but I wasn't sure if the victim of his wrath would be me or Avan.

"Um." My mind was alarmingly blank. "We just got back."

"I see," Reev said evenly, at odds with the intensity of his scowl. At least he looked unharmed. He must have missed the attack completely.

Avan tried to straighten out his tunic with quick, surreptitious movements. I risked a glance at him and winced at his disheveled appearance. I probably didn't look much better. My face burned.

"I should go," Avan said. He brushed his fingers over my knuckles, gave Reev a polite bow, which Reev didn't return, and left the throne room.

The silence that hung in the air after his departure felt stifling. With a hastily mumbled excuse, I patted down my hair and tried to walk past Reev.

"Kai."

I flinched, and then looked at him with as much dignity as I could muster. "Yes?"

"Are you going to explain what that was about?" His voice was dangerously calm.

I straightened my shoulders. I wasn't a little girl anymore who could be sent to bed early, even if my trembling knees had yet to realize that. "You really need an explanation?"

Reev's gray eyes were like granite. "You can't go around kissing—"

"I can kiss whoever I want," I said, taking strength in my renewed anger. I wasn't ashamed by what we'd been doing. I was only embarrassed that Reev had seen.

"You're not old enough to unders—"

"I'm seventeen," I protested. "Eighteen in a couple months. How old were *you* when you kissed a girl?"

The way his scowl wavered was answer enough.

"Besides, I *understand* what I'm doing. It's not like I didn't see enough of it by the docks."

"That's not what I'm talking about, and don't you dare start thinking about doing *that* with him."

I couldn't believe we were having this conversation. "Of course not. But even if I was, it's none of your business."

"Avan isn't safe," he said, raking his fingers through his hair. "None of the Infinite are."

The Infinite were the most powerful—and unpredictable— beings in the world. But I couldn't help feeling defensive. "In case you forgot, Avan gave up his life to save mine."

"I could never forget. But that was the old Avan. That"—he gestured at the doors through which Avan had left—"isn't him.

He's one of *them* now. Mason told me about what happened to the sentinels at the tower." I shook my head, but Reev continued, his voice softer, pleading. "He isn't safe, Kai."

He reached for my hands. Physical contact was something else that had receded between us, and his touch was such a relief that my eyes blurred. I blinked away the tears.

Sometimes I wished that I could sink into the strength of his arms and hold on to the illusion that, as long as we were together, nothing could touch us. But that was a fantasy I'd constructed as an eight-year-old kid with no family and no past, clinging to the only person in the world who would have me. It was a fantasy that had lasted up until the moment Ninu had shattered it.

I couldn't lean on Reev's strength anymore. I had proved to myself that I could stand well enough on my own. But that didn't mean I couldn't take comfort in his presence or his touch. He was still my brother.

I just wished I knew what *he* thought about us. His hands were warm around mine, but the rift between us was still there. I didn't know how to reach across and pull him back.

I sighed. "Avan can't help that his Infinite nature takes over sometimes. He's trying, though. You of all people know what it's like to have something in your head that you can't control."

"That's not the same. Avan isn't being controlled by the Infinite. He *is* one."

Hearing him voice my own doubts made my resolve falter. Since first learning about the existence of the Infinite, I'd encountered five of them. They ranged from tolerable to downright sadistic. Istar, who had been allies with Ninu but left the city after I killed him, had introduced herself to me as Strife and taken particular joy in my discomfort. Like Ninu and now Avan, she had once been human long ago.

Thinking about what Avan could become unsettled me, but at least I knew what the end result might look like. And Avan wasn't yet far gone.

"You do realize," Reev said with measured words, "that you can't be with him. You and I—we're going to change, grow old, die, as any human should. Avan won't." His fingers tightened around mine, forcing me to listen. "He'll remain ageless until long after we're both gone, because he isn't human. And no amount of reminiscing about who he once was will change that. Unless—" He released me, and I backed away into a pillar.

Reev rarely allowed his emotions to show on his face, but for once, they were plain to see. The wariness in his eyes, and the way his hands hovered in the space where I'd been standing, told me enough of what he was thinking. I shook my head.

"Don't worry. I haven't changed my mind about becoming Infinite," I said. Was I tempted by the idea of immortality? By the promise of power I'd only glimpsed in Kronos? Perhaps. If Avan had been allowed to keep his memories, I might even have considered giving in to Kronos.

But after everything they'd done, after everything that had happened *because* of my Infinite side, it was impossible to want anything to do with them.

"It's not about *being* with him. It's about not giving up on the possibility that he might still remember what it means to be human," I said. "I never gave up on you. Even after the terrible things Ninu made you do. Don't you see? I can't give up on him, either."

After a long pause, during which I endured Reev's assessing gaze, he said, "All right. I'll try . . . I'll try to understand."

I squeezed his hand. "Thank you."

"But that doesn't mean I'm okay with you kissing him."

I gave him an exasperated look. "Reev—"

"You should go clean up." His nose wrinkled as he surveyed the damage. Smoke stains streaked my hands, and I had to assume my face was no better. At least Avan hadn't seemed to mind. How had he and Irra come out looking so untouched in comparison? They were in the lobby longer than I was. Were the Infinite fire-repellent?

Probably, I thought sourly.

I left Reev in the throne room and hurried to wash up.

My hand felt sticky and heavy. I fumbled with the blanket, kicking it off my overheated body. Daylight filtered through my room.

My pulse thudded in my ears. My breathing was loud in the silence. I stared up at the canopy drapes, my thoughts scattered. I tugged at the damp warmth of my nightshirt and rolled onto my side.

Reev's sightless eyes greeted me.

My mouth opened, but a scream wouldn't come. Reev lay on his back, head turned to the side, blood flecking his jaw. More blood saturated his tunic, darkest at the center of his chest where a wound gaped at me. I'd mistaken the sticky warmth of his blood for sweat.

I scrambled away, my body shaking. My palms slipped off the mattress. I tumbled backward. Something clattered to the floor beside me.

It was a knife. The blade was stained almost black. I'd been clutching it.

Terror released my voice. I screamed and screamed and—

"Kai!"

My eyelids flew open, my screams echoing in my ears. Someone was standing over me, but all I could see was Reev's mutilated body.

"Kai, look at me."

Mason. My hands clutched at the blankets. I gasped in air. My eyes focused on Mason.

"It's okay," he said, speaking low, soothing. His fingers skimmed over my temple, my cheek, settling beneath my jaw. His touch was firm but gentle, coaxing me into full awareness. "It was a dream."

A dream. I gripped Mason's forearms. *Just another dream.*

"I'm fine," I said hoarsely. I sucked in a breath as my body sagged into the mattress, the tension gradually fading along with the nightmare.

"You sure?" Mason perched on my bed. Behind him, my door was wide open. He must have heard me screaming and rushed in. Probably broke the lock. Great.

I groaned and rolled onto my side to bury my face in my pillow. "I'm fine," I repeated, my voice muffled.

It wasn't always Reev in the nightmare. In the beginning, I'd dreamed that I was in Kalla's tower, reliving that night with my bloodied hands gripping her knife as Ninu bled to death. Then my subconscious had gotten creative. Sometimes I was back in Avan's shop, standing over Avan's body, Kalla's knife dripping onto the dusky tiles. Sometimes I was in the Labyrinth, straddling Reev's waist as I plunged the knife into his chest. Once, I watched myself kill all of them: Reev, Avan, Mason, even Hina, the only other friend I'd made in Etu Gahl. I had dragged the blade across their necks, their arms, their stomachs, carving murals into their skin. After waking from that one, I had barely made it to the bathroom before my stomach heaved.

"Kai?"

I wiped my hands against my pillow, as if I could still feel the sticky warmth of Reev's blood between my fingers. Then I rubbed my face and sat up. I offered Mason a sheepish smile, but inside, I was mortified.

"Sorry you had to see that."

"Does that happen often?"

"No," I lied. He didn't look like he believed me, but I wasn't going to talk about it. "What are you doing in here?" I looked around. It was still early, the light from the window suggesting just after dawn.

He seemed reluctant to change the subject, but he must have realized my discomfort, because he stood. "I was coming to wake you. A messenger arrived at the city gates."

"Messenger?" Maybe I wasn't fully awake, because I couldn't process what he was saying. Where could a messenger possibly have come from?

"Claims she's from a country up north. Looks like we're not alone after all."

CHAPTER 7

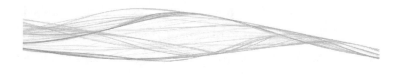

MASON WAITED OUT IN THE HALL AS I SPLASHED WATER OVER MY face and tied my tousled hair back into a ponytail. A million questions raced through my mind as I dressed.

How had they known we were here when we'd never found signs that anyone else had survived Rebirth? Why were they making contact now? And how the drek could someone without a scout have gotten through the Outlands without being eaten by gargoyles? Mason had said the messenger arrived on a horse. A *horse*. I couldn't wait to see that.

As soon as I pulled on a simple tunic, I threw open my door, and we headed down.

Mason explained that the Watchmen had escorted the messenger into the city as far as the palace gates. From there, a sentinel had taken her to a waiting room in the guest quarters of the west wing. It was sheer luck that Mason had been heading out for his morning training when the sentinels brought her in.

We were practically running through the halls, startling the servants as we tore past. I was breathless with excitement.

In no time at all, we'd reached the door to the waiting room. We took a moment to compose ourselves, and then pushed inside. I'd never had reason to be in this section of the palace, so I quickly took stock of the room. It was elegantly furnished with a settee, an armchair, and several upholstered wooden chairs, all of which were empty except for one.

Sitting there, looking self-conscious, was a girl. At least, I was pretty sure she was a girl. She was covered head to boots in a crust of dirt. Her hair was shorter than Mason's, and her heavy riding cloak hid everything from her neck to her knees. Beneath the dirt and dust, her hair might have been brown. Her lips were cracked, and her cheeks and the tip of her nose were red from the heat of the Outlands. Who knew how long she'd been out there?

She sat at the very edge of the seat, as if trying to touch as little of the pale gold upholstery as possible.

The sentinel who'd escorted her stood nearby, watching her with a puzzled sort of look, like he couldn't believe the girl was really here. I could understand. This was crazy.

At our entrance, the girl jumped to her feet. Her hands appeared from beneath her cloak as she wrung them together at her waist.

I addressed the sentinel: "Find Master Hathney and have him arrange for a room and a meal. And bring her some water."

The sentinel hurried away to find the steward.

The girl stared at me with wide brown eyes. I put out my hand, and she rushed forward to shake it. She bowed her head low over our joined hands. Dust from her hair sprinkled down over my knuckles.

"Welcome to Ninurta," I said, and then felt immediately awkward, but I didn't know how else to receive her. "I'm Kai. And this is Mason."

She beamed. Beneath the outer corner of her left eye was a blue tattoo about the size of a pebble. It looked like an eight-point star with the four longer arms pointing north, south, east, and west.

"I'm Yara. It's such a relief to have at last arrived," she said, sounding surprisingly energetic for someone who must have spent quite some time on her journey, judging by the collection of dirt. "I wasn't sure if I was going in the right direction or if I'd find a city here at all." She dropped my hand and rubbed her palms together, releasing another shower of dust. She grimaced.

"Where do you come from?" Mason asked.

"Lanathrill, north of the Yellow Wastes."

"Yellow Wastes?"

"The Outlands," I said. The dirt coating Yara's brow crinkled.

With no outside contact of any kind since Rebirth, it made sense that we would have different names for places. The archived maps in the records hall showed much less desert land prior to Rebirth, and an area that the history texts claimed had contained more wildlife. The Outlands hadn't been big enough to need a name back then.

The door to the waiting room opened. Kalla and Miraya entered, followed by a servant bearing a tray with a flagon of water and a cup. The servant set the tray down on a table against the wall, beside the mantel. No fire had been lit in the hearth, but the room was warm enough with the thick burgundy rug and heavy tapestries to chase away the chill of stone.

At the sight of Kalla, Yara's eyes went impossibly wide. She bent at the waist, her dirt-encrusted cloak falling in stiff layers around her.

"The Pale Lady," Yara uttered breathily. When she straightened, her face shone with reverence. "I never expected to be honored with meeting you."

"How do you know her?" I asked. Yara lowered her gaze. The back of my neck prickled.

Rather than offer an answer, Kalla swept aside the shimmery satin train of her gown and sat with sinuous grace. Miraya sat beside her on the settee, her shrewd eyes taking in every detail of Yara's appearance.

The servant placed a full cup in front of Yara. Yara all but attacked the water. She must have gone through whatever provisions she'd had, not knowing how long the journey through the Outlands would take.

"I think we should hold off on interrogating the poor girl until she's cleaned up and gotten some rest," Miraya said.

Kalla looked unconcerned. "Is that an order or a suggestion?"

The look Miraya gave her was worthy of any Kahl. "It's an order."

Kalla's red lips curved into a smile. "Very well. We will reconvene this afternoon."

I shifted on my feet, annoyed with having to wait for answers even if I agreed that Yara was in desperate need of a bath and probably sleep as well. Resigned, Mason and I excused ourselves as the others waited for Master Hathney.

"I'll see you later?" I said as Mason and I parted ways near the throne room.

He nodded, and then hesitated. Before he could bring up the nightmare he'd woken me from, I mumbled something about finding breakfast and hurried away. I could feel his gaze on me until I rounded the corner and sagged against the wall.

I appreciated his concern, but my nightmares needed to remain solely in my head. Talking about them would make them more real.

I walked into the Hall of Memories and stopped short. Having spent hours in this stretch of stone and history, I knew that something was different. I scanned the rows of carved columns until I saw it: the shadow of one column was darker than the rest.

I inched forward. My feet whispered against the stone, and I thanked Mason for the lessons in how to move like him. I wasn't as light on my feet as he was, but this would do.

The murmur of voices disturbed the space. There was some-one hidden back there. Two someones. Their combined shad-ows had cast the column in darker relief.

Positioning myself behind the depiction of a three-story temple and a long line of warrior *mahjo*, I strained my ears. I couldn't make out much. They were speaking too quietly. A beat of silence fell, and then the two figures stepped out from behind the column. My lips parted in surprise.

It was Reev. He was with a sentinel I didn't recognize. Whatever they'd been discussing must have been serious, because Reev's eyes had an unfamiliar chill. He looked like a sentinel.

What if Reev's badgering yesterday about where I was going hadn't been just brotherly concern? He had warned me to be careful because of trouble with the sentinels.

Had he known there would be an attack on Kalla's tower?

Reev's companion left in the opposite direction. I waited until he was gone before I stepped out from my hiding spot, not both-ering to conceal the sound of my footsteps.

When Reev saw me, he froze. A guarded look flashed across his face before his expression settled into a neutral smile. My stomach clenched.

"What are you doing here?" he asked. He turned away, head-ing toward the corridor that led up to our rooms. I hurried to catch up.

"Who was that?" I asked, trying to sound as casual as I could with my heart drumming in my ears.

Reev took a second to answer. "An old friend."

"Do you talk to all your old friends in dark corners?"

He didn't respond. A muscle jumped in his cheek. I dug my nails into my palms, afraid to ask the question weighing on my mind but even more afraid of the answer.

"Reev," I said. Although I tried to hide my fear, he must have heard it, because he stopped and looked down at me.

His expression softened, and his smile was genuine. I wanted desperately to touch him.

Instead, I said, "Promise you won't keep any more secrets from me."

Reev's smile splintered for a moment, and something flickered behind his eyes.

He continued walking. "Of course," he said. He didn't look at me again.

CHAPTER 8

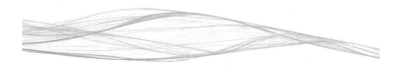

"SOMETIMES OUR BORDER PATROLS CROSSED PATHS WITH YOUR sentinels. Most of them ignored us, but a few were friendly. That's how we knew where Ninurta might be. Or, at least, that's what I was told." Yara's smile was apologetic.

As Miraya had ordered, we were back in the waiting room. Except for Mason, who remained impatiently outside. The only reason I was allowed to be here was because Miraya still hoped I would consent to be her adviser.

Yara had bathed and changed into a faded white-and-red servant tunic. Master Hathney had a tailor bring in some nicer tunics for her, but as a servant herself, Yara had refused to dress "above my station." I'd heard him grumbling about it during lunch.

Without the caking of dust, the other signs of her weariness were visible. There were bruises beneath her eyes that I didn't think any amount of sleep would cure. Bright-red patches of dry, irritated skin covered her cheeks, and I'd caught sight of numerous blisters on her palms that had burst and scabbed over. Miraya had mentioned sending a medic to see her once we were finished here.

"And how did you know about Kalla?" I asked. Something about Yara's explanation felt off to me.

Yara looked at me. She was perched rigidly in her chair, as if afraid to relax in front of Miraya and Kalla. There was a slight tremor in her legs, like she was trying not to collapse into the cushion. The few hours of rest hadn't been nearly enough.

"From the goddess," she said earnestly.

"Goddess?"

"I've never actually seen her," Yara said. "I would never presume to be worthy of such an honor. She presents herself only to my Kahl and his Council."

"And she told them about Kalla?" Miraya asked skeptically.

Yara nodded. "And she promised my Kahl that she would protect me in my journey. Her reassurance gave me the strength to leave home and ride alone into the Yellow Wastes."

I drummed my fingers against the stuffed arm of the chair I was sitting in, and wondered if she could be telling the truth. She and her horse had, after all, somehow escaped being easy prey for the gargoyles.

"I'm ashamed to say that, after a week, I'd begun to lose hope," Yara continued. "But here I am, safely delivered as she promised."

I gaped. "You were alone in the Outlands for a *week*?"

Her face flushed. "I lost my compass after the first day, and I kept circling back on my own tracks. The sight of your great walls . . ." She released a shaky breath. "The sight of your walls brought me to tears. I had begun to fear the Yellow Wastes would see me dead, even though the goddess's promise urged me on."

"Why did your Kahl decide now was the time to make contact?" Miraya asked.

"We haven't seen your border patrols in months. We knew something must have happened, and the goddess confirmed that now was the time to seek you out."

Miraya regarded Yara for so long that the girl began to squirm. I opened my mouth to break the tension as Miraya finally said, "Why are you really here?"

Yara's expression went from nervous to grim. Her weary face grew even more haggard. "Lanathrill needs urgent help. We've been invaded, and we don't have the strength to stop them. We'll be overrun if you don't help us."

"Invaded by *whom*?" Miraya asked.

Yara looked down. "Demons."

I frowned. "What do you mean?"

She picked agitatedly at the dry skin around her nails. "The demons we've always watched from afar have grown bold enough to cross our borders. They've killed everyone they've come across, and our soldiers are no match."

Did she mean the gargoyles? "What do they look like?" I asked.

"Monstrous," she said, lowering her voice as if talking about them would summon one to the palace. "Twice the girth of my horse and twice as tall as well, with horns and scaly skin and—" She closed her eyes with a shudder. "You must know what I'm talking about. Your sentinels, the ones who patrolled your borders—they've seen them."

I had no idea, but those didn't sound like gargoyles. The creatures that had hunted me and Avan in the forest had been overgrown lizards, sleek and long, not nearly the height of our Gray. Maybe these "demons" were some other creature that had been mutated by Rebirth.

"Please," she said, clasping her hands in front of her. "You must believe me. I did not travel all this way only to deceive you."

It was hard *not* to believe her when she had wandered through the Outlands for a week, on nothing but a promise from some nebulous goddess.

"What makes you think we can help?" Miraya asked.

It was a good question. Ninurta wasn't exactly in a solid position at the moment. We had enough problems of our own without adding someone else's.

"The demons never attacked your border patrols," Yara said. "There must be something about your sentinels that they fear. With that kind of help, and with our combined numbers, we might have a chance at running them out of Lanathrill."

Miraya scrutinized her. She still looked more sentinel than Kahl, but this unlikely visit had helped to adjust the mantle of leadership on her shoulders.

Kalla had listened to the entire exchange in silence, her face as still as marble. If Ninu had sentinels patrolling the border— it was a shock that we even *had* a border—then she must have known Lanathrill existed. What else might she be hiding?

"If this is all the information you can offer us, then we will need to discuss the matter privately," Miraya said.

Yara bit her lip, looking despondent.

With the meeting over, I left to find Mason gone. He must have gotten bored waiting. I'd fill him in later.

I headed back to my room to change for a run. Running helped me think. Before Hina had left the city to return to Etu Gahl, she had forced me into daily runs with her, claiming the exercise would improve my stamina. After a while, I grew to enjoy it.

Ninu's oasis—the only place in Ninurta where the trees weren't bare and brittle—held a myriad of wandering paths that made for a peaceful run. On my way there, a noise I'd never heard before drew me away from the path, toward a border of hedges surrounding a small pond.

Drinking from the pond was what I could only assume to be Yara's horse. Two sentinels stood nearby, looking rather mystified with how to handle the creature. I stared blatantly for a long while, watching as the animal's regal head dipped for another drink of water. Its mane and tail were a darker brown than its coat, and I wanted very much to touch the coarse hairs.

Although many of our Grays shared its form, there was no equal to seeing a live horse. It was somehow more intimidating, especially because it was larger than a Gray. I watched the animal wander about the pond a moment longer, and I considered stepping past the row of hedges to actually approach the beast.

"Kai?"

I turned away from the horse to see Avan coming up the path. Smiling, I stepped away from the hedges and back toward the path where he'd stopped to wait for me. He looked nothing less than stunning in a fitted silver tunic with wide sleeves. His expression, however, was curiously somber.

"Hey," I said, trying for a lighthearted tone. "What's up?"

With a glance at my outfit, which he'd come to recognize as my running clothes, he tilted his head in the direction of the oasis. "I'll walk you."

Without a word, we made our way over the cobblestones that wended around the buildings. I looked up at him, watching his dark hair flutter around his ears. My cheeks grew warm when I realized I was thinking about how soft the strands had felt between my fingers.

"How was the meeting?" he asked.

"Informative." I gave him a quick summary. Kalla had excluded Avan from government-related decisions right from the start, which was how I'd known she hadn't been coaching him to become Kahl even before we learned about Miraya. I had initially worried that Avan was meant to replace Ninu not only as Conquest but also as Kahl. "We'll have to wait and see what Kalla and Miraya decide."

"I've learned I'm not very good at waiting. Have I always been impatient?"

"Not at all."

His gaze was unfocused, and his thoughts turned inward. "Sometimes when I'm with you," Avan said, "I get this feeling like I've been waiting a long time for you."

I tucked my hands into my pockets to keep them still as I studied his profile. He had yet to look at me. We continued in silence for another few steps before I looked down at the cobblestones and gave up trying to find whatever it was I wanted to see in his face.

"We're both waiting, aren't we?" I asked. "We're waiting for you to remember."

"*You're* waiting for me to remember," he said gently. "I don't know what it is *I'm* waiting for anymore."

My hands curled into fists in my pockets. Despite the kiss, maybe the incident with his dad and then the fire in the tower had pushed him into a decision. Maybe he thought he'd be happier without his past.

"Doesn't it bother you?" I asked, a sudden gust of annoyance sharpening my words. "Not knowing?"

He'd asked me the same thing once. *Why are you so content not knowing?*

But I hadn't been content. The not knowing had bothered me—it *still* bothered me—and while I had learned to live with the questions, to accept that I might never find the answers, I had never stopped asking them.

"How could it not?" he said. "What I've learned from you has helped, but we both know it's not enough. What good are secondhand accounts of a life I might never remember?"

Avan and I weren't so different. I had been Infinite once, until that life had been taken from me by Kronos. He had left me to a young, confused sentinel when I was eight, and I had no memory from before then. Hadn't I decided that this new life, the only one I'd ever known, was the one I wanted to keep? Avan's existence as an Infinite might have only just begun, but how could I argue with him for making the same decision?

I wasn't ready to let him go, but it was selfish of me to hope that he would pick his old life for me, to think that I held that much weight. He barely knew me.

I hunched my shoulders, as if that might somehow protect my heart from the pain that squeezed it. "Maybe . . ." I tried to shrug. "Maybe you should take more time to think about it. Being around each other all the time probably isn't helping. Maybe you need some space to figure things out."

We stopped before the line of bushes that marked the entrance into the oasis. I awkwardly waited for him to respond.

He reached out, his warm fingers grazing my cheek. I had to resist leaning into his touch. "I think maybe that's what we both need."

I didn't reply, because there was nothing else to say.

"We'll talk again soon," Avan said lightly. "Maybe we'll both have figured things out then."

The moment he turned away, I rushed into the oasis, my legs picking up speed until I was sprinting. Fronds and low branches slapped against my cheeks and snagged my hair, but I didn't mind the stings. What I couldn't bear would've been to watch him leave.

CHAPTER 9

I RETURNED A COUPLE OF HOURS LATER, SWEATY AND EXHAUSTED, to find a summons. Miraya wanted to see me again.

I groaned. Dinner would be served soon, and I was ravenous. I cleaned up quickly, made a short stop in the kitchens to steal a bread roll—the chef liked me because I was excessive in my compliments—and reported back to the waiting room. Miraya and Kalla must not have left since our last meeting.

Yara wasn't present, and I wondered if that meant good news or bad.

"We will not be sending an army to Lanathrill's aid," Miraya said without preamble.

I stuffed my mouth with bread and nodded. There was wisdom in that considering the unrest among the sentinels.

"However, they're the only contact we've had with other survivors since Rebirth, and if we're to be neighbors, then we can't turn them away." Miraya looked unhappy about it.

"Did you know about Lanathrill?" I asked Kalla.

"Yes, but Ninu chose to keep hidden the truth of the outside world," Kalla said. "I know little about Lanathrill beyond the fact that it exists. My priority was to monitor Ninu, and since he'd wanted nothing to do with Lanathrill, I put them out of my concern. Only a handful of his top sentinels know."

"The ones Yara said patrolled the border?" I waited until she nodded, and then said, "Who else knew?" Istar had been Ninu's ally, for whatever reason, so she must have known as well. Had Irra known?

"I don't see how it matters," Kalla said.

"It matters because all of you knew that this entire other country was out there, and no one thought to tell the rest of us."

Miraya coughed pointedly. "What matters *now* is the situation at hand. I want to know what exactly is happening in Lanathrill, and whether these creatures pose a threat to Ninurta. I'll allow Yara to guide a group of sentinels back to assess the situation. If their need is as dire as Yara claims, then I'll reconsider sending reinforcements."

"And what does Ninurta get out of helping them?" I asked.

Miraya glanced at Kalla, whose lips held a hint of approval. Helping Lanathrill had to be about more than cultivating goodwill between neighbors. As Kahl, Miraya would have to put Ninurta's best interests before anything else.

"If communication and travel are opened between the two countries," Kalla said, "it would be the first concerted effort to begin rebuilding your world. A road would be constructed. The exchange of goods and information could be negotiated."

I forgot my irritation in the sudden possibilities that her words unlocked. The prospect of something *new*, of expanding beyond the confines of Ninurta's walls, filled me with a sense of exhilaration. This could be the beginning of restoring human-kind to more than a race of people who cowered behind stone walls and scrounged what they could to get by.

"This would prove to the rebel sentinels and to any other dis-senters that my loyalties lie with the people of Ninurta," Miraya said. "They might finally see reason and support me as their Kahl."

"Sounds like you don't really need an adviser." I brushed bread crumbs off my fingers and settled back into the armchair.

"Actually, I do." She smoothed her fingers along the hem of her tunic. "If you're to be my adviser, then I have my first task for you: I need you to accompany Yara and the sentinels to Lanathrill."

I stared at her. Her gaze was steady. She was serious.

"The sentinels are going only as your guard. You will be my official liaison."

I straightened against the cushions. This was one drek of a first test for a new adviser. "Wouldn't one of the ministers be better qualified?"

"I can't trust them to make the right decisions for Ninurta. They've held their positions for too long. Some of them might view associating with Lanathrill as a threat rather than progress." She looked down into her lap, and the mask of confidence cracked. She seemed uncomfortable again with the power she'd been given. "I'm still working on earning their full trust." She shook her head. "I can't send any of them. It has to be you."

I rubbed my forehead—so many questions and doubts. She wanted *me* to represent Ninurta, and to make the call on whether Lanathrill needed our help. I could be the deciding factor in the formation of the first political alliance in two centuries.

I stood. I felt Miraya's eyes on me as I paced along the side of the room.

What if I decided that Lanathrill was fine? What then?

Although I didn't think Yara would risk her life crossing the Outlands if they didn't truly need help, it was still possible that they'd simply panicked at the sight of demonic-looking creatures on their land. If that was the case, then it should be easy enough to help them rally and strategize their defense. Not that I knew anything about that, but surely the sentinels would?

I couldn't believe I was even considering this. Hadn't I determined that I didn't want Ninurta's problems heaped on top of my own? But I couldn't deny that a part of me liked the idea of going north—that same part of me that had enjoyed mentally mapping the streets of the Lower Alley by getting lost and then navigating my way back to familiar paths, the part that had fallen in love with the forest and the promise of discovery in all its unexplored corners.

But going to Lanathrill meant leaving behind Reev. And Avan.

I swallowed at the reminder of my last conversations with both of them.

"Kai?" Miraya said.

The rug was a blur of colors beneath my feet. I forced myself to stop pacing. She looked as anxious for my answer as I felt. Kalla was, as usual, the picture of poise.

Maybe . . . Maybe leaving could be a good thing. An opportunity to give me and Avan the space we needed as well as a chance to figure out how to reach Reev without constantly questioning our every interaction.

"Do you agree?" Miraya asked.

Before I could talk myself out of it, I said, "Yes. I'll go."

Preparations for our departure began immediately. We would give Yara a couple more days to recuperate before setting out. Having a small contingent of sentinels with us should be enough to deter the gargoyles, but we would also be riding scouts, which were fast enough to outpace them. Yara's horse would have to stay behind. The beast would never be able to keep up.

I'd never ridden or operated a Gray by myself. Unless I wanted to ruin the entire journey by falling off my scout and breaking my neck right out the door, I decided I should probably learn.

The day before our departure, I met with Mason by the stable. It wasn't a stable in the traditional sense—not in the way they were described in the history texts. This stable was a pavilion with no walls, the roof held up by sturdy wooden corner and support beams. The scouts rested in a long line of stalls on one side. They were identical: sleek and catlike, their metal bodies shining from polish and the servants' care. Their construction was more rigorous than the normal Grays, needing to withstand more than the typical deterioration from use. They were compact in size, but they ran on two energy stones to enhance speed and performance.

Mason walked me over to a scout that was lying on its stomach, its head pillowed on its paws. Despite the metal body, it was eerily lifelike. Mason leaned down to touch the controls on the scout's neck.

Its silver eyelids sprang open. I jumped. Mason looked amused by my reaction as he straightened. The scout's luminous eyes had the same red light as the energy stones emanating from the vents in its chest. I stepped back as the scout rose to its feet. It followed Mason out of its stall. The scout only reached Mason's chest. Its length, however, was at least six feet, excluding its tail, which was currently curled around one of its hind legs.

"Scouts are designed for ease of operation in case, you know, we're being chased by gargoyles and don't have time to fiddle with a bunch of dials," Mason said. He motioned for me to move in closer so I could examine the control panel.

I lifted one eyebrow at his instructor tone. Months ago, Mason had trained me and Avan in Etu Gahl in order to prepare us to infiltrate the White Court and rescue Reev. Although his demeanor in the training circle was the opposite of his usual affable self, he had proved to be a demanding but effective instructor.

The control panel was sparse, nothing like the controls on Avan's Gray. There was only a button and a lever.

"Here's the starter. Self-explanatory. Press it again to switch it off. When the lever is in this position, the scout is either at rest or a slow walk. Flip it over one, and you can move the scout into a run. Last setting is only for when you're being chased by gargoyles. That kind of speed burns up too much energy. Everything else is intuitive. The scouts have the most advanced system of all the Grays. It works seamlessly with the magic from the energy stones."

He rubbed his palm up the scout's neck to its ears, and I swear its metal body rippled with pleasure. A contoured leather seat was affixed to the scout's back, along with footrests. Mason slipped his foot in the notch and swung his leg over the scout, settling into the padded seat. He touched both hands to palm-shaped grips on either side of the scout's neck, right above its shoulders.

"Hold your hands here to keep from falling off and to activate the sensors. The scout will monitor your body's signals for where to move and how fast to run. There are two more sensors by your legs. There's also a brake by your footrest for emergencies, but otherwise, that's about it. These things are magic and metal harmony. Anyone could operate them."

"Looks easy enough," I said.

"I'll show you, and then you can try on your own." He adjusted the lever on the scout's neck, and flashed me a grin, his sandy hair falling over his brow. I returned his smile and moved back to give him space.

The scout stepped forward, slowly at first, but then Mason smirked, and the scout leaped into a sprint. Its metal paws barely seemed to touch the floor as it made a wide circle around the stable. It took a corner at breathtaking speed. I expected Mason to crash, but he didn't. They flew past me in a blur of metal and blue tunic as they turned into another lap.

Mason circled back around and brought the scout to a stop in the same place they'd begun. He looked mussed but elated, his blue eyes bright. His enthusiasm was catching.

He slid off the seat and motioned for me to take his place. Heart thudding, I approached the scout. Mason's hands brushed over my waist as I put my leg over the scout and sank down onto the seat. It was warm from Mason's body heat, a pleasant contrast to the cool metal.

His fingers positioned mine on the sensors, his touch featherlight. I adjusted my legs, resting the balls of my feet on the footrests. Backing away, he gave a nod of approval.

"Lean forward a bit to get it moving," he said.

My pulse drummed loudly as I took a steadying breath and leaned forward. The scout stirred beneath me, the motion startling at first but only because I was unsure of what to expect. The scout operated much more smoothly than Avan's Gray. It hardly jostled me, unlike the way I sometimes felt bouncing in the saddle behind Avan. I grinned and leaned in more, my thighs tightening around the metal, urging it to go faster.

The scout sped up, taking great leaping strides down the length of the stable. My hair flapped behind me as I let out a laugh. The ground was much closer than it had been on the Gray, and it was a brown smear as we flew around a corner. The scout adjusted to my body's commands like we were one creature, one mind in shared motion.

We made two laps around the stable, and then I eased back, digging my feet in. The scout slowed, loping forward until it came to stop beside Mason. I flicked the lever to its first setting and hopped off.

"That was amazing!" I said. I felt winded, my limbs vibrating with energy as if I had been the one running.

"You're a natural," Mason said. He rested his hand on one of the sensors and guided the scout into its stall.

"Thank you for showing me. I . . ." As my pulse slowed to a normal pace, the reality of my leaving crept into the space between us, making me nervous all over again. Mason was always such a bright spot amid all the uncertainties around me. "I'll miss you."

"Will you?" he asked with a pleased twist of his mouth. He brushed a strand of hair off my cheek. "Even though I'll be right next to you?"

My eyes widened. "You're coming?" I flung my arms around him. The journey felt suddenly less daunting.

He laughed and lifted me off my feet with a squeeze before setting me down. "I was hoping you'd be glad."

"You volunteered, didn't you?"

He gave a shrug and a half smile that meant he did.

I pressed a kiss to his cheek. "Thank you."

His smile had faltered. His eyes watched me with a cautious tenderness. "Careful," he said. "I might let this go to my head."

I let go of his shoulders. My cheeks felt hot. "Sorry."

He put up his hands. "I wasn't complaining."

With a laugh, I brushed back my windblown hair. "I need to go talk to Reev. I'll see you later."

CHAPTER 10

THE THRILL OF RIDING THE SCOUT SOON FADED AS I SEARCHED for Reev.

Reev had yet to confront me about my part in the journey, or about my new position as the Kahl's adviser. He might have been avoiding me. It hurt, and while it underscored how the time apart might do us both some good, I wasn't about to leave Ninurta without talking about it.

I eventually tracked him down to Irra's lab on one of the lower levels of Kalla's tower. He'd been here often over the past weeks. I pounded against the thick stone door with the flat of my hand so he would hear me.

When no one answered, I pressed both palms against the door and shoved. It opened with the rumble of stone on stone and the screech of old hinges. Steam blasted my face. I wrinkled my nose and waved frantically at the vapors as I peered into the room. Inside was a flurry of cables, levers, and cogs, all of which were obscured by the steam spewing from some hissing contraption in the middle of the room. The diffused glow from several lamps didn't help much, nor did the two vents above the door.

Standing near the steam contraption was Irra, his tall form a sliver of shadow in the hazy room. He was writing on a pad of paper, his head bowed, his face a stark contrast of dark and light. He looked like a madman overseeing his invention.

Reev was fiddling with wires off to the side, his back to me. His damp hair clung to his scalp and his tunic molded wetly to his skin, outlining the muscles in his shoulders and back. He leaned over a control panel not unlike what I'd seen on the Grays, and the angle gave me a clear view of his collar. He still tried to hide it even though we now both knew what it meant.

Neither of them seemed concerned about the damp or the heat. They didn't even look up at me when the door loudly announced my arrival.

"Um," I said, raising my voice above the hiss of machinery. "Busy?"

Irra finished whatever he was writing with a flourish and set his pad and quill pen on a counter. How was he writing on wet paper?

He smiled at me, his brown eyes liquid pools in the soupy light. "All packed for your journey?"

"Yep." I didn't have much to pack. Miraya would see to it that we had enough provisions.

"Thinking about coming along?" I asked, only half joking. Having an Infinite in the party would probably be an asset, and I wasn't about to ask Avan.

"No," Irra said, joining me by the door where it wasn't so steamy. The cool air from the hallway was a relief.

Reev continued working. He had yet to acknowledge me. I had the urge to march up behind him and give him a good shake. Or a kick.

"My role in Ninurta's conflicts has ended now that Ninu is gone. Once I've provided Miraya with an alternative power source for the city that isn't reliant upon magic, I will return to Etu Gahl. When I do, it is unlikely I will come back."

The prospect of never seeing him again hit me with a shock of sadness. When had I begun to like Irra, much less care for him? It had crept up on me, and I hadn't even noticed.

"But I can visit, right?" I felt foolish for needing to ask. "In the Void. You'll open your gates for me?"

Irra smiled. "Etu Gahl will always welcome you."

The tightness in my chest eased. I told myself it was because Hina lived in Etu Gahl, and I wanted to see her again.

"And when you are the Keeper of Time, you will not need me to show you the way," he said.

His words reminded me of Kalla's promise to keep Kronos away so long as I was Miraya's adviser.

"I was wondering . . . If the position of Conquest can be passed to an unexpected successor, can the same be done for Kronos?" Not that I wanted some unfortunate soul plucked out from his or her life the way Ninu had been when he was made Conquest, but it was an alternative I had at least briefly entertained.

Irra smiled at my question. "Theoretically, yes. But as his position is of vital importance, Kronos took strides to prevent such a necessity. He wanted to ensure that he would be present to guide his heir in her duties rather than to allow a newly made Infinite to flounder in her sudden responsibilities."

"But how would you even begin to learn the kind of things the Infinite do?"

"Kronos will teach you," he said patiently, which made me want to roll my eyes.

"Yes, but I mean if I was in Avan's position. Newly made."

"Much of it is inherent. Istar, for example, took up her mantle with ease. She'd been an assassin in her mortal life, so Strife was hardly a foreign concept to her. Stirring the humans to battle and war was a skill she enjoyed honing." He spoke of her with distaste, with which I could only agree. "Avan's disposition is yet to be seen. Conquest was . . . Well, Ninu aside, like most of us, Conquest must learn to exist within his own balance, although the scale could—and often does—tip one way or the other depending on the situation."

I rubbed at my neck, where moisture was beginning to collect from the heat. "Are you talking about good and evil?"

Irra smiled. "A conqueror may become either a benevolent ruler or a hated tyrant."

"I suppose, although it depends on where you're standing. No one ever really *wants* to be conquered."

He nodded, conceding the point. "Enough talk of the Infinite. When does your party leave?"

"In the morning. And what about you? Will you stay until the rebels are dealt with? Miraya might need your help again."

"Perhaps, but the conflict with the sentinels is not my concern." He flicked at a droplet of water that had condensed at the tip of his nose. The steam made his hair stick out from his head even more wildly than usual. "And if I'm not mistaken, it is my presence to which the rebels object. My leaving might mollify them."

"Or give them an opening to attack Miraya again," I said.

Irra shrugged, and the soft spot in my chest for him was elbowed aside by annoyance. Sometimes I forgot that the Infinite—those who'd always been Infinite, like Irra and Kalla—weren't capable of the same depth of emotion as humans. Not that I'd seen anyway. Fortunately, they were good at reminding me.

"Well, if you can spare him, I want to talk to Reev."

Over by the control panel, Reev stilled. "Give me a minute," he said quietly.

Irra walked past me, his damp robes making a squelching sound as they slapped against the door. "You may talk here. I'll be back in a bit."

I watched him leave. Then as I waited for Reev to stop stalling, I wandered cautiously around the room. I didn't know what any of the objects did. A metal tube ran from the steam contraption across the floor into the wall where, through a vent, I could see the red coals of a furnace. I stepped over wires and stray cogs, listening to the hiss of hot water and the well-oiled tinker of turning gears. There was a spark here and there, like the beginnings of a flame except blue instead of red.

I fanned myself, but it was useless. This was worse than being in the bathhouse in Etu Gahl. My clothes had begun to suction unpleasantly onto my skin.

"We're working on a replacement power source for the Grays," Reev said. He finally looked at me. "The Grays will have to be completely redesigned, and the finished model won't be nearly as smooth, but it should work. We're just modifying the same technology that used to move the trains."

"I see," I said, although I didn't. His face was fuzzy through the mist, so I moved closer until only a few feet of space was between us. I felt hot and uncomfortable, and I didn't want to dance around the topic now that we were talking. "Why haven't you said anything about my leaving?"

Reev tilted his head back, running his fingers through his wet hair. "Would anything I say change your mind?"

"No."

"Well, then."

"So you say nothing at all?" The frustration boiled over. Maybe it was the heat. Or the fact I was leaving soon and I wouldn't have to face the consequences of my words, but I couldn't stand the awkwardness between us anymore. "Why won't you talk to me? If . . . If you want to be free of your responsibility to me, then—"

His hands gripped my shoulders, startling me. Suddenly, I was wrapped in his arms. I hugged him back, a lump forming in my throat.

"Never," he said into my hair. "You went into the Void and back for me. I'm not worried about a little trip up north."

I pressed my lips to his damp shoulder. I believed him, but there was more to it than he was saying. "I heard that Miraya asked you to go with us."

Reev was silent for too long. I eased out of his arms, our wet tunics peeling apart. I caught a stormy look on his face that brightened too quickly for me to be sure I'd seen it.

"I have things I need to do here," he said. "Whatever you find in Lanathrill, I know you'll be fine. You don't need me looking out for you anymore."

I rested my hands against his back and looked up, studying the line of his jaw. I wasn't worried about Lanathrill. The demons would be a danger, but my excitement to see the world north of the Outlands had only grown in the last two days. My concern was about whom I'd be leaving behind. Knowing that the distance might benefit all of us didn't make going away any easier.

That evening, Mason and I took scouts around the White Court to ensure that I felt comfortable with steering. If we ran into gargoyles, I wanted to feel in control of the scout. Mason led me through areas of the White Court I hadn't even known were there—narrow passageways between the barracks and a tunnel that ran beneath the Watchmen Academy. We ended up racing down the main road and laughing at the way the Watchmen glowered at our recreational defiance of regulation speeds.

The next morning, our group of seven gathered outside the palace gates. The scouts were lined up along the street, drawing quite the attention. Our supplies had been secured in compartments hidden within the scouts' bodies, which could be accessed by either unlatching our seats or sliding open a slot in the scouts' hindquarters.

I didn't recognize any of the sentinels accompanying us. There were four in addition to Mason. Yara, who'd been given riding lessons of her own, bounced on her heels, eager to set out.

She waved when she saw me and rushed over, looking considerably better than she had a couple days ago. The irritated patches on her cheeks had been eased by heavy lotions, and although she still had weary smudges beneath her eyes, they had lightened somewhat. The blue tattoo high on her left cheekbone wrinkled a bit as she grinned.

We exchanged greetings before I glanced over my shoulder, at the footpath that led through the grounds to Kalla's tower. Mason called me from the gates, and I reluctantly looked away. I had said my good-byes to Reev, but I hadn't seen Avan since our talk outside the oasis.

I squashed the disappointment. Seeing each other again would have just muddled things even more.

Mason glanced at my riding outfit. "You look ready for an adventure."

I smiled. I was covered from neck to toes in a fitted gray tunic, matching pants, and leather boots. The fabric was light enough for the heat of the Outlands, but when the temperature dropped at night, I had a thick hooded cloak in my bag. The cloak was something I would have loved during my first venture into the Outlands.

The sentinels had on their standard leather, and Mason wore a flattering navy tunic. He had met the sentinels already, so he made quick introductions for me. Of the four sentinels, only two looked excited about leaving. The others, two women named Gret and Winnifer, grumbled to each other about the long journey ahead.

"All right, boss," Mason said to me, settling into his scout's leather seat. "Ready to . . ." His eyes focused on something behind me.

I turned. Avan was coming down the footpath, his dark hair and crimson tunic unmistakable. I sucked in my breath and held it. *Calm down*, I told myself firmly.

As he neared, his steps grew less hurried. He hunched his shoulders a bit, as if embarrassed by his haste. I walked up to meet him so that our conversation wouldn't be overheard.

"Hey," he said, sounding a little out of breath.

"Hey," I echoed, unable to keep from smiling.

"I was worried you'd left already," he said, looking down and then back to me. "I wasn't going to come, but . . . I had to."

"Thank you for seeing me off," I said. We stood there for a few seconds more as I held on to so many things that couldn't be said.

Too often in these last few months, I'd caught myself smiling at a memory of us from school or in his shop or in Etu Gahl. The first couple of times, he had asked what was so funny, so I'd told him. His eyes had grown remote, as if saddened by his inability to share those moments with me.

Now, I was reminded of that night months ago when we had prepared to leave Ninurta for the first time. How hastily we'd made the decision, and how adamant Avan had been about coming with me. So many times I wished I'd had the good sense to steal his Gray and leave on my own. But it wouldn't have done any good. After his deal with Kronos, he probably would have found another Gray and followed me.

His lips tightened. "Please be careful. You don't know anything about Lanathrill or the people there."

"That's why we're going," I said, my smile broadening.

"Promise me you'll be careful."

Once, he would have told me, "Stay safe."

I nodded and murmured, "Of course."

"Kai!" Mason called from the street. I waved, knowing everyone was waiting for me.

Avan met Mason with a slight frown and a nod, and Mason answered the gesture with equal enthusiasm. I didn't understand the wariness between them. The two had exchanged no more than half a dozen words since Avan was made Infinite. I had expected Mason to share my conflicted feelings—or to at least possess some empathy for what they'd done to Avan. But Mason had taken Reev's position on the matter. Mason's loyalty to the Infinite began and ended at Irra, but his outright distrust of Avan still surprised me.

As I was turning away, Avan caught my hand. Seeing the concern in his face was almost like looking at my Avan.

"I have something for you." He reached into his pocket and withdrew something small, cradled within his palm. He uncurled his fingers and presented it to me. It was a silver leaf brooch with the barest shimmer of translucent green. "For your cloak."

My fingertips brushed against his palm as I took it from him. The silver was warm from being in his pocket. "Thank you."

"It's weird, but I thought . . ." His fingers picked absentmindedly at his tunic, right above the spot on his chest where three green leaves adorned his otherwise stark tattoo. "I thought a leaf would be right."

He'd told me once that the leaves of his tattoo symbolized the start of something new—something *good*—in what had been a rather bleak life. And that each new leaf added would represent gradual changes toward something better.

My fist tightened around the brooch, its ridges digging into my palm. Did he realize the significance of those leaves on his chest? Or the leaf he was giving me? I doubted it, and yet some part of him must have remembered.

He gave me his crooked smile. "I'll see you when you get back." Neither of us said good-bye.

CHAPTER 11

WE WERE A SPECTACLE LEAVING THE WHITE COURT.

Seven scouts on the main road drew a lot of attention. Other riders craned their necks to watch as they passed us on the opposite side of the road. People gathered along the sidewalk. They muttered among themselves, probably speculating as to what we were doing.

After the Watchmen had led Yara into the city on her horse, news of her arrival had rapidly spread. However, I doubted that anyone outside of Miraya's immediate council—and our group—knew where Yara had come from or why. I didn't think even the ministers had been informed.

Leaving under so much attention felt less exhilarating and more apprehensive. I wished we'd arranged to meet at the city gates instead.

Beneath the curiosity, I could sense the hostility—the distrust of the White Court and the sentinels, the certainty that our party could mean nothing good for them. In their position, I would have felt the same.

There was nothing I could do to put their fears to rest. So I kept my hands on the sensors and my eyes forward. Someday, maybe, Miraya could fill the chasm between the White Court and the North District.

Up ahead, the Watchmen threw open the city gates. Like that night Avan and I had left Ninurta, the open gates provided an unobstructed view of the Outlands: flat, cracked earth with low, craggy rock formations to break up the monotony. How had Yara been able to stand a week out there with only her horse as a companion?

According to Yara, her horse had been bred for speed and endurance, but she had still needed to stop often to rest and water the animal. On our scouts, as long as we didn't run out of energy stones, we'd be much faster. Scouts could outpace a gargoyle, but they weren't meant to maintain those speeds for long periods of time. It would cause too much strain on the creatures' joints and gears. Our actual pace would probably match Avan's Gray, which had been modified to be faster than regulation.

Still, we'd be traveling twice as fast as Yara had, and we could conceivably reach what Yara claimed to be Lanathrill's border in only a day's time.

The Watchmen saluted us as we rode through the gates, Yara and I in the lead with Mason directly behind me. The knots in my stomach grew tighter as we spilled into the Outlands. Yara directed her scout northward, and the rest of us followed. She was grinning, her face aimed into the wind. Her short hair fluttered against her forehead. My own hair was braided tight and coiled into a bun at the base of my neck, as Hina had taught me.

Crossing the Outlands on my own Gray was starkly different from riding behind someone else. I couldn't rest even for a moment, no matter how tired I was or how stiff my arms and legs grew. I could shift a bit on the seat, but it didn't do much to alleviate the numbness seeping into my butt.

We spotted gargoyles, but they kept their distance. Their large flat eyes watched us pass. They seemed disinterested in our party.

At noon, we stopped for a short lunch and to stretch our legs. My eyes and ears remained alert. I mostly took my cues from Mason and the others, whose senses were sharper than mine. Thirty minutes later, we were back on our scouts.

A couple of hours after, Mason rode up beside me. He flicked his head, indicating something to our left.

More gargoyles. Their lizard-like bodies darted over and around a gathering of boulders. However, something about these gargoyles was different.

I stared at them a moment longer but couldn't pinpoint what was wrong.

Then one gargoyle opened its mouth and its torso seemed to expand. My fingers tightened on the sensors as I watched it roar at the other gargoyles. Its mouth was massive. These gargoyles didn't have neck frills. Instead, what looked like bony spines protruded from beneath their jaws up to the crowns of their heads. The longer I looked, the more differences I could pick out. Even their front legs seemed longer to account for their heavier upper bodies.

Maybe these gargoyles had evolved differently from the ones near Ninurta. The thought was alarming because it also meant they might behave differently. These gargoyles might not hesitate to attack us.

I was on edge for hours, my eyes fixed on the slowly changing landscape around us, searching for movement. It didn't help that Yara seemed just as aware of the danger. She stared ahead, her fingers white where they gripped her scout. She was mouthing something I couldn't make out, but I'd be willing to bet she was praying to her goddess.

We rode until daylight was a golden blush across the horizon. The bright-red light from the chests of our scouts illuminated our way in the descending dark. We'd been riding for almost ten hours, and my body ached all the way from my shoulders down to the backs of my thighs.

An hour after nightfall, Yara slowed her scout and declared she would fall off if we didn't stop. We made camp by an old, scraggly tree, the branches of which we used for kindling. Winnifer got the fire going, then we circled our scouts around the flames and slept alongside the metal bodies so that, if gargoyles showed up, we could be riding away in an instant. After a dinner of dry sandwiches and vegetable soup, Mason and the sentinels agreed to take the watch in rotation. I hoped we'd left those strange-looking gargoyles far behind.

I pulled out my cloak to use as a blanket. The thick material made a good barrier against the cool air. Mason slept a few feet away, upright, his back against his scout's side. Firelight leaped across the bridge of his nose, his cheekbones, the swell of his bottom lip. His lowered lashes cast shadows beneath his eyes.

"You should sleep," he murmured. I looked away. I hadn't realized he was still awake. "You'll be tired in the morning."

"I know." My body was exhausted, but my mind refused to rest. My gaze shifted to the darkness beyond the reach of the fire, wondering what might be lurking there.

It was reassuring that Mason and the sentinels had excellent night vision. They would see and hear the gargoyles coming well before I did.

"There's nothing out there right now," Mason said.

I curled onto my side, tucking the cloak around my shoulder. "Right now," I echoed.

"Right now is all we have to work with." He looked at me. "Unless you can speed up time?"

I shook my head. I tried envisioning the threads, tried to imagine running my fingers along the delicate strands. My hands traced the hem of my tunic, as if the physical sensation might help. It was useless.

Low laughter reached us from across the campfire. Yara was grinning as she talked with a sentinel named Dennyl. She seemed to get along well with them.

"Do you know any of them?" I asked Mason with a nod at the sentinels.

"Not very well."

"What about your teammates? Were you able to find them?" I asked. Irra had first captured Mason when he and his team had been scouting the Void for Etu Gahl. Other hollows had cornered Mason and taken him back to the hidden fortress, where Irra had severed Mason's connection to Ninu, freeing him.

Despite the warmth of the firelight, Mason's face looked cold and hard. "Yes. But they were damaged beyond repair. Irra suspects the injuries to their minds were punishment for returning from the Void without me. He could do nothing for them."

His voice was quiet but terse, and I decided it was probably best to leave the topic alone.

"I'm sorry," I said.

He sank lower against the side of his scout, and his face was doused in shadow. Across from us, Yara and Dennyl both settled into their own blankets to sleep. Winnifer and Gret slept between me and Yara, their bodies curled together within the cradle of their two scouts. Their voices were a soft murmur over the snap of burning wood. Winnifer's hand rose in the darkness, her fingers brushing back the messy fall of Gret's hair.

"Don't look so sad," Mason said.

I forced my gaze away from the couple. "I'm not sad."

"Are you regretting coming?"

"No. I'm just . . ."

He flicked a pebble. It skittered through the dirt. "Thinking about the last time you were out here?"

I looked at him again, surprised, although I shouldn't have been. Mason was always too perceptive.

"Time to make new memories, I think," he murmured.

I tucked the cloak tighter around my shoulders. I thought about Avan: the angles of his body fitted to mine, his arm a pleasant weight around my waist, and his body heat warding off the chill of the Void. Avan might not remember, but I didn't want to forget.

New memories didn't have to mean replacing the old ones.

Aylis, the sentinel on watch, woke us when daylight began to seep across the Outlands.

When I tried to stand, I let out a surprised yelp. My stiff muscles ached. Gret looked unimpressed, and I glared at her. I was in decent shape, but I was no sentinel. I rubbed my palms into my lower back with a groan. Nearby, Aylis smothered the embers of our fire with dirt as Winnifer unpacked us a breakfast of crusty bread and cheese.

Mason was running a few laps around our camp to warm up his muscles in preparation for another day of riding. My sore back and legs would probably benefit from doing the same, so I jogged over to join him.

"Morning," I said as I matched his pace. My body relaxed into the movement.

"It is, isn't it?" he said, smiling. "Sleep well?"

He made the question sound casual, but I knew what he was really asking. I'd awoken sometime in the middle of the night to Mason's voice, calling me from my nightmare in a whisper to keep the others from waking.

I had opened my eyes and, for the span of a blink, the threads had fluttered around me, beckoning. But they had vanished just as quickly, and I didn't know if I'd seen right or if it had been merely a trick of the firelight. I'd wondered for a while now if my nightmares might somehow be related to the loss of my powers, as the two had happened at approximately the same time, but I wasn't sure how.

"Well enough," I said vaguely.

"Doesn't happen often, hmm?"

"Not particularly," I said, determined not to talk about it. I winced as the backs of my thighs twinged with pain.

I could practically see the internal struggle waging behind those perceptive blue eyes. After a moment, he seemed to concede, because he looked away.

"You'll get used to it," he said, meaning the ache in my muscles.

Funny how even the hint of Mason's instructor tone made my back snap straight. He seemed to realize it, too, because he smirked. I kicked out at his leg, but he easily dodged with a laugh.

Yara, bright-eyed and cheerful, walked around looking perfectly recovered. I knew Mason was right. But it would suck in the meantime.

We ran two more wide laps before joining the others. Things got a bit awkward when we all had to turn our backs to wash up, but then we regrouped for breakfast before I had to sink grudgingly back into that leather seat.

Yara kept her compass close at hand, determined not to lose it this time. Although we didn't have a map, she knew we had to head north, so north we went. The farther we traveled, the clearer it became that we were finally leaving the Outlands.

The rock formations grew higher, and there were copses of trees instead of lone skeletal ones. Some of the trees had leaves, although they were brittle and brown. Patches of yellow grass and weeds pushed out through the cracks in the earth, and I even spotted tiny blue wildflowers. The landscape was rapidly transforming, and I could feel Yara's anticipation grow stronger the more land we covered. She was eager to be home.

A few hours into the morning, there was actual grass beneath our scouts' feet. Not bright, healthy green grass but a pale frost green, each blade outlined in brown or yellow. Probably more weeds than grass—still, it was welcome. Trees became more frequent, their branches the same sickly green as the grass. Black birds with yellow-tipped wings took flight from the upper boughs as our passing scouts startled them.

And in the distance, becoming ever clearer against the horizon, were the jagged peaks of mountains.

The sight left me breathless. The excitement returned, fluttering through my stomach. I had known, rationally, that the Outlands had to end somewhere, but I'd never tried to imagine what lay beyond for fear there was nothing but more of the same emptiness.

The world suddenly didn't feel so alone.

CHAPTER 12

WE APPROACHED A BROOK. I'D NEVER SEEN A REAL ONE. I slowed my scout as we crossed. The water burbled merrily over the stones, cloudy but not nearly the brown murk of the river in Ninurta. I grinned at Mason, who was leaning over his scout to dip his fingers into the water.

Shortly before noon, Yara pointed ahead at a thinly wooded area we were fast approaching. "Lanathrill!" she shouted, beaming. "The woods mark our borders."

Mason threw me a mischievous smile. Then he leaned over his scout and rushed ahead in a burst of speed. I moved the lever on my scout's neck to its final setting, and then lowered myself over its powerful body as its legs sped up to follow Mason. Our scouts tore through overgrown weeds as we raced for the woods.

With a laugh, we broke through the trees, the metal paws of our scouts scattering dirt and leaves in our wake.

Crossing into Lanathrill lifted a weight from our party. Even Gret and Winnifer were in a better mood. The landscape changed more quickly now. Flat earth became cresting hills and deepening slopes. The grass remained dry and overgrown, but I noticed a few scattered patches of green. We passed a series of connected ponds, the water dark with algae. Frogs, fatter than the ones that hid in the muddy river in Ninurta, rustled through the reeds that sprouted in the shallows along the bank.

Trees stood in abundance. They were old, their scarred trunks tall and thick, gnarled about the roots. Their branches soared high above us, but their leaves, while dense, were speckled in yellow. Still, these trees had survived the war, clinging to life even now.

Warm air lifted loose strands of hair from my neck. I lifted my palm into the wind. The air tumbled and slid through my fingers, a meager imitation of the threads against my skin. My throat felt suddenly tight, and I lowered my hand.

We traveled more slowly, all of us wanting the opportunity to take everything in. This was nothing like the rich green forest bordering the Void, but it didn't matter. This was new and wondrous, and those far-off mountains loomed ever closer.

A half hour later, we came upon the first sign of human life. It was a farmhouse, made of wood with a thatched roof. The farmhouse was connected to a barn, and both buildings were encased by a low cobblestone fence.

A pall of gravity settled over us as we drew closer. A portion of the roof was caved in, leaving a gaping hole and shredded straw thatch. We ambled along the fence, peering inside at the abandoned farming equipment lying haphazard in the dirt. Behind the farmhouse, I could make out what had once been distinct rows of crops. Now, they were shriveled and half-hidden beneath the untamed weeds.

I exchanged an uneasy look with Mason as we circled the buildings. Yara had gone alarmingly pale.

The front door to the farmhouse hung crookedly from a single hinge, as if it had been ripped open. The beams were splintered around the windows, and long scratches scored the wood and earth beneath the door.

Claw marks.

"We should move on," Yara said, her voice thin with fear.

The others murmured their agreement. I rode up alongside Yara as we left the abandoned farmhouse behind.

"Is this the work of those demons?" I asked.

"The Council calls them chimera. I said they were demons because that's what we call them among the servants."

The gargoyles were chimera as well. Before Rebirth, they'd been native reptiles, but the war and Ninu's experiments had changed them. If creatures like the gargoyles we'd seen yesterday had done this, maybe she hadn't been exaggerating after all. Although we'd seen only one farmhouse, there were no doubt others.

We eventually came to a road, the first we'd seen since leaving Ninurta. Grooves had been worn into the earth from wagon wheels and carriages. Some of the ministers liked to travel in coaches pulled by Grays, but otherwise, wheeled vehicles weren't something we saw much of in Ninurta.

"This is the Silver Road," Yara said. The tension drained from her body as her eyes fixed on the mountains. "They say that, before the war, if you climbed the grandfather trees at sunset and gazed down at the road, it would be lit up like silver trimming."

"Have you ever tried it?" I asked, smiling at the whimsy even though I wasn't familiar with what she meant by "grandfather trees."

"Once, when I was little. I didn't get very high, though," she said. "The road will take us to Vethe."

"Tell me about Vethe," I said. We'd barely had time to speak since our first meeting in the palace.

"For what we've been able to accomplish, it's a beautiful city," she said. "Stone sculptures, glimmer glass light posts, and cave blossoms everywhere."

I looked between her and the mountains. There were three mountains, not quite a range. Their jagged silhouettes had sharpened into focus, but one of them was so tall, its peak pierced the clouds.

"Is Vethe beside the mountains?" I asked.

She shook her head. "Vethe is *inside* the mountains." She pointed at the smallest of them, although "small" wasn't exactly accurate. "We call it the Kahl's Mountain. But it wasn't always so. The original Vethe is *that* way." She pointed to our left. "The ruins are still there. But it's a sad place. I don't like to see it."

I watched plumes of fog drift across the rocky sides of the mountains, the beauty of it calling to the wanderlust inside me.

A scream pierced the air.

We all drew up, spinning in circles to pinpoint the source. A second scream echoed from our right. The sentinels took off, their scouts diving into the trees. I followed a beat behind them, with Yara so close to my side that our scouts nearly grazed each other. Her face was white with terror.

Through the scatter of trees, I could see another farmhouse up ahead. This one was larger than the last, a two-story stone building. We stopped short of the fence to take in the scene. My knees pressed into the sides of my scout, and I had to fight the urge to turn and run. Beside me, Yara made a sound like a stifled moan.

More shouts issued from inside the house. For a moment, all of us were frozen, watching the creatures rake at the walls.

There were two of them. They were three times the size of the gargoyles that Irra had tamed. Short pointed horns protruded from their leathery skin in uneven rows along their jaws. Layers of bony ridges sloped back from their brows into more horns that rose from the tops of their heads and then continued down their spines. They stood differently from the gargoyles, their bulkier upper bodies supported by forelimbs that were thicker and longer than their hind legs. Long claws slashed at the sturdy house with intimidating force. One of the chimera had shattered a window. Its head was too large to fit through, so it had wrapped its body around the corner of the house and thrust its arm into the window, clawing at what it could reach.

Like the gargoyles' frills, these creatures' bony spines quivered as they reared and roared. Their mouths were huge, and their jaws looked powerful enough to crush our scouts.

Mason and the sentinels snapped out of their shock and dropped from their mounts. Each withdrew a torch blade from the compartments beneath their seats. Miraya hadn't wanted them leaving without weapons, and I was glad for it. My eyes found Mason. He already had his weapon in hand and was circling around the fence to attack from the other side.

By now, the chimera had noticed our arrival. The one not trying to dig through the window turned away from the house. Its upper body puffed up in an aggressive stance, its mouth opened wide to reveal daggerlike teeth as long as my fingers.

Gret, Winnifer, and Aylis converged on it. The chimera lunged at them, its head battering at the nearest body, its rows of horns as deadly as its teeth. It was slower than a gargoyle, which meant the sentinels were better able to dodge. Normal human soldiers, however, wouldn't have stood much of a chance against these creatures.

Aylis swung his torch blade into the creature's tail. The weapon seared through thick lizard skin, and the chimera roared. It whipped around, its swinging tail slamming him off his feet.

The other sentinels jumped into action, striking fast and then darting out of range. It was dizzying to watch them fight. They moved almost too swiftly for my eyes to follow, their swords arcs of light that drew blood and frenzied roars.

Gret cried out as the chimera's claws caught her leg. She stumbled. Winnifer dived to her side, lugging her out of range before the chimera could do more damage.

Helplessness gripped me. My fingers dug into the metal of my scout's shoulders, and my legs itched restlessly. I needed to do something, but Mason had taught me how to defend against a torch blade, not how to use one. I had a simple dagger stored beneath my seat, but it would do little good.

I grappled for threads that weren't there. Where my power had been, only a hole remained, siphoning away a little more of me every time I reached instinctually for the threads only to be confronted again with their absence. I'd never felt their loss more keenly.

At the other end of the house, where the second chimera focused on trying to force its way inside, Mason had leaped onto its back. The chimera's bony spines made for convenient hand- and footholds as Mason clung on and tried to angle his torch blade for a strike to the neck. The chimera flailed and bucked wildly. Mason's grip broke. He tumbled off, rolling and skidding through the dirt. Dennyl tried to distract the creature, but it charged after Mason.

I jumped from my scout, running as soon as my feet touched the ground.

Mason's sword hand jerked up as the chimera bore down on him. The blade pierced the chimera beneath its chin, burying into its skull. It gave a guttural cry and then collapsed in a heap at Mason's feet. Puffs of dirt shot into the air around its heavy body. Mason rolled away, clutching his bleeding arm.

I shouted for Yara to remain where she was as I crossed the yard. Mason was already on his feet, pulling his weapon free of the chimera's skull. A furious roar and the scrabbling sound of claws digging into the dirt made me spin around to keep the other chimera in my field of vision. In an instant, Mason was in front of me, the gentle brush of his fingers on my shoulder a wordless command to stay behind him.

Aylis and the others had taken the chimera down. It lay on its side, its body twitching. Winnifer stabbed her torch blade into its chest, and it went still.

Mason sheathed his weapon just as the front door opened a crack. The door was wood, but reinforced with metal. That was probably the only reason the chimera hadn't been able to break it down as easily as they had the other farmhouse door. A frightened face peered out at us.

"It's okay," I said, approaching carefully. I put out my hands so she'd see I wasn't carrying a weapon. "The chimera are dead."

The door opened wider, and a woman stepped out, wearing a dirt-stained dress and stockings. She surveyed the mess of her yard. Her cheeks were still wet.

"Who are you?" she asked, her voice hoarse from screaming.

"Friends," I said hastily. "Are you and your family all right? It's safe to come out now."

Her chin trembled. Fresh tears spilled down her cheeks. "We'll never be safe until these monsters are gone from Lanathrill," she said. Someone in the house behind her rested his hands on her shoulders, attempting to comfort her.

I looked to Yara, wan and unmoving against the backdrop of the trees. A regular army of soldiers should have been able to handle a few chimera. But if Yara was telling the truth—that Lanathrill would be overrun—then there were more than just a few of these out there. Maybe Lanathrill did need Ninurta's help. I would have to see what their Kahl had to say about it.

"Kai!"

Something in Mason's voice made me tense. I hurried over to where he and the others were standing over one of the chimera. I gave him a quizzical look before seeing for myself what had caught their attention. I snatched at Mason's sleeve to steady myself.

Beneath the ridges at the crown of the chimera's head were the red markings of a collar.

CHAPTER 13

MY CONFUSION WAS REFLECTED IN THE FACES AROUND ME. I turned back to Yara.

"When did you say the chimera began attacking your people?" I asked.

Yara had dismounted from her scout. "A few months ago. Before then, they had remained in the Yellow Wastes. We figured it was because they were territorial. But then the first attack happened, and the rest began crossing into Lanathrill. There've been a dozen within the last month."

Ninu must have branded these creatures to use them as the Outlands' border guards. The history texts claimed that he'd lost control over the experiments and unleashed them into the Outlands, but maybe that was what he'd wanted us to think. The chimera would keep the outside world at bay, and the gargoyles would keep Ninurta and its people isolated.

When Ninu died, these creatures had been freed from control, like the sentinels. Now, they were running loose, a danger to everyone in their path.

This was Ninu's doing, which meant this was now Ninurta's responsibility. Anger rushed through my limbs. Even now, I wasn't free of him.

"How far is Vethe?" I asked, stalking across the yard to reach my scout.

Yara jumped back onto hers. She looked more composed. "We should reach the capital in a couple of hours."

"You should pack up and head for Vethe as well," I said to the woman still cowering in her doorway.

Mason and the sentinels mounted up, and we turned into the trees toward the Silver Road.

The Kahl's Mountain rose above us like a path into the clouds. The Silver Road sloped upward as the terrain grew rockier and more treacherous. Yara quickened her pace and shouted, pointing ahead.

Set into the mountain was a pair of imposing metal doors, greater even than the ones that had greeted us in Etu Gahl.

As we approached, the doors groaned open. The earth beneath us shuddered. Loose pebbles and debris cascaded down the mountainside. The dark abyss into which the doors had opened was less than inviting.

But once we were standing directly in front of the doors, I could see a bright glow from deep within the mountain. Coming up the tunnel was a man on horseback, a torch of some kind in his hand. Behind him was a contingent of guards. They emerged from the mountain, and the man on horseback paused in front of Yara, his soldiers fanning out behind him on foot.

I admired the glossy brown coat of the horse before studying Lanathrill's soldiers. They made for an impressive lineup. They wore a combination of leather and metal armor. Thick leather breastplates matched the layered leather pauldron on one shoulder. A metal pauldron that shone silver covered their other shoulder, presumably their sword arms. The same starburst as Yara's tattoo was finely rendered into the metal of their vambraces. Broad swords with hilts nearly a foot long were strapped at their waists.

The rider was dressed differently from the others. His breastplate bore the starburst, the design branded into the sturdy leather. The detailing in his armor was more intricately engraved. A heavy silver cloak draped down his back, and on his head sat a simple circlet, its single white gem glittering in the daylight.

Yara had scrambled off her scout at the sight of him and was now bowed so low that her forehead practically touched the ground. It was a safe bet that this was Kahl Emryn.

His eyes narrowed at our lack of deference. I gave him a polite nod, but that was all he was getting from me.

His soldiers stared at our scouts with a mixture of fascination and wariness. Emryn's horse shied away, uncertain of the metal beasts, but he steadied the creature and passed Yara, approaching me instead. He had rough features, plain if not for the slight offset of a crooked jaw, with brown hair that dusted his shoulders and sharp green eyes set in a face that was young but hardened by the weight of leadership.

Emryn held a metal rod, topped by a cluster of radiant crystals. I wasn't sure now if it was supposed to be a scepter or a makeshift torch. He looked us over, taking note of Mason's and Gret's wounds with a furrow of his brow. They were no doubt healed by now, but the bloodstains remained as evidence of our recent scuffle. No one spoke.

He nodded curtly. Then he turned his horse away and trotted back into the tunnel. His soldiers parted, forming a path for us to follow him. Yara climbed back onto her scout and moved forward.

"It's okay," she said, looking over her shoulder at us.

The rest of us followed her, single file, into the darkness. Our scouts' steps echoed faintly in the cavernous space. Specks of light high up on the walls held off the darkness. I squinted to try to make them out. They looked like crystals, similar to the ones that Emryn was holding.

We traveled in silence for several minutes, the light from inside the mountain growing brighter as we neared what I could only assume was the city.

Up ahead, more soldiers stood guard at another pair of doors, these ones already open. When I peered through, my eyes widened.

We emerged on a path that led down into the city. From this vantage point, the city lay sprawled before us, so vast that I could barely see to the other side. The rocky ceiling rose high above, obscured by mist.

A glance at my companions showed that they were as speechless as I was.

Roads had been chiseled out of the stone, dissecting the city in perpendicular lines. Two- and three-story buildings with paneless windows rose on either side of us. They were stocky and uniformly built from the same gray stone as the mountain. Except some had been personalized with patterned sheets suspended from windows or splashes of colorful paint.

Lampposts lined the roads, but instead of firelight, they were topped by crystals. I peered up at one as we passed, studying its glass-smooth facets. They were bright enough to illuminate a sizable area, with subtle hints of blue and green at their cores.

"Is that magic?" I asked Yara, gesturing to the crystals.

She shook her head. "Even before the Mahjo War, glimmer glass was one of Lanathrill's most prized exports. The crystals have been mined from our mountains for centuries. Now, they're less decorative and more functional." She smiled. "Still pretty, though, right?"

"Yes," I said, craning my neck back to take in as much as I could. Enormous glimmer glass crystals jutted out from the stone that enclosed the city. They had to be a hundred times the size of the ones that lit the street, and they blazed as brightly as the sky during the Week of Sun. Undertones of violet and yellow shimmered beneath their wide facets.

People gathered alongside the road to watch us, and horse-drawn carriages and wagons filled with barrels pulled to the side until we'd passed. The people wore sleeveless dresses and slim tunics with leggings. They looked clean and healthy and in good spirits, a far cry from the people in the North District.

All of them bowed to Emryn, before gawking at the rest of us. They didn't really look at *us*, though. They were transfixed by our scouts, watching their metal bodies move with the same fascination that I felt observing their mountain city.

"Look," Mason said, pointing down.

Remarkably, plants sprouted from the ground. They grew in ribbons across the road and between houses. Fronds and skinny green leaves and brilliant purple blossoms as big as both my hands cupped together. Cave blossoms, just as Yara had said. I didn't know how they could exist down here, but like the glimmer glass, sometimes nature could be more mysterious and magical than anything the Infinite could do.

"The roots," Yara said. She'd noticed us staring at the plants.

Mason and I leaned over our scouts and tilted our heads to get a better look. Sure enough, the plants were growing not out of the mountain itself but from roots that snaked through the stone like veins.

"From the ancient grandfather trees aboveground," Yara said. "They've survived for this long because their far-reaching roots have found stability in the mountain and nourishment from Hiyamun, the burning waterfall." She pointed to our right.

Great clouds of water vapor rose from some indistinguishable point beyond the stretch of buildings. I couldn't see the waterfall, but the evidence was there. That must have been why the ceiling of the city was covered in mist.

I realized then that it was quite warm. I tugged at the collar of my tunic. The burning waterfall—whatever that was—kept away the chill of being underground.

"This place is incredible," Mason said, and the rest of us murmured various forms of agreement. I wished Reev had come with us. He would've loved to see this.

We passed beneath a tall arch, which had horses carved into the stone. The arch seemed to mark a border of sorts, not unlike the train station in the Alley, because once we passed through, the buildings became noticeably larger and more elaborately sculpted. Curling roofs were adorned by whimsical, winged stone creatures. The windows of a three-story building were braced with bright-blue shutters. Elegant vines and flowers were carved into front doors.

The people here wore clothes that were clearly more finely constructed. Women in colorful gowns that billowed as they walked and men in tailored tunics all bowed as Emryn passed. Many of them were accompanied by servants. The servants were dressed more plainly, and they remained a step behind their masters. They were marked by a blue starburst tattoo beneath their left eyes.

I looked at Yara. I had initially thought the tattoo was a personal choice, like Avan's. I hadn't realized it was a mark of servitude. I wondered how she felt about being forced to wear her rank on her face. That wasn't much different from a collar.

We traveled farther into the city until the ground began to slope upward. At the end of the road stood a wall, about ten feet high, and iron gates. Beyond was a black palace that rose high into the mist like a shroud looming over the city.

"The citadel," Yara said, her voice hushed with reverence.

"What is it made of?" Mason asked.

"Shadow glass," she said. "It's what glimmer glass becomes after its light has faded. It darkens into a glossy black crystal that can be melted and reformed like metal."

The citadel was made up of several wings with pointed dome roofs and towers capped in glimmer glass. It was a beautiful structure, like something that might have emerged from the enchanted fog that veiled Etu Gahl. I couldn't imagine how much work went into constructing it.

Soldiers swung open the gates, which arched into spiked peaks at the center. We passed through into a courtyard. Emryn swung down from his horse, and a servant rushed up to take the reins from him. The rest of his soldiers fanned out around us.

He addressed Yara: "You were supposed to bring back an army."

Yara flushed and dipped into another low bow. "Please forgive me, Your Eminence." She gestured to me. "This is—"

"Do these people need a medic?" he asked Mason brusquely with a nod at the sentinels.

Mason looked at me, allowing me the chance to respond as our party's leader.

"They're fine," I said. "My name is—"

"Who's in charge of this sorry lot?" he barked, looking past me.

I ground my teeth together and slid off my mount. His soldiers gripped the hilts of their sheathed swords. In response, Mason and the sentinels went for their torch blades. I wasn't worried. The sentinels had taken down two chimera. These people didn't stand a chance.

I stalked up to Emryn, so close that he *had* to look at me. Or rather, try to glare me into submission.

I spoke very carefully. "Talk over me again, and I will take my 'sorry lot' and leave your country to the chimera."

I'd had enough of people in power trying to manipulate me, to subdue me, to threaten me. I didn't care that he was Kahl or that he didn't seem to like me, but he would damn well listen to me.

"Y-your Eminence," Yara stuttered, aghast. "She meant no offense."

I absolutely meant to offend him. They needed *our* help. I wouldn't have us treated as if they had to suffer our presence.

Emryn stared at me, his green eyes as hard as the mountain. A closely trimmed beard framed thin lips, which had flattened with contempt.

I didn't intimidate him. He was a Kahl, and I was just some foreigner in whose hands he was supposed to place the future of his country. I tried to sympathize, but mostly I was annoyed.

"Very well," he said, voice tight with restraint. "We'll see what use you are against those beasts." He pivoted on his heel and marched away, barking orders to have us housed in the citadel.

I stared at his retreating back, drawing slow breaths to calm my anger. Around us, his soldiers broke away, still wary but no longer prepared for a fight. The sentinels relaxed and dismounted from their scouts. It was a rather inauspicious start to our visit.

Mason clapped a hand on my shoulder. "That was beautiful," he said proudly. I blushed at the compliment.

"I can't believe you spoke to him like that," Yara said, wringing her hands. She glanced nervously in the direction Emryn had gone.

It struck me then that Yara could be held responsible for my rudeness. "He's not going to punish you for what I said, is he?"

"Oh no!" Yara said, dropping her hands to her sides. "He would never. I've just never heard anyone speak to him that way. It's unheard of." She sounded incensed.

"Well, maybe someone should," I muttered.

"I volunteer Kai," Winnifer said, and the sentinels all snickered.

Yara frowned. "You must forgive him," she said sternly. "He is a fair and kind Kahl. But he loses more soldiers every time there's an attack. He's had to bury both his best friend and his uncle, the former captain of the guard." She lowered her voice, as if worried someone might overhear. "I think he has lost hope."

"That doesn't mean I have to put up with his drek."

Yara grimaced but didn't say anything else.

We parked our scouts along the inside of the citadel's walls, across from the stables. *Real* stables with more *real* horses. And real smells too. I wrinkled my nose. The novelty would soon wear off, I was sure.

Then we gathered up our things, and the servants showed us where we'd be staying. We were on the second floor, our party taking up almost the entire wing. The guest rooms were stunning. I could see my reflection in the glossy shadow glass walls. Glimmer glass grew from the walls and ceiling, seemingly without pattern. A bundle of crystals even jutted out from the floor beside the bed, casting a gentle glow across the canopy drapes. Colorful rugs lay scattered across the floor to cushion bare feet. The furniture was clean and polished, but the slightly puckered corners of the damask upholstery revealed its age. I'd bet these had been recovered from the ruins of the original Vethe.

A single window in my room overlooked the courtyard and the front gates. It also provided a magnificent view of the city. I could see the great clouds of steam from the waterfall and even the distant rock face with the open doors through which we'd arrived. Giant glimmer glass protruded from the mountain walls, extending in all directions like crystal netting.

In the courtyard below, Kahl Emryn stood watch over his soldiers as they ran through drills, not unlike what Mason used to do with me and Avan. His arms were crossed, his back straight, as he growled corrections. He was a very hands-on Kahl, I'd give him that.

As if sensing my irritation, his head turned and our eyes met. The corners of his mouth turned downward.

I held his gaze a moment longer, so he'd know I wasn't embarrassed to be caught staring—although maybe I was—and then moved away from the window.

I didn't bother unpacking. I hadn't brought much, just a few changes of clothes aside from the provisions. I left my bag beside my bed. I wanted to be able to leave at a moment's notice.

Even though the city outside these black walls begged to be explored, exhaustion from the long hours of riding crept into my legs and back. I spread out on the bed, the pillow cool against my cheek. I could release the canopy drapes to shut out the light from the glimmer glass, but I liked looking at the muted colors shifting beneath the facets.

I reached into my pocket and took out the leaf brooch that Avan had given me. Riding a scout for hours on end hadn't provided much opportunity to examine it. The leaf was beautifully detailed and finely crafted. Tiny veins had been etched into the silver. The translucent green gave the leaf a subtle gleam.

This was Avan's fourth leaf, and he had given it to me. I didn't know what to do with that fact.

I drew whorls across the leaf's surface with the tip of my finger, imagining the threads twining around the bit of metal as if to keep it safe. I sighed, feeling that hole inside gape ever wider.

I pinned the brooch to my shirt and rolled onto my side. The comfort of a soft bed beckoned me into unconsciousness.

CHAPTER 14

I STARTLED AWAKE FROM A NEW NIGHTMARE.

I'd been in the arena again, with Avan standing over me, shielding me. Instead of Reev delivering the killing blow, however, it had been a chimera. Its claws had ripped through Avan, slicing him open. Without my powers, I could do nothing but watch. I had denied the threads, and so they had abandoned me.

I threw my arms up over my head. *This is getting ridiculous*, I told myself. *Stop it.* I didn't think talking to my subconscious would actually work, but I was exasperated enough to try.

A clock above the mantel indicated it was still early, so I dragged the armchair over to the window and watched the streets beyond the citadel's wall gradually fill with activity: servants carrying baskets of bread, rattling carriages, wagons laden with vegetables. There was even a whole section far from the citadel that looked like pens for livestock.

I had an adjacent washroom, so I ran the bath and soaked my sore muscles until the morning reached a more reasonable hour. Then I finished cleaning up and changed. As I was tying a belt at my waist, a servant arrived to escort me to the guest dining hall for breakfast.

Apparently, we were the only guests in the citadel, because the guest dining hall was otherwise empty. I wondered where the important people ate.

Mason and I sat in front of a platter of fresh rolls and cream-stuffed pastries. Fruit drizzled in honey was arranged artfully on a silver tray. The sentinels eagerly piled their plates with mounds of egg, cheese, and bread.

Aylis poured himself a cup of an amber sweet-smelling drink. "It must get depressing having to sleep and eat surrounded by shadow glass," he remarked.

Possibly, but I thought there was something soothing and elegant about it. Besides, all the rooms were well lit by the glimmer glass that grew randomly from the walls and ceilings, providing both function and beauty.

I watched with a critical eye as Mason slathered a heap of golden butter onto his roll.

He took a bite. His lashes fluttered shut. "Okay, that's good."

"Better than Rennard's?" I asked. Rennard was the chef in Etu Gahl. He kept its army of hollows exceptionally well fed.

"Not quite," Mason admitted, "but this is close."

I selected a cream pastry and bit down on the flaky dough. Sweet cream and buttery crust filled my mouth. *Delicious.* I swiped some cream from the corner of my lips with my thumb and then licked the sweetness from my finger.

Mason made a choking sound. I glanced at him, but he'd quickly looked away.

"Um," I said, uncertain.

He cleared his throat. "You slept through dinner last night."

I grabbed a linen napkin this time to wipe my mouth. "So that's why I was the only one who needed an escort down here."

He dipped a spongy-looking cake into honey. "I considered waking you, but I think you must have needed the rest."

I did, but I wished my subconscious had felt the same and left me to sleep in peace.

I devoured two buns and a bowl of honeyed peaches before I washed it all down with a glass of cider. I had become way too accustomed to filling meals, and it always made me feel a little guilty, with people starving in the North District.

After those first few weeks in Ninurta's palace, I had tried to convince the chef to prepare less elaborate meals, but the suggestion didn't go over well. So instead, I asked Avan to tell Kalla to order the Minister of Law to instruct the Watchmen to deliver our untouched leftovers to the Labyrinth. I heard back through the line of communication that the Minister of Law thought I was a meddling status leech—the ministers hadn't known why I was staying in the palace or that Kahl Ninu hadn't died in a tragic *accident*—and that I should be dumped back in the gutters where I belonged.

I didn't really care what the minister had to say as long as he followed through with Kalla's orders, and he had. The man was allowed his opinions, even if they made me want to strangle him. Now that I was adviser to the Kahl, however, I wasn't sure how much good a man like that would do for Ninurta, considering his disregard for how the Watchmen operated in the North District. That would have to be revisited later.

As expected, the people of the Labyrinth had refused the food. The first few times, they'd tossed it back at the Watchmen. Pride and distrust for the White Court went deep there. I refused to stop trying, though, and after a while, some kids gave in. It had created a ripple effect, and now the Watchmen were practically welcomed at their daily drop-offs. I had even convinced the chef to prepare larger meals so there'd be more to hand out.

But there were many inside the Labyrinth who still refused assistance from the White Court, and I didn't blame them. Still, a bridge, however minor, had formed between the East Quarter and the Watchmen, when before there had been only hostility and hatred.

It was a beginning, and that was something.

"I was talking with some of the soldiers last night," Mason said, buttering his sixth bun. "They have an interesting social system here. The wealthiest people in the city are the farmers, because they provide the majority of the food and—"

A loud knock interrupted him. A woman stood in the doorway, scanning the room. She was dressed in a servant's gray tunic and marked with a blue tattoo on her face. Her eyes rested on me, and she walked over.

She bobbed her head and said, "His Eminence, Kahl Emryn of Lanathrill, will see you now."

I wondered if that was how Ninu used to make people introduce him.

"Should I come with you?" Mason asked. The others murmured their agreement that I shouldn't go alone.

We'd witnessed firsthand that Lanathrill needed our help. And after I'd pressed that point yesterday, I didn't think Emryn would risk doing anything else to lose Ninurta's support.

"I'll talk to him alone," I said. Emryn had underestimated me yesterday, and although I'd made my point, I was pretty sure he still didn't think much of me. If we were alone, he might relax his guard enough to let something slip. Not that I thought they were somehow deceiving us, but just because these people needed our help didn't mean I was going to trust everything they said.

Mason didn't look happy about it, and even Gret looked concerned, but I waved good-bye and followed the servant from the room.

The citadel was immaculately kept. Every shadow glass surface gleamed. A thick runner covered the length of the halls, cushioning our steps and muting the echoes. Paintings, oversized vases, and heavy draperies decorated the long stretches of black, but like the furniture in my room, they had an aged sort of opulence to them. They were clean and polished, but the attempts at restoration couldn't quite hide the marks of time. Maybe Emryn liked it that way: a reminder of where they'd come from and what they'd survived.

We took one more corner and then came upon a metal door. The servant gave it a single firm tap.

A voice from inside called, "Come in."

She pushed in and bowed her head low. Then she stepped aside and gestured for me to enter. I thanked her, and moved into the room. She shut the door after me.

It was a small council room. Maps lay scattered and unfurled over every flat surface, their curling ends weighted down by piles of books topped by scrolls that looked ready to topple at the slightest nudge. More maps had been fastened to the walls, many of them overlapping. Tables lined the walls, half-buried beneath the clutter. In the middle of the room was a wide table, also covered by heavy tomes, manuals, discolored scrolls, and loose papers. Bent over the table, studying some lines drawn on a map, was Kahl Emryn.

I was reminded of the first time I'd met Irra, in his study bent over a miniature sculpture of bread bites. It seemed Kahl Emryn had an obsession with maps the way Irra did with lamps and sugar.

At my entrance, Emryn straightened and clasped his hands behind his back. He looked much the same as yesterday, but I noticed other details now that I wasn't distracted by his city. He had a white scar along his temple that disappeared into his hairline. A matching scar ran down his crooked jaw, a pale sliver through his dark beard.

"I was told your sentinels killed two chimera yesterday," he said, not bothering with pleasantries. I didn't mind. "And yet they came away nearly unscathed."

"We were lucky," I said, approaching the table. Directly above, glimmer glass grew down from the ceiling like the stalactites I'd seen in the history texts. They cast lights and shadows throughout the room.

Emryn's mouth curved into a humorless smile. "I doubt that. We've taken down a dozen chimera in the last two months, but we've suffered three times the losses."

Although he spoke calmly, it was easy to hear the strain in his voice, the emotion underneath that he kept tightly leashed. It was hard to tell whether he believed our presence would make a difference.

"My soldiers have seen Ninurta's sentinels patrol the Yellow Wastes on their silver beasts. The chimera have never attacked them." His finger tracked an imaginary line down the map.

I tilted my head to get a better look at it. Although the map was upside down, I recognized the lower half as the Outlands, the forest, and the very edges of the Void, but everything beyond was new to me. The lands as they were now looked very little like the archived maps in the records hall. Where there had once been a mountain range stretching from one side of the continent to the other, now only a few lonely mountains remained at either end. I couldn't wrap my head around the amount of magic and devastation it must have taken to level mountains.

"The chimera have learned to fear your sentinels," Emryn said. "We've discovered that they're quite intelligent. They're able to observe and adapt, which is why the same strategy never works on them twice. Am I wrong?"

Actually, the chimera had never attacked the sentinels because they'd been under Ninu's control. But I wasn't about to tell Emryn that.

Besides, his assumption was just as accurate. If the gargoyles were anything to go by, it was no surprise that the chimera were also clever.

"How many chimera would you say have entered Lanathrill?" I asked. I leaned over the map, my eyes following the coastline eastward. The name *Lanathrill* was inked onto the map in curling script. To the east, a square plot of land that shared one border with the sea and the other with the Void was labeled *Peshtigo*.

"More sightings come in weekly," he said. "Given the frequency and location of the attacks, I'd say more than two dozen. They're making their way closer to Vethe."

I looked up at him. "You're worried about the city."

His eyes flashed with annoyance. "Of course I am."

"But you live inside a mountain," I said, not sure why I needed to point this out. What could be safer than the walls of a mountain?

Emryn scowled. "The chimera are burrowing creatures."

I raised an eyebrow, not quite believing him. But then I thought about those powerful forearms with large paws and long, curved claws. Perfect for digging. A weight sank in my stomach.

"It would take time," Emryn said. "The mountain is strong. But eventually, they would break through, and we would have nowhere to run."

I remembered the chimera raking their claws against the walls of the farmhouse, gradually shredding through the stone. It would certainly take a while for them to dig through a mountain, but they could do it. And if the chimera made it into the city . . . I shuddered at the thought.

Given that it had taken five people to kill two chimera—*not* unscathed—we would need a small army of sentinels to defeat two dozen of those creatures.

"The chimera live and travel in packs," I said, thinking of the gargoyle nest at the top of Etu Gahl. "They must have an underground burrow, a nest of some kind that they all return to after they've finished hunting for food."

Emryn nodded. "The Fields of Ishta. The majority of their attacks occur in that area. I can take you and your sentinels there to investigate."

"That'd be fine," I said. Something nagged at me, though, something I was overlooking.

I studied the room, the maps, the scrolls, and what might have been black chess pieces scattered around a tower of books. This was a war room, but where were the rest of his officers?

I'd watched him run his soldiers through drills yesterday in the courtyard, something his captain of the guard should have done. Yara had mentioned the position belonged to his uncle, who'd been killed by the chimera. How could Kahl Emryn have lost all his officers in the last few months while he, himself, walked away with little more than a couple of minor scars?

Maybe as Kahl, he remained behind the shield of his army in a battle. But he didn't strike me as the sort. He would be at the lead, charging in first to inspire his soldiers to bravery.

Then again, I wasn't exactly the best judge of character. I could be wrong. Or the answer could be something as obvious as Kahl Emryn being an exceptionally talented fighter.

But I wanted to be sure.

"Kahl Emryn," I said, "how—"

"Just Emryn will do," he told me.

"Emryn, how have you been keeping the chimera at bay so far?"

He understood what I was asking, because his lips pinched and his shoulders tensed. I crossed my arms and leaned back against a desk, waiting.

"May I ask you something first?" he said, retreating to a table in the corner where some scales and writing instruments were strewn.

"I guess." At least he was being polite now.

"Was it true that your Kahl Ninurta was *mahjo*? That he could wield magic?"

I frowned, looking for a trap in his words. Ninu had deceived everyone into believing he was *mahjo* when really, he had been Infinite.

"Having seen your silver beasts up close," he continued, "I believe such creatures could exist only through magic."

"Kahl Ninu possessed magic, yes."

"Then you'll understand when I say that I'm the same."

"The same?" Emryn wasn't Infinite. He couldn't be.

"I'm *mahjo*." He held out his hand. The air around his fingers distorted, rushing and swirling and snapping his sleeve against his wrist until he held a miniature windstorm right there in his palm.

CHAPTER 15

MY GAZE DARTED FROM EMRYN'S FACE TO THE TEMPEST IN HIS hand.

How was this possible? The Infinite had stripped *mahjo* of their magic.

But there was no denying that this *was* magic. I moved around the table, stepping closer.

In my experience, there was always something about the Infinite that gave them away, from Kalla's pale, unnatural beauty to Irra's aura of hollowness to the fire that burned in Avan's eyes. Nothing about Emryn's physical appearance suggested he was anything but human.

"These last few months have been a period of many changes," Emryn said, closing his fingers into a fist, extinguishing the storm. The violent winds dispersed in a rush of air that whipped my hair against my cheeks and sent a pile of scrolls cascading to the floor. The last traces of his magic fluttered around my hands, sending an unexpected jolt of envy through me. I rubbed my fingers to get rid of the sensation while waiting for Emryn to explain.

He removed a book from a chair and sank heavily onto the seat, his strength spent. "It was said that *mahjo* came into their powers at different times in their lives," he began.

"Yes," I agreed, remembering what I'd read in school. I realized what he was implying. "But it was almost always during their teen years. It rarely happened with anyone older than twenty."

"Maybe the Mahjo War changed that," he said, opening and closing his fist.

If Emryn's magic had appeared only within the last few months, then that couldn't be a coincidence. But I didn't see how Ninu's death could've had anything to do with this. Then again, the Infinite were good at covering their tracks.

"Have you always known you were *mahjo*?" I asked.

He lifted his chin, and even from his seat, I got the impression he was looking down his nose at me. "The Kahls of Lanathrill have always been *mahjo*. My great-grandmother, Kahl Bael, was the only surviving heir after the war. She was younger than you are now, but she rebuilt Vethe here, within one of the last mountains of the Leluna Range. Lanathrill had once been home to the greatest craftsmen and miners on the continent, and enough of them remained after the war to help relocate the capital. However, my great-grandmother never came into her magic the way our ancestors had. None of her children did, either. Until my grandfather first saw your silver beasts in the Yellow Wastes, we had believed the war had extinguished magic altogether."

He wasn't wrong. I rubbed my forehead. "How is this happening?" I muttered.

"The goddess has promised us many things," he said. He rolled his shoulders back and straightened in his chair. His strength seemed to be returning.

"Yara mentioned a goddess."

"The *mahjo* of old were said to have spoken directly to the deities."

Only because the Infinite were meddlesome. Like this goddess. "What exactly has this goddess been promising you?" I asked. "And does she have a name?"

The way Emryn's lip curled told me he wasn't going to be as forthcoming as I'd hoped.

As expected, he said, "The nature of the goddess and her secrets is kept between the Kahl and the Council of Vethe, and no other."

"Then what *can* you tell me?"

He scratched his beard, right next to where his scar cut through the dark hair. "It is our belief that the world is finally righting itself."

I doubted it. Someone would have noticed if the sentinels and hollows, all of them *mahjo*, suddenly began throwing magic around. Still, how could I be sure? Maybe their collars had altered them too much, and they couldn't wield magic anymore. There was no way to tell.

I needed to talk to Irra.

"It must be true," Emryn said. He sounded pretty convinced, so I didn't bother arguing. "The Council of Vethe have come into their powers as well."

I'd been studying the glimmer glass overhead. Now I turned to stare at him. "There are more of you?"

"Four others."

I gaped. *Five mahjo?* And you still need our help with the chimera?"

"Our magic is weak," he said curtly. I imagined he didn't like having to admit it. "Only myself and one other possess the control to fight the chimera, and even then, we would never be able to face more than one at a time." He sighed, his eyes closing. When he opened them again, his gaze was hard. "Which brings us back to our dilemma. Ninurta *must* send help."

It wasn't that simple, not with everything Miraya was currently facing, and I was annoyed that he thought he could order me around. While I agreed that Ninurta would have to do something—the chimera were Ninu's fault, after all—I still had to make sure that Miraya got what she wanted out of a deal with them.

"This is the first official contact between our countries," I said. "If Kahl Miraya sends reinforcements, she would expect you to agree to an alliance to expand our relationship as neighbors."

"I expected no less," Emryn said, standing. He walked around me, returning to the central table where he braced his hands against the surface and leaned over the map again. His hair brushed his jaw, held back from falling into his face by his circlet. "We've wanted to discuss an alliance with Ninurta for some time now, but we were never welcome," he said.

"And now?"

He looked at me over his shoulder. "Now that we know the Yellow Wastes can be crossed safely, opening communication would benefit both our countries." Some nameless emotion lit his green eyes. "We have each survived the destruction of this world. But together, maybe we can repair it."

The servants found me some paper and a pen, and I wrote a letter to Miraya.

First, I explained the situation with the chimera. Lanathrill needed help and only a contingent of sentinels would be of any use against the creatures. Second, Emryn had agreed that once the chimera were dealt with, he and his Council would return with the sentinels to Ninurta to meet with Miraya and begin discussing their alliance. One of the things he'd mentioned was the construction of a road between the two countries, and a shared patrol to keep travelers safe from gargoyles.

I then drew a clean sheet of paper from the stack. This letter I addressed to Irra. I told him about Emryn's magic and how he and the Council members had developed these powers right after Kahl Ninu's death. I didn't have any theories about why their magic had manifested, so I needed Irra's opinion.

At the bottom, I added, "Don't patronize me by giving me roundabout answers like you always do. Tell me the facts or I'll come back to Ninurta just to yell at you."

I drew a third sheet of paper. I wrote Reev's name at the top and then paused. What should I say to him?

I decided simply to tell him we had reached Lanathrill safely and ask that he keep me updated on how he was doing. Thinking about him filled me with homesickness, so I finished the letter and set it aside. I considered writing a fourth letter to Avan, but it had been only a few days, and I had no idea what to say to him.

I folded all three letters together and sealed them with wax. Dennyl had volunteered to return to Ninurta to deliver them. I wandered down the hall to his room to drop them off. He would leave in the hours before dawn and reach Ninurta well after sunset. It was a long ride, but Dennyl assured me he'd be fine.

We were leaving to see the Fields of Ishta in a couple of hours. Mason and I spent the time in between exploring the city. We followed the streets without direction, stepping over ribbons of flowered roots and stopping to pick purple blossoms. Near the western boundaries of the city was a glimmer glass garden. Crystals grew in profusion from the ground, some as tall as three times Mason's height, while others were as tiny and delicate as raindrops. The whole garden sparkled like a thousand miniature beacons.

I smiled as we passed two girls on a bench, holding hands and whispering to each other with shy smiles. Nearby, a boy and girl giggled between light kisses before they disappeared around a shiny arch. The garden was a popular romantic spot, it seemed.

Couples were concealed beneath every crystalline canopy and behind every luminous cluster. Mason and I snickered a little too loudly at the fourth pair we came across, earning us a glare from a boy who turned long enough for me to glimpse the red curls of the girl with him before her gloved fingers nudged him back around.

The shade of those curls made my heart jump. I let Mason lead me away as I calmed the irrational desire to intrude again on their privacy to get a better look at the boy's partner.

I was reluctant to leave the garden, but Mason wanted to explore further, so we continued on. Eventually, we ended up at Hiyamun, the burning waterfall. Neither of us had ever seen a waterfall before, although the river that divided the North District from the East Quarter ended in one just south of the city.

Hiyamun had to be as high as the wall surrounding Ninurta. Glimmer glass shone from behind the surging waters, transforming the waterfall into something otherworldly. A metal guardrail had been installed twenty feet away from the deep, bubbling pool that the waterfall poured into. We couldn't talk over the roar of the water, but we lingered at the guardrail for a few minutes, which was the longest I could stand the stifling heat. This was worse than being in Irra's workroom, especially as the spray from the waterfall could still reach us and the droplets burned.

A series of narrow canals carried the liquid from the pool to a communal bath where people could soak in the naturally heated water. Mason wiggled his eyebrows at me, but I punched him in the arm. While the hot water was tempting, public bathing was a little too much for me. I'd learned to guard my privacy well in the Labyrinth.

"I've been thinking," he said casually as we walked, away from the communal bath.

"That's always reassuring."

He elbowed me, and I snickered, shuffling a few steps out of range.

"I've been thinking about your nightmares," he said.

My good humor fled, and I looked at him. "You shouldn't."

Ignoring me, he said, "One of my teammates—his name was Bolin—had a training accident about a month after he received his collar. He still remembered too much, and he was angry all the time. While sparring with one of the newly branded sentinels, he lost control of himself and ended up crushing the poor kid's ribs. Killed her instantly."

I fingered my ribs, grimacing. "That's horrible. Did Ninu punish him?"

"Not really. Just scheduled him for accelerated cleansing. But every night leading up to his cleansing, I'd catch him muttering apologies in his sleep. A few times, he woke the whole team with his shouting."

"Mason, I'm not suffering from—"

"Guilt is a powerful emotion, Kai."

"I don't feel *guilty* about k—" I stumbled on the word, but forced it out, my voice rising. "About killing Ninu." Collecting myself, I clamped my lips together and picked up my pace.

"That's not what I mean," he said. He hopped into the street as we hurried around two women on the sidewalk wearing full skirts.

"Don't push it, Mason," I said. He seemed to sense the unspoken warning in my words, because he gave me a long-suffering look and fell silent.

He wasn't entirely wrong. That day in the tower haunted me, chasing me into my dreams, and whether that was guilt or just a stubbornly fixated subconscious, who could say for certain? The only thing I knew was that I had no desire to discuss it.

His silence lasted only a minute, but at least he was done trying to analyze me.

"What's your theory on the *mahjo* here?" he asked. After my meeting with Emryn, I'd returned to the dining hall to finish my breakfast and to inform Mason and the sentinels about Lanathrill's *mahjo*.

"Wouldn't have believed it if I hadn't seen it with my own eyes," I said. "But I don't have any theories. Could be anything." I gestured to the glimmer glass all around us. "Could be something in the crystals for all we know."

"Well, if I start spontaneously setting things on fire, I'll let you know."

I grinned. "What kind of magic do you think you'd have?"

He looked thoughtful, reaching back to touch the raised red lines of his collar. "I've never told anyone, but I've always felt a . . . well, a connection of sorts with plants."

"Plants," I repeated, somewhat surprised. He stooped over to run his fingers along the satiny petal of an open bloom.

"I know," he said wryly. "Seems odd. But sometimes . . ." He closed his eyes with his fingertip still resting against the purple blossom. "Sometimes when I touch the flowers in Irra's garden, I get glimpses of places—a forest, a field, an open sky—as if the seeds can remember, and they want to show me."

"That sounds wonderful," I said, watching with keen interest the way his face relaxed as he spoke.

He opened his eyes and straightened up again, looking embarrassed. "It doesn't happen very often."

"Why didn't I ever see you in the courtyard?" I asked. In Etu Gahl, Avan and I had spent time every day in the courtyard because it had been the only place in the fortress with green growing things and a view of the sky.

"I didn't want to intrude," he said as we continued walking.

"You wouldn't have been intruding."

One corner of his mouth twitched into a brief smile. "I don't think Avan would have agreed."

I sucked in my cheeks, uncertain how to respond. It was true I'd cherished those quiet moments with Avan in the courtyard. It hadn't occurred to me that Avan had felt the same.

"Where to next?" Mason asked, sparing me from having to reply.

I gestured with my chin to the citadel. I supposed it was time to meet the other *mahjo*.

CHAPTER 16

THE TEMPLE OF THE COUNCIL OF VETHE WAS A SQUARE BUILDING
that stood in the shadow of the citadel. A brief set of stairs led up
to a wide entrance with no doors. Directly following was a gallery. The room had a series of shadow glass pillars at either side
that rose as high as the ceiling. I looked up and gasped. Every
inch of the ceiling was covered with glimmer glass, flooding the
gallery's black walls with light.

The black floor was embedded with chips of colored glass.
With the light from above, the glass chips glittered like star-
dust. At the end of the room, a table with four occupied seats
rested on a raised platform. Behind them, a mural of stained
glass occupied the length of the wall, depicting a cityscape with
a white castle that looked quite a bit like the citadel. That had to
be the original capital—Vethe as it had been before the war, the

city set against the backdrop of giant, ancient trees and looming mountains.

Only one of the four people at the table looked up when I entered. The girl who stood to greet me appeared to be the youngest of the group. She wore a modest blue gown beneath blue robes with gold starbursts embroidered along the hem. The starburst, I'd learned, was Lanathrill's emblem. The other Council members wore matching robes.

The girl's long auburn hair was pulled back into a braid, which I'd noticed was a common style for the women. Or at least the women who weren't servants. Men or women, the servants wore their hair short.

My footsteps echoed through the gallery, bouncing off the high walls and the glimmer glass ceiling. As I approached the platform, the girl extended her arm, indicating that I should join her up there. I did, and she held out her hand.

"I'm Cassia," she said. "It's so good to meet you, Kai."

I shook her hand, and she introduced me to the other members: Brienne, Finn, and Henna, all of whom looked like they'd been sucking on lemons. I could already tell we would get along spectacularly.

"Lanathrill thanks you for coming to our aid," Cassia said.

"Don't thank me yet." All I'd done so far was write a few letters and watch from the sidelines as the others saved that farmhouse from the chimera.

Emryn had said one other *mahjo* was strong enough to fight the chimera. As Cassia rattled on about their gratitude, I looked between their wearied faces and wondered which one of them he'd been talking about.

But something else caught my attention. They all looked . . . ill. They were too thin, their cheeks hollow, their eyes sunken. Henna's weathered hands had a grayish tint that I didn't think had to do with his age, and there was an unhealthy pallor to Finn's brown skin.

"Kahl Emryn tells me that you wish to see the Fields of Ishta," Cassia said, breaking my scrutiny.

"He thinks the chimera's nest might be there. Their attacks mainly happen at night or in the mornings, so we're hoping they'll be asleep at this time of day."

"May the goddess protect us today."

"Have you always worshipped the goddess or is this a new thing?"

Cassia looked affronted, and the other Council members bristled. "We have always looked to the goddess for guidance," she said.

I held up my hands. "Sorry, I didn't mean to offend you," I said, which seemed to placate Cassia. "I'm trying to understand—has she always been able to communicate with you?"

Cassia's lips tightened. "We do not discuss our connection to the goddess. Such knowledge must be protected, kept within the Council."

"But what makes you so certain she's the reason you have magic?"

"We would never presume to understand or question the will of the goddess."

Of course they wouldn't. I wanted to believe that, even prior to meeting the Infinite, I wouldn't have put such blind faith in a deity that promised so many good things without asking for some form of repayment. But I suspected I might have—the part of me that had wanted to know who I was, that had yearned to believe that my magic had been given to me for a purpose.

In the end, I *did* have a purpose—to kill Ninu. But now, here I was again, potentially in the middle of some Infinite's manipulations, and I didn't even have my magic to rely on anymore.

Footsteps echoed through the hall. Yara walked briskly through the gallery until she reached the bottom of the platform. She smiled when she saw me, but she addressed Cassia.

"I've readied your horse," she said.

"Thank you, Yara," Cassia said, sweeping her robes aside and descending the stairs.

"You're Cassia's servant?" I asked Yara. When she nodded, I looked at the back of Cassia's auburn head. "*You* ordered her into the Outlands?"

Yara's eyes went round. When Cassia turned to me, Yara gave a tiny shake of her head. Maybe she was worried about being punished this time.

"Yara did what had to be done for Lanathrill."

While you sat safely here inside the mountain? The words were at the tip of my tongue, but Yara's desperate eyes begged me to stop.

I managed to say politely, "She was very brave."

Cassia's expression softened. "Yes, she was."

Yara blushed as Cassia rested her fingers against Yara's shoulder.

When Yara realized I was still watching, her cheeks grew even redder. She mumbled down at the floor, "Kai, I wasn't sure if you'd be wanting a horse or if—"

"I'll ride my scout," I said.

"Are you ready?" Cassia asked me.

The rest of the Council members had moved on to discussing other things and were completely ignoring me, so I hurried down the steps. "You're coming along?"

"My magic is an asset to your team, no matter how skilled your sentinels are."

I guessed that meant Cassia was the other *mahjo* Emryn had mentioned. Maybe that was why the others deferred to her.

Emryn was in the courtyard, already mounted and waiting. When he saw me, he pushed his horse forward.

"We should take more soldiers with us."

"No," I said. I didn't need a bunch of people tromping through the grass and drawing attention.

"If the nest is really there, then it's too dangerous with just—"

"Emryn, have you seen the way my sentinels move?"

His nostrils flared. He wasn't used to being interrupted. "Yes," he said. "I observed them sparring this morning."

"I'm sure you have brave, well-trained soldiers, but mine are faster, stronger, and can walk, run if necessary, without making a sound. Anyone else—you, me, Cassia—is a risk, and I'd like to keep those risks down. I wouldn't even want Cassia along except she's right: her magic might be helpful if we run into trouble."

Emryn fell silent, which must have meant he'd gotten the point.

It took mere minutes for me and the sentinels to mount up. Everyone in the vicinity stopped to watch our scouts stir and rise from what looked like sleep. Their rippling sheets of metal produced a startling imitation of life.

Emryn and Cassia led the party through the city, back toward the tunnel built into the mountainside. We had to pace our scouts to match Emryn and Cassia's much slower horses. Once we'd descended from the mountain and the Silver Road leveled out, I took the opportunity to get a better look at Lanathrill's landscape.

Beyond the enormous trees with trunks so thick that even the huge Grays in Ninurta would probably fit inside them, the land rose and fell in gentle hills. Farmhouses stood amid fields of wheat that stretched across countless acres, interspersed with patches of other crops. I didn't know much about farming— okay, I knew *nothing* about farming—but plants needed sunlight to grow strong and healthy. How were they able to maintain so many crops with the sun hidden behind clouds for the majority of the year?

I had often worried that the production district in Ninurta might actually be relying on Kalla's magic to produce the quantity of food necessary to keep the city fed. I'd never confronted her about it, but if it were true, what would happen when she left? With Ninurta surrounded by the Outlands, farming would never be a viable option. If we could find a way to get safely down the cliff to the sea, we could try to revive the fishing industry. Maybe Irra would teach us to build that pulley system he'd installed in Kalla's tower. That was assuming the sea still had fish in it. Who knew what havoc the war had caused to the life there?

We turned off the Silver Road onto a dusty path that narrowed until it disappeared into the weeds. Emryn and Cassia led us past farms several times larger than the ones we'd encountered on our way to Vethe. Servants hurried through the yard between multiple buildings, feeding livestock and going about their daily chores. I lingered along the borders of a pasture, watching animals graze. If asked, I wouldn't have been able to name what they were, but I was charmed by their furry bodies and how their jaws gnashed the grass. Nearby, a farmer was herding more animals into pens.

I could only imagine the struggle these people faced between choosing to stay and work or to flee to the safety of the mountain. Maybe Emryn had ordered them to stay. He still had a city to feed.

We traveled single file along a depression in the waist-high grass until we passed through a copse of trees, younger than the ones by the Silver Road. When we emerged on the other side, Emryn and Cassia drew their horses to a stop. I pulled up beside them, taking in the view.

The Fields of Ishta stretched out before us in rippling waves of yellow-green grass. I urged my scout a few steps forward. The grass rustled against my legs and prickled the backs of my hands.

I understood why Emryn thought the chimera nest might be here. I could feel the echo of *something* in the way the wind breathed through the dry grass, the way the blades whispered of memories held within the earth around their roots. It wasn't anywhere near as powerful or oppressive as the Void, but it was still a physical presence.

"What is this place?" I asked, although I suspected I knew. Had the chimera been drawn here because the traces of old magic felt familiar to what they'd known under Ninu's control?

"A battlefield from the Mahjo War," Emryn said.

CHAPTER 17

"AS THE STORY GOES, NO ONE SURVIVED THE BATTLE," CASSIA said. Her gaze swept across the Fields as if imagining the bodies strewn through the grass. "The warriors fought as though crazed, driven so mad by magic and bloodlust that they turned their swords on their own comrades, screaming the name of their god Ishta even as they lay dying."

"Bet that made for a pleasant bedtime story," Mason muttered from behind me. I suppressed the smile that tugged at my mouth.

"Well," I said, "let's have a look around." We'd already discussed what to look for: areas in the grass that might have been recently trampled, chimera tracks, and scratched tree trunks. The chimera weren't as fast or agile as the gargoyles, but they were just as powerful, and with their extra bulk, they would definitely leave evidence of their comings and goings. "If you see chimera, run for backup. Don't try to fight them alone," I told everyone.

The sentinels split off on foot. They kept low to the ground so that I could see only the very tops of their heads moving through the grass.

I remained on my scout as I retreated into the trees to search along the perimeter. A moment later, Cassia joined me.

"Is there anything I can do?" she asked.

"You can stay alert," I said.

Somewhere to my right, deeper into the woods, I could hear the crackle of Emryn's horse stepping through the dry under-brush. He and Cassia were trying to be silent, but every snap of twigs and crunch of leaves made my nerves bunch tighter. The paws of my scout moved much more quietly than I'd expected, seemingly understanding my desire to step lightly.

"He's a good Kahl," Cassia said, her voice almost a whisper.

"I'm sure he is."

"You shouldn't have scolded him."

I almost rolled my eyes. "I don't think it's possible to scold a Kahl."

"Emryn is doing the best he can. His father wanted nothing more than to restore the glory of Lanathrill, and when he died, he left all his ambitions to Emryn. If Lanathrill was to collapse under his rule, the shame would kill him."

I wasn't sure why she was telling me this. I understood that Emryn had a lot on his shoulders. He was Kahl. That kind of responsibility came with the job description. I'd told Emryn that the three of us were liabilities because we weren't like the sentinels, not because I was picking on him.

A shout rang out. My body snapped into motion, my hands clenching the sensors as my scout surged forward. Emryn and Cassia's shouts faded behind me, their horses unable to keep up. We wove through the trees and burst out into the open.

Aylis was trying, and failing, to fight off two chimera. His tunic was dark with blood, even while he ducked into a roll to avoid the deadly swipe of claws. Gret and Winnifer were sprinting through the grass toward us, but they were still too far away.

Aylis's torch blade rested in the dirt a few feet from me. I reached for it. I had no idea how to use a sword, but Mason had always said I was fast. Without the threads of time, I hoped speed would be enough.

One of the chimera circled around to attack Aylis from behind. He shuffled sideways, trying to keep them both in sight without giving either of them his back. It was impossible. The chimera nearest me puffed up, preparing to lunge at him. I attacked first, striking its flank.

Blood splattered the torch blade. The chimera screamed and rounded on me. I dived into the grass, the chimera's jaws snapping at the spot where my head had been. I rolled, dodged the lash of its tail, and then pushed to my feet, stabbing the blade into its other flank. I yanked the blade free just as its claws swiped at me, scoring the blade and my forearm.

Pain tore through me. The torch blade slipped from my hand. I tried to make a grab for it, but the chimera's massive mouth snapped at me again. I leaped away. My feet tangled in the grass, and I tumbled. I landed on my arm. Fire ripped up my shoulder. My vision blurred. *Focus!* I choked back the bile and scrambled backward. The chimera reared up, its shadow falling over me.

Someone shouted my name. A second later, the chimera roared and whipped its head to the side to face its new attackers. Mason and Dennyl had stolen its attention.

Drek! Fury at myself gave me the strength to regain my feet. My right arm hung uselessly at my side, but I limped forward, searching for the torch blade. A short gasp made my head snap up. *Mason!*

But he was fine. He stood with blade drawn, his eyes on the chimera that was . . . floating. It was suspended in the air, its arms and legs thrashing at nothing.

Cassia had reached us on her horse. She held her arm outstretched, hand up and fingers splayed, keeping the chimera trapped. A glance at Aylis confirmed he, Winnifer, and Gret had taken down the first chimera.

Cassia's arm began to tremble. Her control was slipping. "Kill it," she commanded.

The chimera let out a final shriek as Mason buried his torch blade through its pale underbelly. Cassia dropped her arm, and the chimera's body crashed into the grass. My own body sagged.

Strong hands caught me. "I've got you," said a rough voice.

I turned my head, surprised to see Emryn. I stared at the scar on his jaw for a few seconds—unless we were fighting, I didn't like being in such close proximity to anyone I didn't trust—until Mason and the others gathered around us. Mason collected me into his arms, hooking his elbow beneath my knees and lifting me against him.

"Mason, that's not necessary," I said as he carried me through the grass. My face grew warm in spite of the blood dripping wetly through my fingers.

He didn't answer. He looked angry, his blue eyes narrowed into icy slits.

"We need to get out of here," I said, pushing against his chest with my good arm. I wasn't sure where he was headed until he reached my scout. Winnifer had realized his intent and retrieved a vial from the compartment beneath the seat.

Irra had ensured I was equipped with healing tonic, and Reev had gone so far as to insist it was stored in every scout in case mine was somehow destroyed or out of reach.

Mason set me on my feet with embarrassing gentleness. I accepted the vial from Winnifer. It tasted as awful as I remembered, but I swallowed every drop. Almost immediately, the pain began to recede. My arm tingled and then itched like crazy as the broken skin knit back together. Mason reached for my hand, his fingers carefully turning my arm for his inspection.

"How is it?" I asked, grimacing from the aftertaste.

"You'll need another tonic in a bit," he said. "But the bleeding has stopped." He drew a ragged breath. "What happened to not fighting alone?"

I'd never seen him this angry. Actually, I'd never seen him angry at all.

"I wasn't going to watch Aylis die," I said. I searched for Aylis among the sentinels. He was on his scout, his arm curled over his side. When our eyes met, he nodded to let me know he was fine.

Emryn broke through the wall of sentinels around me. His gaze fell on my arm, which Mason was still holding.

"What is that?" he asked, meaning the vial.

"Healing tonic," I said.

His lips thinned, and he turned away. I could imagine what he was thinking. Healing tonic would have come in handy these last few months. It might have saved a lot of lives.

Unfortunately, I doubted Irra would want such a powerful remedy in anyone's hands but his own.

"We need to get out of here," I repeated. "There are bound to be more chimera, and we've been loud enough to attract the whole nest. We can come back another time."

"We found the nest, actually," Gret said. "Bunch of mounds that way." She pointed in the direction from which she and Winnifer had come when Aylis shouted for help.

I nodded, grateful we wouldn't have to make another trip here until we were ready to flush out the chimera.

My arm still hurt when I flexed it. The vial had healed my injury into a red line down my forearm. The blood made it look raw. Too much tonic at once would make me sick, so I had to wait a few hours for the next dose.

I rinsed away as much blood as I could with a canteen of water, glaring at the wound and the proof of how much I relied on my powers. In Ninurta, it had been easy to ignore the absence of the threads. There'd been little danger in the palace. But here, the frustration grew daily. I hadn't yet learned how to fight without the reassurance of their presence. It made me feel not only useless, but foolish and guilty—foolish because I'd allowed this part of me to fade and hadn't had the good sense to try to keep it, and guilty for missing something that had caused so much pain.

Cassia rode beside me, looking worse than I did. Her complexion had taken on an unhealthy gray pallor, and her forehead was bright with perspiration.

"Are you okay?" I was reminded of how Emryn had looked after demonstrating his magic in his war room, and of the haggard appearance of the other Council members.

She smiled weakly but didn't look away from the road. Her hands shook.

"It's the magic, isn't it?" I asked.

"It drains us. Even the slightest use leaves us weakened."

The tremors spread into her shoulders and back. She looked ready to fall off her horse.

"You should ride with Emryn," I said.

She gave an unsteady shake of her head. "I can manage."

I agreed but remained close in case she pitched off her saddle. Magic wasn't supposed to drain *mahjo*. That had never been a mark of its use.

If their goddess had somehow granted them magic, then their powers defied the very balance that Irra and Kalla were trying to restore. These *mahjo* weren't meant to possess magic, and they were paying the price for it.

CHAPTER 18

I DREAMED OF AVAN.

"Do you remember that time at school . . ." he was saying.

When he trailed off, I said, "You're going to have to be more specific."

He smiled. I wanted to brush my thumb against the curve of his mouth. So I did. He turned his face into my touch, lips pressing the lightest of kisses against the pad of my thumb.

"You didn't let me finish," he said good-naturedly.

I gestured for him to continue. Judging by the branches tangled above our heads, we were in the forest. Beneath us, a carpet of moss and yellow blossoms cushioned the ground. Broad, leafy ferns curled around us like petals. It was like being cocooned within a half-bloomed flower.

"Do you remember that time at school when you discovered Dani had dropped out?" he said, cocking his head at me with that endearing smile. "I made you skip class so we could find her and try to get her to come back."

"Yes," I said, nudging aside his knee so I could shift positions in our little haven and lie beside him. I rested my head against his shoulder, my fingers playing with the lines of his tattoo. "That didn't go as planned."

While coming up the street, we'd seen Dani leave the old *mahjo* temple at the center of the North District. Her father and two younger brothers had been with her. They were following a procession of mounted Watchmen and the temple caretakers. I hadn't needed to see the closed wagon amid them to understand why Dani had quit school.

With two brothers to support, she would have to find a full-time job to help her dad now that her mom was gone. We'd turned back around before she ever noticed us.

It had been unfair of me, but on the way back to school, I'd made Avan promise that he would finish school. If I had to do it—because Reev would never hear otherwise—then he'd have to as well.

"You kept your promise," I said, looking up at the vines hanging just beyond our hiding place. "You didn't forget."

His arm tightened around my shoulder. "I would never."

The dream faded away like smoke on water. I awoke with a dull headache in my temple, but I remembered every detail of my dream and of Avan.

"Fantastic," I muttered as I rolled out of bed. My subconscious had conjured up a new way to torture me.

I thrust a torch blade, pointing downward, into the space between me and Mason. "Teach me how to use this."

After waking from my dream that morning, I had intercepted Dennyl in time to ask him to leave his torch blade for me. He could pick up a new one in Ninurta.

"Why?" Mason said. "So you can get yourself killed next time?"

My fingers clenched around the handle. "Don't you *dare* baby me. You of all people know what I can do."

"Yeah," he said, knocking my hand aside as he leaned in close. "So why didn't you?"

"Why didn't I *what*?" I asked, my vision suddenly filled with clear blue eyes flecked in gray.

He lowered his voice. "Why didn't you use your power? You could have died."

Emotion broke through the hard set of his mouth. He drew back, scowling at the brief crack in his control. An ache bloomed in my chest as I touched his cheek. Mason had become my dearest friend, and yet I hadn't considered what losing me might mean to him.

"I'm sorry for worrying you," I said.

His hand came up to cover mine. "Why didn't you use your power?" he pressed.

All around us, the courtyard buzzed with activity: men and women training or sparring, servants carrying buckets of laundry or bushels of vegetables for the day's meals or running from one task to another. Emryn was standing in his usual spot, arms crossed as his soldiers ran through drills. But he was looking at me and Mason.

I looked away from Emryn. He was too far away to hear.

"Because I can't," I said, meeting Mason's questioning gaze.

"Why are you worried about the sentinels finding out what you can do? You killed Ninu—they've already figured out that you're different. Cassia and Emryn would have questions, but they're *mahjo*. They would—"

"No, I mean I *can't*. I can't . . . do it." I stared at his chin as I dug my heel into the dirt. "Anymore."

Mason's mouth opened, closed, and then opened again. "But that's impossible," he finally said. "It doesn't just go away, not for someone like *you*."

"Someone like *me*?"

He gave an impatient shake of his head. "You know what I mean. You're not *mahjo*, but you're not quite Infinite, either. You're different. Your powers can't *disappear*."

"How do you know? If I'm different, then there's never been a precedent. We don't *know* what's normal for me."

"Okay, fine, you have a point." He tilted his head, as if he could figure out what was wrong by studying me. I elbowed him to make him stop, and he smiled. "Have you told Irra?"

"You're the first."

"When did it start? I mean stop?"

I took his arm and led him farther off, toward where our scouts were lined up against the wall that faced the stables. "Little over a month ago."

"Why didn't you tell anyone? Maybe Irra could have helped."

"I didn't want help," I said, leaning my back against the wall and crossing my ankles. In the stables, a pair of servants were grooming the horses. I watched them work as Mason mimicked my position, his shoulder purposely jostling me.

"Why?" he asked.

"Because." I waved my fingers, imagining the way the threads had once caught against them. Even I could hear the sadness in my voice when I said, "Maybe it's better this way. If it wasn't for my powers and what they meant about me, Reev wouldn't have been found and Avan—"

"That's drek." Mason shifted to face me, his shoulder still resting against the wall. He drummed his fingers against his thigh. Then he slapped his palm against the stone beside my head, boxing me in.

I blinked rapidly, caught off guard by how close he suddenly was. Although we weren't touching, his broad shoulders almost completely blocked out the stables.

"I know it's none of my business," Mason said, "and I know you don't want to talk about it."

I frowned. I didn't like where this was going.

"But I'm your friend," he continued, "and I've held my tongue long enough. What happened wasn't your fault. Avan made his own choices. Nothing you could have said or done would have stopped him from helping you, and not because of his deal with Kronos." His eyes shifted to my left. "It was because he loved you."

I turned my head away, glaring stonily at his shoulder. I didn't know what to say, but it was just as well. I couldn't speak past the lump in my throat.

"When I mentioned guilt yesterday, I meant . . . taking a life, *anyone's* life, is a difficult burden."

"Mason—"

"It's not something you can just get over because he happened to be a terrible person."

"What would *you* know?" I snapped.

"More than you," he said. Anger punctuated his words although his expression changed little. "And you're going to listen this time instead of running aw—"

"Or what? You'll sic the chimera on me?"

"*Don't tempt me.*"

"You two require a room? Because there are plenty." It was Emryn.

Mason scowled in exasperation. My face burned at how we must have looked. He pulled away to look at Emryn, while I turned my back to collect myself.

"We were having a private conversation," Mason said.

"I could see that."

When I could face them again, I forced my mouth into a smile. My fingers gripped the torch blade I'd somehow forgotten

I was holding and raised it again at Mason. "Before you began talking about *feelings*, I was asking you to teach me how to use this."

Mason drew his own torch blade from its leather sheath at his waist. He flicked his weapon, striking our blades together. "Fine."

We found an unoccupied area in the courtyard for him to teach me some basic moves: different stances, footwork, how to block a strike aimed at my various body parts, and a few simple offensive strikes. Emryn volunteered to help Mason demonstrate each move. Afterward, he stuck around and watched me go through the motions, offering insight and criticism where he saw fit.

I didn't know why Emryn had suddenly warmed up to me, but after a couple of hours, having *two* remorseless perfectionists as instructors made me want to run screaming from the citadel, if only to see how they'd react to such a spectacle. Fortunately, Emryn seemed to sense this and returned to his own soldiers. Mason sparred with me for another hour, and although I tried my hardest to take off his head—only because I knew I wouldn't succeed—I could tell he was holding back. But he still tripped me half a dozen times for giving him the opening. The sentinels eventually came around to spar with me as well, taking turns as my partner.

By dinnertime, I was hot and sweaty and covered in bruises. But the thrill of being able to swing a sword without fear of injuring myself overshadowed the fatigue. I rushed back to my room to clean up and change, then I headed for the Temple of the Council of Vethe.

Cassia and the other Council members lived in chambers built on either side of the gallery. I had no idea which room was hers, but luckily, she was coming down the front steps just as I reached the Temple.

Her face brightened when she saw me. She looked better than she had yesterday, but the effects of her magic remained visible.

"I know you don't usually eat with guests, but I was wondering if you might want to join me and the sentinels today," I said. She had helped us at the risk of her own health, and I had yet to thank her. Plus, it would be a good opportunity to get to know her better and learn more about Lanathrill.

She looked surprised by my invitation. "Oh. Thank you. I'd like that."

Either invitations to dinner weren't common here or Cassia had as limited a social circle as I did. I figured everyone would be clamoring to gain her favor. That's how it had seemed in Ninurta with the mail carrier delivering a dozen invitations daily for Kalla. She rarely attended anything unless Miraya specifically asked. Having the support of the Kahl's former adviser—and executioner—gave Miraya considerably more influence.

Cassia and I made our way briskly through the palace. Her blue robes, worn today over a plain cream-colored gown, billowed behind her as we walked.

"Where do the other Council members eat?" I asked.

She wound the hem of her robes around her fingers before catching herself and dropping the wrinkled fabric. As we passed clusters of glimmer glass, light shifted over her wan face before the stretches of shadow glass doused it in darkness again.

"With their families. They're all married."

"Oh." I tried to estimate her age. I would have said no older than twenty-five except her frail appearance made it difficult to be sure. I might as well ask. "How old are you?"

"Nineteen."

My footsteps slowed. She noticed the hesitation and cocked her head at me.

"What?" she asked, looking self-conscious.

"Nothing," I said quickly. "You said the others eat with their families. What about you?"

She kept smoothing her palms nervously over her waist and the skirt of her gown. "My parents died some time ago from sickness. And my brother was killed two months ago on a patrol. I have no other family."

Now I wished I hadn't brought it up. "I'm sorry," I said. "I lost my parents when I was young, too." Kronos was my father, but whatever affection I might have once held for him had vanished along with my memories.

She gave me a small smile, and for a moment, the understanding of loss connected us.

"I like to think that my parents would be happy with what I'm doing," she said. "My brother always spoke of leaving a legacy that might make them proud."

"He sounds like a good brother."

"He was. He and Emryn were best friends. Caylum's loss devastated both of us."

"We'll stop the chimera," I said, because it was better than offering another useless apology. "Thank you, by the way. You know, for what you did yesterday."

My gratitude seemed to confuse her. "I only did what was necessary," she said.

We entered the guest dining hall. The sentinels grew quiet when they noticed my companion. Cassia paused, but I greeted them as usual and led her over to the table. When they realized this wasn't an impromptu meeting, their attention returned to their food. Mason sat farther down with Aylis, watching us in slight puzzlement. I smiled to let him know that Cassia was here only as a friend.

Today, the table was set with savory vegetable platters, pasta, fresh fruit, and sweet desserts. The chef had learned that we didn't eat meat—not because we had anything against it, but because we weren't used to it—and began preparing elaborate vegetable dishes instead. The aroma of the meat *had* smelled alluring, so I'd tried it, but the flavor and texture, while not unpleasant, had been a little too strange.

I helped myself to a thick stew of hearty root vegetables and spices, and a couple of rolls of cheese-crusted bread. If Cassia found it unusual that we didn't have a single meat platter, she didn't remark on it.

"Could you tell me about Ninurta?" she asked once we were settled. She twirled her fork in her bowl of noodles. "Is it very different from Lanathrill?"

I wasn't sure what I was supposed to say in this instance as the Kahl's adviser. So I decided to answer simply as myself.

I left out choice pieces of information about my past, but I told her about the East Quarter and the Labyrinth where I grew up. The mixture of horror and fascination on her face amused me.

"How did you come to be the Kahl's adviser?" she asked.

I kept it vague. "I did something for the last Kahl when he died. It was kind of a big deal." Before she could press for details, I added, "It's complicated. And a long story."

She got the hint, because she nodded politely for me to move on. I told her next about the White Court and how starkly different it was from the North District.

"Sounds like our farmers," Cassia said when I mentioned how lavishly the people in the White Court dressed and how they spent their credits on indulgences like parties and the theater and flashy Grays.

"How does that work?" I asked. Mason had said something previously about their farmers being the wealthiest.

"The people who work the land benefit the most from it," she explained. "Every citizen of Lanathrill is required to work and contribute to the city. The farmers are our most valuable workers because they provide the majority of the food. That's another reason the chimera are such a problem. Many of our farmers are now afraid to remain on the surface during planting season, and the crops suffer for it. Without that food, Vethe will starve." She shook her head, as if to dispel her fears. "Every citizen is given a monthly ration of flour, but the farmers get much larger rations as well as the occasional bonus, depending on the bounty of their harvest."

It sounded like a great system, but not one I could see Ninurta implementing without mass objection from the White Court. I didn't know what those people did for a living. They would probably revolt if they were expected to *earn* their places in the upper class.

"And what if you can't find work?"

"Then the Council would step in and assign you work. Although most people are pretty good about staying employed, because the last jobs available are usually the undesirable ones," she said with a grin.

"I bet you could think of a few people you'd want to have assigned those jobs," I said.

Her grin twisted into something more mischievous. "Yes, but I'm glad it's never necessary. The promise of fresh bread can be a powerful motivator for work."

"Oh, I know." I shoved a roll under my nose and took a deep breath before sighing happily. We both laughed.

She grabbed for her own roll and ripped it open before bringing it to her nose. "Mmm. I could live on the smell of fresh bread alone."

"I'd rather eat it," I said. We both took huge bites of our bread, grinning at each other and snorting with laughter when a hunk of chewed bread fell from her mouth.

Her face had flushed pink, temporarily chasing away her pallor. Her eyes sparkling with humor, she looked every bit the young, healthy girl she should have been. I'd never been the best at making friends, but conversation with Cassia came surprisingly easy. Laughing with her made me miss Hina.

I moved onto dessert, selecting a slice of sticky, sweet pie. "How do your farmers grow so much food without the sun?"

"We were fortunate in that the mountains became a barrier of sorts during the war, taking the majority of the damage that would have otherwise fallen on Lanathrill."

Most of the mountains had been crushed into dust. Had Lanathrill not been protected by the mountain range, the country would probably be as barren and useless now as the Outlands.

"The ill effects on our soil were manageable," she continued. "We could still grow a little food. But the farmers who served under Kahl Bael were ingenious, and they developed a new kind of grain, a sturdier one that could survive cooler temperatures and wouldn't need direct sunlight to flourish."

I wondered if Ninurta might somehow be able to use their sturdier grain. I made a mental note to add it to the list of possible trade crops. "Your farmers are also quite educated, I take it."

"They receive the best of everything, including access to all the tomes recovered from the University of Vethe. It was one of the largest universities on the continent, second only to the

Westlin Academy of Science in Peshtigo." She sighed wistfully. "To have seen or even attended those schools . . ."

I felt a pang of that same wistfulness. So much had been lost to the war.

"Anyway," she said, "the farmers plant twice a year, working on rotation. Those who work the land in the spring are allowed respite in Vethe for the winter. When they're here resting, they tend to enjoy competing with one another for who can hold the most glamorous party of the season. Quite the spectacle."

"I suppose they've earned the right."

"No one would dispute that," she said. "But they flaunt their wealth, which doesn't carry very well into the middle class."

"Anyone can learn to farm," I said.

"Sure, but it's a trade skill. Who would risk her own position by teaching them? And where would they work? Requests for land have to be granted by the Council, which rarely happens now. Lanathrill's lands are limited, and farming has become an inherited occupation."

I scooped up a chunk of fleshy red fruit dressed in a thick syrup. "So the farmers who owned those farmhouses we passed on the way to the Fields of Ishta also have a fancy home here in Vethe. And when the harvest is complete, they'll switch places with another farmer and return here to relax and throw parties until their turn to plant comes around again?"

She nodded. "Speaking of which, Mrs. Gabrien is holding a ball tomorrow. Please say you'll come."

Even though I'd been living in the palace, I'd never attended a ball. Kalla had shuffled a few invitations my way, but I had ignored them. Except for the ministers, no one outside the palace grounds even knew who I was or that I was there. I had no desire to change that.

However, as the Kahl's adviser, once Miraya had her coronation, everyone in Ninurta would know who I was. The idea of that much public recognition made me want to take my scout into the forest and never come back.

"I don't think that'd be a good idea," I said. "I'm kind of new to this adviser thing, and I've never been to a fancy party. I'd probably embarrass you."

"But you must," she said. She set down her fork and leaned toward me. "I have to attend a few events on behalf of the Council for the sake of appearances. Come with me. Just being there will be good practice for when you return to Ninurta."

I couldn't deny that I was curious. A ball could be fun. Would it be anything like the party the hollows had thrown me and Avan? Either way, Cassia had a point that I needed experience before being thrust into the middle of the White Court.

I scraped the last bits of fruit and pie from my plate and said, "Okay."

CHAPTER 19

"KAI, WAIT!"

I paused with my door opened partway. Mason was coming down the hall, footsteps silent over the glossy shadow glass. Living in the same wing as the sentinels was a bit unnerving. I hardly ever heard them walking around. I'd been startled more than once when I'd thought I was alone.

"What's up?" I asked.

"Why was Cassia eating with you?" He slipped his hands into his back pockets and shifted on his feet, as if there was more he wanted to say.

"Because I invited her."

When I didn't elaborate, he said, "Okay, then. She seems nice."

"She is."

"Not as intense as Emryn," he said, brow furrowing in imitation.

My lips twitched. I instantly felt ashamed for being amused. "We shouldn't joke. He's lost a lot."

Mason shrugged. "So has everyone."

I touched his arm. Mason had lost a lot to Ninu and the Infinite—his family, his team, his free will—but he still managed to find the humor in every situation.

"You're pretty intense sometimes, too, you know. Like whenever you're teaching me something," I said.

Mason looked pleased with himself. "Force of habit. Ninu had me train the new sentinels. They were always a little disoriented after the branding, and they responded best to a firm hand."

What must that have been like for him to usher in each new sentinel, knowing they would someday be reduced to mindless soldiers? Had the task bothered him or had he been too far gone himself to care?

He pulled his hands out of his pockets and looked down. "So . . . about what I said earlier—"

"I'm really not in the mood to talk about that again." I pushed into my room, but Mason's hand came up to stop me from shutting the door in his face.

"I know. I wanted to say I'm sorry."

I gave him a dubious look. He laughed.

"I'm serious," he said. "I know it's complicated, and it's none of my business anyway. But I'm worried about you, and I can't just *stop* being worried."

I scratched my fingernail against the corner of the wooden door, uncertain how to respond. "I don't want you to worry, but I have to figure things out myself. Like you said. It's . . . complicated."

"I still think you should tell Irra about what's happened to your powers," he said.

"Maybe." I stepped back and swung my door open wider. "I don't want to do this in the hall."

"Haven't heard that one before," he said.

I smiled and grabbed his arm, tugging him inside. Shutting the door, I gestured to the overstuffed armchair in the corner. He dropped onto the cushion while I settled on my bed, folding my legs beneath me.

"Cassia says there's a party tomorrow." I fiddled with the leaf brooch that I kept pinned to the hem of my tunic. "You should come. And the others, too. Maybe you can ask them?"

"They respect you," he said. "Even Winnifer and Gret. If you asked, they'd be happy to go."

"But I don't want it to sound like an order."

He laced his fingers in his lap. "Yeah, okay, I can bring it up to them."

"Thanks. So you'll come?"

"Are you asking me on a date?"

"Mason!"

"It's a legitimate question!"

We both laughed. He lifted his brows at me as if to ask, *Well?*

I looked up at my canopy, thinking it over. "I don't know," I said. "I've never asked anyone on a date before."

"Not even Avan?"

"We sort of just mutually agree to be in the same places together."

He leaned over, hanging his head between his knees. His shoulders shook with silent laughter.

"What?" I asked defensively, although I was laughing again, too.

When he straightened again, the silence between us lingered for a beat too long, and his smile began to fade. I could almost feel the tension rising. I braced myself for whatever he would say next.

"Is he ever . . . the way he was?"

The sadness in his eyes surprised me. In my own grief, I had failed to notice that Mason missed the old Avan, too. They had become friends in Etu Gahl. Maybe not in the way Mason and I were friends, but they had joked and trained and planned that going-away party for us and helped Rennard bake that enormous cake.

Ever since Avan's resurrection as Conquest, Mason treated him like an unwelcome stranger. It had never occurred to me that maybe it hurt him to see Avan like this.

"Sometimes I get glimpses of the old Avan," I said, looking down at my hands. They lay limp in my lap. I curled them into fists. "It gives me hope that he'll come back someday."

I didn't say that every time I glimpsed my Avan, it hurt like I was losing him all over again. Sometimes, I wondered if maybe it would be better if there was no hope. So that I could let go.

But those sorts of thoughts were fleeting, born of pain and weakness. As long as Avan wanted to remember, I would never stop hoping. Still, the question remained: *Did* he want to remember?

I looked up as Mason stood. He crossed the room and sank to his knees in front of me so that we were eye level. He touched the knuckles of my clenched hands.

"Back in Etu Gahl, I knew how you felt for him. It was obvious to everyone," he said with a smile that made me squirm self-consciously. Had I really been so transparent? "And it was pretty clear he felt the same. We'd only just met, so I wasn't going to get in the way of that. I doubt I would have been able to steal your attention even if I'd tried."

His words made my heart pump faster. I didn't think I was ready to hear them.

"But . . . things are different now. I'm your friend. And no matter what, I will always be your friend." He looked down, the gold fan of his lashes shielding his eyes. "Can I allow myself to hope?"

It wasn't difficult to understand what he meant. My skin tingled where his fingers touched my knuckles. I held my breath and then released it slowly. I'd suspected that, in the beginning, Mason's feelings for me might have been more than friendship. But until now, he had never given any indication that those feelings remained.

I'd be lying if I said I'd never thought about it. Mason was brave and honest and loyal, and I couldn't help the way those blue eyes and broad shoulders sometimes left me feeling flustered. It wasn't so easy to dismiss him. I wished it was.

He waited patiently for my response. His face was close, his cheekbones and the shape of his lips outlined by the light of the glimmer glass. I wrestled for something to say.

"Kai," Mason whispered.

"Yes?"

"You're staring at my mouth." That same mouth stretched into a grin as I leaned back, blushing from my chest to my cheeks. He nudged me forward again with a hand beneath my chin. "You should tell me to get out. Because if you don't, right now, I'm going to kiss you."

I swallowed, my gaze drawn back to his mouth. The words rose in my throat and then stayed there, trapped. Mason's thumb brushed against my lower lip. He leaned forward.

His lips were soft. Heat sang through me, and my heart beat a chaotic tune.

His fingers slid along my jaw, pushing into my hair. I gripped his shoulders as he deepened the kiss. A tremor raced through me. His muscles contracted beneath my hands.

His arm circled my back, gathering me closer.

A rush of panic filled me, closing my throat. I turned my head and pushed at Mason's shoulder. Immediately, he pulled back, his hands falling away.

"Are you okay?" he asked. He looked torn between reaching out and giving me space.

"I'm . . . sorry," I managed to say. "I can't."

"I understand," he said, but sadness still lurked behind his eyes. "You don't have to."

I drew a shaky breath. "Promise me something?"

He smiled. "Anything."

"Promise you won't wait for me."

Pain flickered over his face before he hid it behind a rueful smile.

"Mason," I said, taking his hand and squeezing it until his eyes met mine again. "I don't know when I'll be ready. You weren't willing to get between me and Avan, and I can't get in the way of something wonderful happening for you."

His free hand brushed my hair behind my ear. "You're something wonderful." Before I could respond, he continued: "But okay. I promise. Now promise me something in return."

"What?" I asked.

"Promise you'll keep practicing with that torch blade before you accidentally impale yourself with it."

His face cracked into another grin. With a shout, I grabbed the nearest pillow and whacked his shoulder with it.

"Do you remember our first kiss?"

I leaned into the narrow space between us. The scent of crushed moss and wildflowers filled our little haven.

My mouth touched Avan's, and I whispered, "How could I forget? You told me about how you weren't used to anyone having the power to hurt you anymore. But that it wasn't a bad kind of hurt."

His hand cupped the back of my head, tilting my face so that I looked up at him. Our breaths mingled in the warm air.

He grinned. "That's not the part I was remembering."

CHAPTER 20

THE NEXT MORNING, I ENDURED THE TAILOR'S POKING AND prodding as he took my measurements for the gown he meant to construct for me for the ball. I had no idea how he planned to finish it by that evening, but I kept my doubts to myself.

I occupied my mind by mulling over my latest dream. Obviously, the kiss with Mason must have sparked the subject matter, but I'd awoken again with the impression of threads shivering just out of reach. If Mason's theory about my nightmares—that they were connected to my guilt—was correct, then maybe these ones about Avan were somehow related.

After the session with the tailor, I spent a few hours training with the torch blade as Mason repeatedly corrected my form. When he allowed me to leave, I washed up and headed out into the city. That morning, Cassia had mentioned that her favorite bakery resided a few blocks down from the stone arch that divided Vethe between the farmer upper class and everyone else.

I avoided eye contact with the farmers dressed in fine tunics and damask gowns strolling by at a leisurely pace. In contrast, all the servants walked briskly, their eyes averted. I probably would have looked like a servant if not for my long hair and the fact I didn't have a servant's tattoo.

While the farmers reminded me a bit of the White Court citizens, now that I knew to look, I could see the evidence of their work in the rough texture of their hands, when they weren't covered with leather or lace gloves. These people provided food for Vethe, and they appeared to wear that duty proudly.

A carriage rattled by with a family crest painted on the door. Everything felt so novel. I could sit on one of the benches off to the side of the road and be content simply watching the vehicles and horses pass. The buildings rose and fell along with the rough terrain of the mountain, looking much more cramped and crooked from ground level. With the abundant glimmer glass as Vethe's main source of light, the city was always well illuminated.

As I neared the arch, I scanned the shops. On the corner ahead was a building with elegant curls carved into the window frames. Painted into the smooth stone in bright pink was the name *Patriya's Bakery*.

I pushed inside. A bell jingled above the door. The aroma of fresh baked goods and sugary sweets wafted around me. I smiled.

Platters and trays of pastries, breads, scones, and cookies were displayed on tables and racks all around the shop. I selected a cookie in the shape of a flower and a cream-stuffed pastry, and nestled both inside a paper box. Then I took my purchases to the counter. A pair of women chatted ahead of me in line. I tapped my fingers along the sides of my box while I waited, unable to help overhearing their conversation.

"For six months," one of the women was saying. A purple hat with tufts of gauzy black lace sat at an angle on her head. "I've been writing every week, but I haven't heard a word."

The other woman clucked her tongue in sympathy and pressed a satin-gloved hand to Purple Hat's shoulder. "It's horrible, isn't it? I wish they'd make peace and bring our children home."

Purple Hat bobbed her head in agreement. "Kahl Emryn did say in his latest speech that we've pushed Peshtigo back behind their own borders. That's something! It'll be over any day now, I'm sure." She chewed her lip, not looking very confident.

Peshtigo? Where had I heard that name before? I mulled it over as the women left and the clerk rang up my order.

I munched on the cookie as I headed back to the citadel.

"Kai?"

I stiffened at the voice. Emryn rode up, probably returning from checking in with the guards outside the mountain. He was dressed in his armor, his cloak draped immaculately over his horse's tail. Two of his men flanked him.

He handed his reins to the soldier on his left. "Return her to the citadel for me."

The soldier nodded as Emryn dismounted and joined me on the sidewalk.

Ever since the chimera attack in the Fields of Ishta, his demeanor had changed around me. He wasn't so brusque. He actually smiled sometimes. While I was glad to be spared his constant superiority, it annoyed me that seeing me in danger had caused his change. I wasn't some defenseless kid who needed protecting.

"Hello, Emryn," I said, continuing down the sidewalk. Everyone on the street who'd been ignoring me before now openly stared.

Emryn didn't seem to notice. He was probably used to it.

He pointed to the box I was carrying. "My best friend and I used to buy sweet buns from Patriya's Bakery every morning when I was a child."

I didn't have any similar stories to share considering my first taste of cake had been a few months ago in Etu Gahl, and I'd never really had a best friend. So I waved my half-eaten cookie at him and said, "They're really good. Would you like the other one?"

He declined the offer with a polite shake of his head.

"Returning to the citadel?" When I nodded, he said, "If you decide to explore the westernmost neighborhoods, one of your sentinels should accompany you. It's not safe there by yourself."

"I grew up on streets a lot worse than this. I think I can manage."

"I don't doubt that," he said. I couldn't tell if he was patronizing me. "But I'd feel better if you weren't alone."

Since he seemed determined to walk with me, I ignored him and finished off my cookie. For a few blocks, neither of us said much. He pointed out some buildings, like the noodle shop that he claimed made the best pasta, the city square where he gave a speech every couple of months to keep the people apprised of pertinent matters, and the elaborate tangle of roots nearby in which the children liked to climb and hide.

I had to grudgingly admit he was interesting company.

The ground began to slope upward as we neared the gates to the citadel. I paused and turned around to look down on the crowded sprawl of buildings. Emryn stopped next to me.

A woman was crossing the street, clutching the broad-rimmed hat on her head. She reminded me of the women in the shop.

"What's Peshtigo?" I asked Emryn.

"Where did you hear about Peshtigo?"

"In the bakery."

After a moment, he said, "Peshtigo is a country to our east."

That's where I'd seen it. The name had been on Emryn's map. Cassia had mentioned it as well.

I sat on a stone bench beside the road. Emryn did the same, but he followed slowly, as if reluctant to linger. I wasn't going anywhere until he told me more about Peshtigo and whatever conflict might be happening with them.

"Have you been there?" I asked.

"A few months ago. Its lands suffered less damage than ours, but I imagine it would have been a sight more impressive before the Mahjo War."

I watched a wagon filled with hay rattle past, and then asked, "Why's that?"

"Because Peshtigo was once the center of trade on the continent. Its ports saw ships carrying goods from all over the world, and its capital of Westlin was home to both the Academy of Science and the Temple of Light."

I'd read about the Temple of Light. It had been the largest and most revered *mahjo* temple in the world. Young *mahjo* had journeyed there to learn how to control their powers and, if they were lucky, to someday be given control over one of the many *mahjo* temples across the continent.

"That would have been a sight," I agreed. "Why did the women in Patriya's make it sound as if you're at war with them?"

He scratched his beard. He did that a lot, I'd noticed, particularly when I was asking him questions he seemed loath to answer. "Because we are. Peshtigo is a country of madmen. Their kingdom borders a place of darkness. An endless stretch of black earth and a raw emptiness that eats you from the inside."

"The Void," I said.

He looked at me. "An apt name."

"And living so close to the Void drives them crazy?"

"Maybe, but it's worse than that. Peshtigo's Kahl and his people have taken to consuming the soil."

With the toe of my boot, I nudged a patch of green fronds sprouting from a tree root. "Because they're starving?"

He snorted. "That would be a better reason, but no. It's because they think the magic residue that keeps the earth from healing will restore their own magic. And in doing so, help them to reestablish Peshtigo. In reality, it's only driven them mad. They suffer hallucinations that make them believe they've recovered their magic, but it's only in their heads."

"That's terrible." And sad. I'd taken to imagining the threads as they'd looked when I could touch them. Would that seed of longing grow with age and someday curve into madness? Maybe the world was better off without magic.

"I was in the east helping to defend our borders, but fighting people who are half-crazed isn't particularly easy."

I rubbed my thumb along the sharp edge of the box in my lap. "When the chimera began to attack the farmers, you came back."

"Yes. And now our army is divided between the ongoing conflict with Peshtigo and defending against the chimera."

That would explain the distinct shortage of soldiers in the city. There were still enough for a sizable army—enough to defend the city—but not nearly the numbers I'd been expecting.

"Why wasn't this mentioned when we first discussed an alliance?" I asked. He had to realize how suspicious it looked that he'd failed to mention the country was at war with its neighbor.

"It's . . ." He gave a jerk of his head. "It's not something I'm particularly proud of."

"*Embarrassment* isn't a good reason to hide a war." The only time a ruler would want a war kept secret was if he was doing something questionable—like Ninu and his campaign to find Irra's fortress.

"There's nothing more to tell," Emryn said, looking placid. But he was touching his beard again. "Peshtigo continues to assault our eastern border, and we continue to hold them off. We've tried to petition for an audience with their Kahl, but we've always been refused. There was nothing sinister or deceptive about my omission."

I wasn't so convinced. I stared down at the flowers, bright ribbons against the harsh gray, wishing I'd known all this sooner so that I could have included it in my message to Miraya.

"You've fought in a war," Emryn said. It wasn't a question.

"I wouldn't call it a war, but . . . yes. I've fought an enemy." *And killed him.*

"The way you move is practiced, like you've been trained to fight unarmed."

"Mason has been my instructor for a while now."

He was silent a moment. Then, "That was very brave of you—jumping in to save your sentinel without even knowing how to use your sword."

Unless it was my imagination, there was respect in his voice. Maybe I was wrong about his change in demeanor. It wasn't because he thought I needed protection. It was because I had earned his respect.

I looked away. Not enough respect to warrant the truth about this war with Peshtigo. "Thanks," I mumbled, touching my waist where my torch blade would have been. At the moment, it was back in my room in the citadel. "But next time I'll be prepared."

"Next time I hope you'll think twice before facing a chimera alone," he said wryly. "But, yes, at least you'll be prepared."

I pushed to my feet, holding my box against my stomach. "I should get back."

It didn't take long for us to reach the courtyard. While Emryn explained how they never culled the roots unless they threatened the stability of the city, my thoughts kept returning to the war with Peshtigo. There was more to it that Emryn wasn't telling me. I was certain of it.

CHAPTER 21

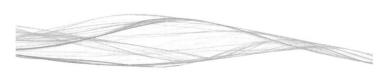

CASSIA CAME RUNNING OUT THE CITADEL'S DOORS A FEW HOURS later, shouting my name. I was in the middle of sparring with Aylis, but she grabbed my wrist without a word of explanation and dragged me back to my room.

She bounced on her heels, teeming with excitement, and I had no idea why until I saw my new gown draped across my bed. My breath caught. Cassia squealed and clasped her hands together.

I was almost too afraid to touch it, but I reached out and carefully held it up. The gown was sleeveless. The front of the bodice was constructed of cream satin with gold embroidery. Delicate gold leaves, blossoms, and lace accents had been hand-sewn into the fabric in flattering patterns. The back of the bodice was sheer, but the gold embroidery continued in leaflike symmetrical patterns across the shoulder blades. A line of tiny pearlescent buttons ran the length of the spine.

The skirt was like nothing I'd seen, not even in the White Court. Layers of cream tulle and chiffon were draped in waves. The top layer was barely a foot long, its thick folds giving dramatic volume around the hips before the elegant draping continued down into the full skirt.

Would I even fit through a door in this?

Two servants blew into my room, an older woman and a young girl carrying a basket filled with bottles and lacquered pots. Cassia greeted them warmly, but I watched with rising apprehension as the young girl set the basket on my dressing table and began unpacking its contents.

"Well, let's see then," the older woman said. She grabbed my arms and held them out from my body as she scrutinized me with a slight curl of her lip. I wanted to cover myself despite being fully dressed. "Hmm. A bit thin."

I snatched my arms away. If she thought I was skinny now, she should have seen me a few months ago when I'd still been scraping by in the Labyrinth, eating little more a day than a sandwich, dried fruit, and whatever Avan could give me for free from his dad's shop.

"Kai, this is Madgie," Cassia said. "She usually helps me prepare for parties, but I thought she could assist you today since it's your first time."

"Undress," Madgie ordered.

I didn't like being barked at, but Cassia only smiled, her eyes bright with amusement. This must have been Madgie's usual manner. Madgie huffed and reached for my tunic.

"I can do it," I said. I sneaked behind the paneled dressing screen in the corner and shed my simple gray and blue tunic and pants.

"Everything!" Madgie snapped from the other side of the screen. With reluctance, I also slipped off my undergarments.

The next couple of hours was a whirlwind of lace and satin, creams and perfumes. The servants jostled me back and forth as they closed buttons and tugged at my hair and applied powders and charcoal to my eyes. As they worked, I fidgeted, picking absently at a scab on my leg where Mason had nicked me during a spar. Was this what the upper class did every day? If it took this much effort to look rich, why bother at all?

And what if none of it worked on me anyway? The gown was exquisite, but I might wind up looking like one of Irra's puffy bread bites.

And yet, as Cassia giggled out of view, I had to admit this was kind of exciting. I'd never done this before—at least not to this extent. There was this girl from school who liked to stain her lips and line her eyes with charcoal. She'd let me wear her makeup when we hung out at her house. Like all my friends, though, once she stopped going to school to work full-time, we lost contact. I had delivered a package to her house once when I was still working for the DMC, but she hadn't been home.

Cassia came to stand beside me. I was sitting on a stool, layers of fabric piled around my hips, with my back to the mirror as the servants manhandled me. "You're going to look beautiful," she said.

I couldn't move my head to look up at her face. So I smiled at her waist instead. "Or like a painted doll."

"Nothing wrong with that," Madgie muttered. I snorted softly.

Cassia brushed her robes aside, and I noticed a fine dusting of black sprinkled over the skirt of her gown.

"You have soot on you," I said.

Cassia swiveled away, brushing her fingers over the fabric. "Oops. Got too close to the fireplace."

A few minutes later, Cassia had to leave to finish preparing for the ball herself. An interminable amount of time later, Madgie and her servant fitted dainty heeled boots on my feet and finally stepped back.

"Stand," Madgie ordered.

I did, her gaze inspecting me. She gave me a terse nod and gestured for me to look in the mirror.

Nerves flitting through my stomach, I looked. And then I gaped.

My hair had been pulled back and arranged into artful curls at the back of my head, leaving my neck bare. Gold flowers and leaves nestled among the dark curls. My eyes, which I'd always thought of as watered-down blue—something else I'd inherited from my father—stood out like fragments of ice, or glimmer glass, against the charcoal darkening my lashes and the smoky gray on my lids. My cheeks were a healthy pink and my lips were stained burgundy.

I lightly fingered the lace peeking out from the gold flowers on my bodice before brushing my palms over the full skirt and its thick layers of folded tulle and chiffon. I had the strange desire to twirl but resisted, because as stunning as the girl in the mirror was . . . she wasn't me. This was the most elaborate costume I'd donned yet. Maybe things weren't entirely the same in Lanathrill, but I'd always thought people in the White Court lived in an illusion—an imaginary world of beast-like Grays and crystal-studded gowns, where their next meal would be more than what Reev and I had eaten in a week in the Labyrinth. It wasn't real.

I sighed and pressed a hand to my abdomen, the delicate flowers soft against my palm.

"You don't like it?" Madgie asked. She looked perplexed and a little insulted.

"No, no, it's . . . astounding. I've never looked like this before. Thank you." I nodded to her assistant as well. "Really. Thank you."

Madgie seemed satisfied, because they began gathering their bottles and pots and vials into the basket.

"Lady Cassia will be back to collect you," Madgie said before they left.

Once the door was shut, I stretched out my fingers and took a deep breath before daring to look in the mirror again. I tilted my head, marveling at the transformation. What would Reev say if he saw me?

What would Avan do?

I retrieved my tunic from where I'd draped it over the changing screen and fumbled through the fabric until I found the leaf brooch. Returning to the mirror, I fixed the brooch to my right hip so that it sat nestled within the first layer of tulle.

Now there was a little bit of me in this costume.

CHAPTER 22

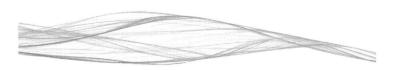

WE TOOK A COACH TO THE BALL. THE RATTLING OF THE CARRIAGE, the rumbling of wheels, and the clomping of the horse's hooves made me appreciate how smooth and silent our Grays were. Not even the sentinels would be able to move around undetected in one of these.

Outside Mrs. Gabrien's house, the street was jammed with coaches lined up to drop off their passengers. I peered out the window at the house up ahead. It was a sturdy three-story home with elegant curling architecture adorning the flat roof. At each corner was a cluster of glimmer glass that cast a bright glow with faint purple undertones down the walls.

I gripped my seat as we bumped along over the road, my skirt gathered around my legs. Across from me, Cassia was dressed in a blue gown of slick satin. The gold starburst of Lanathrill was embroidered into the center of her chest with threads radiating outward down the curves of her waist and over her shoulders into a sheer cape that hung to the base of her spine.

Her hair had been swept up into a similar style to mine with a blue-and-gold metal clasp that hugged the side of her head. With all the creams and powders concealing the shadows beneath her eyes, she looked almost healthy. But even makeup couldn't erase the slight hollows of her cheeks or the weariness that dulled her eyes.

"Will Emryn or the other Council members be there?" I asked as our carriage clattered nearer to the house.

"No. Emryn doesn't attend purely social events."

The forlorn quality to her tone made me tilt my head. "But you wish he would?"

Her ears turned pink, and I grinned. It was somehow comforting to know even someone in Cassia's position suffered from unrequited infatuation.

"Does he know?" I asked.

"Goodness no," she said, horrified. "And you won't say a word. It wouldn't be appropriate."

"Why wouldn't it? You're allowed to like who you want."

"As a representative of Lanathrill, I'm expected to behave a certain way. Besides, Emryn has enough to occupy his mind without my affections weighing on him. And he has no interest in romance anyway. Lanathrill's welfare is the only thing that matters to him. When you've been adviser for a while longer, you'll learn that the welfare of your country is *always* more important."

I propped my elbow on the open window. *Not to me,* I thought, which was why I'd been hesitant to accept Miraya's offer in the first place. Nothing would ever be more important than my friends and family. If I had to choose between Reev or Ninurta, it wouldn't be a choice at all.

"All right," I said to appease Cassia. "What about the others then? The Council—will they be there?"

"No. I'm the voice of the Council, so I represent all of them. But to be honest, they're as dull at parties as they are in meetings."

I laughed in surprise at her candor.

The coach rattled to a stop in front of the walkway. A servant opened the door and extended a hand to help me down. My nervousness and the warm air had me fanning my bare neck. My stomach fluttered. I almost laughed at the ridiculousness.

I had fought an Infinite and won, and yet I was anxious about going to a party in a fancy dress.

Cassia linked her arm with mine, and we entered the house, walking into a foyer. A short hallway led into a series of rooms, filled with milling guests. We roamed through each room, taking everything in. The stone walls had been painted in a curling silver pattern, highlighted by dozens of glimmer glass stands that illuminated every shadowy corner. Each room connected to a central great room where the space had been cleared for dancers.

Women in gowns more elaborate, colorful, and voluminous than mine glided across the dance floor in clouds of satin and lace. The men were dressed in high-collared tunics or brocade vests and slim jackets, paired with tailored dark pants.

This was completely different from the party in Etu Gahl. There, everyone had shouted and laughed, and there had been no room for pride or hesitation. Here, even the dancing looked choreographed as the couples twirled and dipped to the music from the orchestra in the second-story balcony.

Trotting at the end of golden leashes or folded in the laps of a few women were petite horned creatures. I studied one of them as we passed. I gasped in recognition. I'd seen its likeness from a column in the Hall of Memories. It was a fauhn.

Fauhns looked like miniature deer, no bigger than a rabbit, with brown-and-white dappled coats and knobby, hoofed legs. Their most remarkable trait was their double set of horns. The first set sprang out the sides of their heads, right above their ears, and curved back like a halo, tapering into sharp points. The other set rose from the crown of their heads, arching slightly and growing nearly twice the height of the creatures themselves, with the ends transforming into full branches. The carvings in the Hall of Memories had shown fauhns with horns of all lengths: some with short branches, some long and interwoven and adorned with silvery leaves that sprouted from crystalline buds.

Cassia noticed my gawking and whispered, "There were fauhn herds in the forests of Lanathrill before the war. We were able to rescue a few and preserve their species. There aren't enough left for a herd, and the land isn't fertile enough to support them. So the wealthiest of our farmers breed and raise them as pets."

I didn't want to seem rude by continuing to stare, but I couldn't help it. If these creatures had survived the war, who knew what else might still be out there?

Cassia took me around the room, introducing me to a few of her acquaintances. Everyone treated her with a reverence that was part fear and part awe. They were friendly enough on the surface, but it was easy to tell that a wall stood between her and everyone else.

When we found a corner to stand in, I said, "So these people want to gain your favor and your ear, but they don't want to be your friend."

Cassia's cheeks grew red. "It's not their fault. Not only am I the voice of the Council, but I'm *mahjo*." She tried to brush it off, but clearly their behavior bothered her. "*Mahjo* have always lived separate lives from everyone else, even before the war."

"Things are different now," I said. "How we lived before the war doesn't really apply anymore."

Cassia bit her lip, looking contemplative, but she didn't respond.

"I wanted to ask you about something," I said. "I'm sorry for bringing it up now, but I forgot to mention it earlier with all the"—I waved at myself—"primping."

"Go on," she said.

"I wanted to ask about Peshtigo."

Cassia's eyes widened, but she quickly recovered. "What about Peshtigo?" she asked casually.

I felt a tick of annoyance. She would give nothing away until she knew how much information I had. "Why wasn't I told about the war?"

"Our war with Peshtigo is little more than a series of scuffles and conflicts along our eastern border. We keep the military posts well manned in case they somehow unleash a greater, coordinated attack."

"If it's such a minor concern, then why don't you call back your troops to support the fight against the chimera? They're kind of a more pressing issue, don't you think?"

"Kahl Emryn made his decision," she said, and there again was that condescension she'd worn the first time we'd met. She didn't think it was my place to question Emryn. "The time for discussion has passed."

"So if he decided to have all the wheat tossed into the sea, you'd just do it because the decision was final?"

"That's hardly a fair comparison."

"Fine," I conceded, "but my point is that you're his *Council.* So why don't you *counsel* him that, right now, a better use for his army would be to protect his country from the chimera?"

"How?" she asked, brows rising imperiously. "Nothing we have done so far has been effective. What would bringing in more soldiers accomplish except to raise the death toll?"

I rubbed my forehead. There was logic in her arguments, but her words just didn't ring true to me, especially given Lanathrill was so desperate that they had reached out to a country they had no reason to believe would actually help. There would indeed be heavy losses, but with a greater force, they could overcome the chimera. Not to mention more soldiers could be stationed around the countryside to protect the farmers and Vethe's main source of food.

But it was clear that either Cassia was refusing to question Emryn's orders or she thought I would be placated with half answers. Either option annoyed me.

"I should have been told about this 'conflict.' Keeping secrets isn't exactly the best start to an alliance," I said.

"I'm sorry we kept it from you. Our intention wasn't to be deceptive."

I wanted to believe her, but if they weren't going to give me straight answers, then I would find those answers myself.

"Can I have the next dance?"

We both turned. Mason had come up behind me, looking absurdly attractive in a blue tunic with an asymmetrical collar that buttoned at his left shoulder. His hair had been combed into submission, and the shade of his tunic made his eyes appear impossibly blue.

"You look great," I said. Mason's smile grew taut, and I clamped my lips together. An awkward beat passed, my mind trying desperately *not* to remember what his kiss had felt like.

I searched over his shoulder for the other sentinels. Winnifer was dragging Gret onto the dance floor, but instead of joining with the coordinated movements of the other couples, they dived through the dancers with shameless laughter. I hoped they wouldn't get us thrown out. Cassia looked entertained by their antics.

Mason nodded at my outfit. "You don't look so bad yourself. So what do you say? Dance? You did pretty well the first time."

The "first time" being when we'd danced at the party in Etu Gahl. I nodded, and Mason pulled me into the flow of dancers. Instead of focusing on his nearness, I concentrated on the music and the steps of the dance. The tempo was fast, and the couples moved in fluid synchronization. Fortunately, Gret and Winnifer had wandered off to explore other parts of the house.

There'd been a time when I wouldn't have dared draw this sort of attention to myself. Reev and I had preferred to keep our heads down and survive as best we could. The world had been simpler then. Smaller. Narrowed down to just me and Reev.

I tripped over Mason's foot. My fingers dug into his shoulder to stay upright as his hand tightened at my waist.

"Sorry," I said, my feet shuffling and stuttering their way through the dance, nothing like the effortless glide of the other dancers. Mason didn't appear to mind. *He* knew what he was doing. When did he have the chance to learn this kind of dance in Etu Gahl? Then again, he was probably a really fast learner.

"You're doing fine," he said. I smiled, grateful that he hadn't allowed the kiss to alter our friendship. I knew there were still things we'd need to talk about, but those things could wait for another time.

"You're humoring me."

"A bit." He grinned. "When do you think Dennyl will return with a reply?"

"Hopefully tomorrow," I said, trying to relax into the movements. Why was sword fighting so much easier than dancing? "What do you think Miraya will say?"

"I think she'll understand that it's our responsibility to defend these people against Ninu's creations. She'll send help."

"You sound confident."

"The alternative would be to leave Lanathrill to fight a horde of chimera alone. It wouldn't exactly be the best start as neighbors, and there's a lot at stake."

I didn't think Miraya would jeopardize a possible alliance, either, but it was nice to know that he agreed.

"Speaking of our start as neighbors," I said, leaning in so that my mouth hovered at his ear. I could feel him tense, but I gave him a quick summary of Lanathrill's conflict with Peshtigo.

"With the way Emryn first greeted us, the others don't trust him anyway," Mason said quietly. "After we're done in Vethe, maybe we should head east and see this Peshtigo."

"Maybe." That was probably the only way we were going to get any real answers.

"I'll keep my ears open in the meantime, though."

"Emryn seems eager for the chance to talk to Miraya," I said. We made another pass around the room. My feet didn't feel quite so clumsy this time, at last picking up on where to step and how to turn into the motions. Mason's strength helped, carrying me through the dance with typical hollow grace.

"He's warmed up to you," Mason said.

I recalled the conversation we'd had that morning in the city. "He has."

When we'd first arrived, Yara had said that she thought he'd lost hope. Maybe it wasn't just his demeanor that had changed. Maybe Emryn had begun to hope again.

A racket rose to our left. The commotion was coming from one of the adjoining rooms. Mason and I identified Winnifer's and Gret's voices at the same time, and we fled the dance floor in mutual silence.

"Stay here," I said to Mason before squeezing through the guests who'd gathered around to watch the exchange. When I emerged into the circle that had formed around the pair, I looked between them to the man who'd caught the short end of their tempers.

"What happened?" I asked, shouting to be heard over the clamor of arguing and the music still playing in the other room.

Winnifer noticed me first. "This oaf thinks we're not fit to be here," she said, jabbing her thumb at the man who was looking down his long nose at Gret.

The man was immaculate, from his polished boots to the lace at his throat to the way his hair was combed back from his forehead, and he regarded me with similar disdain. I might look the part, but I hadn't yet learned to project the kind of self-importance that would convince these people I belonged here. Winnifer and Gret, although dressed in beautiful gowns and styled with the same precision as every other woman here, hadn't even bothered pretending to fit in.

"If we allowed just anyone to attend, our events would hardly be exclusive, would they?" the man was saying to Gret. Bejeweled rings ornamented each of the fingers he stabbed at her. Judging by the darkening look on Gret's face, he was about to lose those fingers if I didn't intervene.

I brushed past Winnifer to step between the man and Gret. "I'll thank you to keep your snobbery to yourself," I said over Gret's protests.

It was the wrong thing to say, because the man sneered at me, unimpressed. "Who are *you*?"

Our arrival in Vethe had been rather public, but without knowing what these people had been told about our presence in the city, I wasn't sure how to answer him.

"And where did you get that dress?" he demanded, a note of suspicion in his voice. "Steal it?"

"Really?" I asked, because there was no other way to respond without physical violence. Maybe I could understand now why the middle class took issue with the farmers. This man was worse than most of the people I'd met in the White Court—people whose superiority I'd become practiced at brushing off—and my restraint was fast dwindling.

The way Gret kept digging her nails into my forearm, however, helped to remind me that the last thing I needed was an incident between our countries when we hadn't even signed any papers yet. As Cassia had said earlier of her own position, I was a representative of Ninurta and I was expected to behave in a certain way. So I would grit my teeth and be as diplomatic as possible.

"I am adviser to Kahl Miraya of Ninurta, and we're here as the personal guests of the voice of the Council," I said, trying and failing not to take pleasure in the way the man's face paled at the mention of Cassia.

He attempted to scoff, but several bystanders interjected that they had, in fact, seen me arrive with Cassia. At that, the man took two large steps back, which Winnifer and Gret observed with snorts of laughter.

"Let's get back to enjoying this party, shall we?"

At Cassia's interruption, everyone jumped to attention, scattering almost instantly. That was some impressive crowd control.

"Well done, Kai," she said with a slight smile.

"Were you watching the whole time?" I asked before waving off Gret and Winnifer, the latter of whom at least looked somewhat sorry for causing a scene.

"I wanted to see what you'd do," Cassia admitted. She touched my elbow and guided me back into the center room with the dancers. I searched for Mason, who stood near the entryway, waiting.

"And what's your verdict?" I asked Cassia dryly. Mine was that I hadn't the disposition to be a foreign liaison if this had been a preview of future conflicts. Physical fights were so much simpler.

She smiled. "You'll make a fine politician."

CHAPTER 23

IT WAS LATE WHEN WE LEFT. I DOZED IN THE CARRIAGE. WE WERE dropped off at the gates of the citadel, a servant appearing to help us down.

I smothered a yawn and bid Cassia a good night before heading inside. Another servant met me outside my bedroom.

"Madgie asked me to help you out of your gown," the girl said, hovering at my shoulder as I pushed into my room in a groggy haze.

"Just unbutton me," I said, presenting her with my back.

Her nimble fingers went to work, loosening the row of buttons. The material sagged off my shoulders.

"Thanks. You can go. I'm sure you'd rather be sleeping." I stepped out of the gown and draped it over my armchair, too tired to care about modesty. I rooted around for my nightshirt.

"Very well. Also, your sentinel arrived about an hour ago."

I tugged the shirt down over my torso before looking at her over my shoulder, blinking the fog from my eyes. "What?"

"The one you sent to Ninurta. He's returned. He's gone to bed for the night, but he had a message with him. It's on your dresser."

I whirled around, my eyes focusing on the folded slip of paper I hadn't noticed before. Dennyl must have rested for only a few hours in Ninurta before making the return trip.

"Thank you," I said, dismissing her.

I sat on the stool and broke the wax seal on the paper. I was wide awake now, my heart pounding as I unfolded the letter.

The handwriting was unfamiliar, but Irra's name was signed at the bottom. Strange that Miraya hadn't written a response herself. There was only one sheet. Disappointment shot through me. What was Reev doing that he couldn't even scrawl down a quick message to let me know that he was okay? Keeping in contact had always been a strict rule set by him, but now with half a continent between us, he didn't even bother?

I have things I need to do here, Reev had said. Like talk to old sentinel friends in shadowy corners? I swallowed, uncomfortable with where my thoughts were leading me. Reev had nothing to do with those attacks.

I smoothed out the letter's creases and pushed away the doubts as I focused on the neatly written words:

Kai—Miraya sends her apologies for not replying person-
ally. She has been kept busy. There was another attack.
As to the mahjo *and magic, we have a theory.*

He had written something else and then scratched it out.
Below the scribbled ink, he wrote:

Avan pointed out that your threat to return to Ninurta and
demand answers in person was not an idle one, so I decided it
would be prudent to explain our theory.

I smiled at the brief mention of Avan.

Although we stripped the mahjo *of their magic after the*
war, magic never just disappears. All that raw, unleashed
power had to go somewhere. Allowing it simply to soak into
the world could have been as devastating as the war itself. Who
knew what it would do or how it would manifest? So we created
a container. We call it the sepulcher.
If Lanathrill's mahjo *have regained their magic, then it's*
possible that something has happened to the sepulcher. It's a
troubling thought.
None of my hollows or the sentinels have regained magic.
Their collars were designed to amplify the last traces of magic
in their blood. I would know if their full powers returned.
However, there is no way to tell from here if this is isolated to
Lanathrill or if the reappearance of magic has spread elsewhere.

Kalla and I must return to our realms to verify the safety of the sepulcher. The sentinels will remain in Ninurta. Miraya needs them here. There are many who have already promised to serve her of their own free will. They will keep her safe.

As to the chimera, I will send for the hollows in Etu Gahl. They should arrive to assist you in two days.

I set down the letter. Help was coming. Relief seeped through me, and with it, the lull of sleep.

I crawled into bed and closed my eyes. No doubt Emryn had already been informed of Dennyl's return, but letting him and the others know about the contents of Irra's letter would have to wait until tomorrow.

Questions swirled in my head, battling my desire for sleep. This "sepulcher" had to be strong enough to contain the magic of every *mahjo* in the world. Could such a thing be broken?

And if it *could* break, what would happen to all that magic? Would all the living *mahjo* suddenly manifest powers or would the magic be released into the world as Irra had said and rain another cataclysm down on us?

I pushed my face into my pillow and told my brain to shut up so I could sleep.

But while the questions quieted, the disappointment remained. Reev hadn't written to me. I was a little hurt that Avan hadn't said anything, either. Clearly he had read my letter, or been informed of it.

Some nights, when I was half-asleep, and the world was soft and surreal, I would reach out over the bed, expecting to find Avan and twine our fingers together as we had during our time in Etu Gahl. But there was nothing, and the sudden reminder of his loss was like a fresh wave of grief that startled me awake, gasping for air.

Would Avan leave with Irra and Kalla? Irra had said that he was unlikely to come back, but what about Avan? He had nothing to hold him in Ninurta, except for me, and that was hardly enough. He'd been all but ready to move on when I'd seen him last.

I muffled a yawn with my pillow. I would see Avan again. I had to trust that he wouldn't leave without saying good-bye.

The next morning, although I was still tired—and somewhat disappointed that I hadn't dreamed of Avan again—I rose an hour before dawn. I brushed and braided my hair, changed into a gray tunic, tugged on my soft-soled boots, and made my way down to Emryn's war room. I hadn't been in this area of the citadel since I first arrived, but memory guided my feet to the familiar metal door.

I knocked first and waited a few seconds for a response. When none came, I tested the doorknob and was surprised to find that it wasn't locked. I supposed no one would dare enter without permission. Lucky me. I felt a thrum of guilt, but not enough to turn back.

I slipped inside and shut the door behind me. The room looked the same as last time: desks and tables shoved against the walls with stacks of books, maps, and scrolls littering every available surface. The glimmer glass that dangled like a crystal chandelier from the ceiling illuminated the table at the center of the room. I moved in to get a closer look at the map that had been left open across the tabletop.

The map showed current landmarks and borders, although the cartographer had taken creative rein when constructing the lands beyond Lanathrill's reach. The Outlands covered less area than it should have, and Ninurta was in entirely the wrong place. I focused on the parts of the map that had to be accurate.

Lanathrill was a large country, stretching halfway into the continent. The Kahl's Mountain was at the western rim of what had once been the Leluna Range. North of Vethe was the Marrow Sea. I placed my finger on a river that bisected Lanathrill—a river we'd missed on our way here by probably half a day's ride—and followed it eastward through the forest to where it emptied into a lake. A series of *x*'s had been marked in ink along Lanathrill's eastern border. I wondered what they were meant to signify. Guard posts? Battles?

Peshtigo was much smaller in comparison. The country looked as if it had once been much larger, but the Void now swathed the land, marked on the map with dark black ink. A sketch of ruins had been drawn in the corner of land where the Void met the sea, labeled *Westlin*. If Peshtigo's capital had been home to the Temple of Light, then it made sense that this would be where the Void originated.

The Temple of Light would have held the greatest population of *mahjo* in the world, and since it was also a school, it would have housed some of the most powerful *mahjo* as well. Alongside the Westlin Academy of Science, Peshtigo had all the makings of the kind of destructive power that had created the Void.

I was getting sidetracked. I brushed aside the map and shuffled through the other papers on the table. A skim of their contents revealed they were ration and inventory lists. There were some reports on local conflicts within Vethe and between farmers, but nothing related to Peshtigo.

I went from table to table, flipping through papers, unrolling scrolls, skimming the titles of books—none of them were about Peshtigo. I bit the inside of my cheeks as I scanned the room in frustration. A piece of metal flashed in the light from the glimmer glass.

My eyes fastened onto what looked like a handle peeking out from behind an unfurled map. I flipped up the corner of the map to reveal a drawer. I'd taken stock of the contents of the other desk drawers in the room, but they had contained only more of the same information on Lanathrill's day-to-day procedures.

I tugged on the handle. Locked.

The only locked drawer in the room. I knelt and gave the handle another firm tug. The drawer didn't budge. *Drek.*

With all the information about Lanathrill's various assets lying strewn about the room for anyone to see, a locked drawer seemed rather conspicuous. I looked around, searching for something to pick the lock. I didn't actually know how to pick a lock, but I might as well try.

I spotted a metal divider lying underneath some bound scrolls. I snatched it up and knelt in front of the drawer again. I inserted the sharp tip of the divider into the keyhole and wiggled it around, hoping to loosen something.

It didn't work. I tossed the tool aside and glared at the lock. After everything I'd done since leaving Ninurta, I wasn't going to be defeated by a stupid little lock. I gave the handle another frustrated yank.

There was the sound of metal snapping, and then the drawer slid free. I froze.

I'd broken it. I wasn't the smoothest of criminals, but that wasn't exactly a bad thing, right?

I opened the drawer wider. More papers were stacked inside. I pulled them out, my fingers brushing off a smattering of soot that obscured the top page. It didn't help. I couldn't read it. The words were in a language I didn't recognize from the history texts. Maybe this was old Lanathrillian.

A word caught my eye: *gahl.* I frowned. It was possible for the same words to exist from culture to culture, but a word from the language of the Infinite? I skimmed the paper for anything else that might be familiar, but there was nothing. If this wasn't old Lanathrillian, then maybe there was a translation somewhere. I dug through the drawer, shuffling past papers.

A loud knock shattered the silence. I gasped, my body seizing tight.

"Your Eminence?"

I held my breath, staring at the door.

"I told you he's not up yet," said another voice, sounding put out.

The man who'd spoken first sighed loudly. "Well, if he'd call for us to dress him in the mornings, he'd be a lot easier to locate. He said he'd be here today."

Their footsteps receded. I released my breath, my arms shaking. I was so not fit for this kind of thing. If Emryn was supposed to be in here this morning, then I couldn't stay a moment longer. My fingers hesitated over the page of foreign script. I swore as I shoved it and the rest of the papers back inside. A broken lock wouldn't necessarily arouse suspicion, especially if the lock had been old enough to snap so easily. But missing papers would definitely draw attention.

I listened at the door, straining to hear past the pounding in my ears. There was only silence on the other side. I cracked the door open. The hall was empty. I darted out, shut the door behind me, and then raced as quietly as I could back to my room.

Emryn would keep his secrets for a while longer.

CHAPTER 24

THE HOLLOWS ARRIVED THE FOLLOWING EVENING. SINCE THERE were quite a few of them, they declined the offer to be placed inside the citadel, choosing instead to set up camp in the woods at the base of the mountain. Emryn, Mason, and I rode down to receive them. Some of them I recognized from my stay in Etu Gahl, but while they greeted me warmly, they swarmed Mason, carting him off to celebrate their reunion.

Mason looked so happy to be among them. I wondered if he would leave with them when this was over.

"We're so glad you came," I said, shaking hands with the designated leader of their army.

Jain was an older woman with graying hair and fine lines around her bright-gray eyes. Despite her age, her body was strong and wiry. All the hollows, regardless of their age, were in perfect health.

"Irra said you needed help, so we gathered up some volunteers," she said. "Most of us have never been this far north. It's been an adventure."

I smiled gratefully. "Thank—"

Emryn grabbed my arm, jerking me back. I protested, gripping his wrist, but the look on his face made me reach for my torch blade and turn toward whatever had caught his attention.

A gargoyle was wandering through the camp, its head swinging from side to side as if taking in its new surroundings. I relaxed, releasing the handle of my torch blade.

"You brought gargoyles?" I said to Jain.

"We would have been fools not to," she said. "If we're fighting something similar, then we've got an advantage having our own giant lizards, don't you think?"

"Those things fight *for* you?" Emryn looked bewildered.

"Someone get him back to the pen!" Jain shouted, laughing at Emryn's reaction.

Several hollows jumped to obey, leading the gargoyle with firm pats on its head and offerings of food. Its frills trembled with what I could only describe as pleasure.

Emryn watched the gargoyle disappear behind the trees before that stoic expression he always wore snapped back into place. "How did you tame them?"

"We didn't," Jain said with a wink. Emryn gave her a blank look. "They're our comrades, not our pets."

He looked skeptical.

"Is Hina here?" I asked eagerly. She'd left Ninurta almost two months ago, homesick for her boyfriend and the fortress.

Jain shook her head. "She's sorry she couldn't make it, but she's gone and gotten herself with child. She can't be fighting giant beasts with a baby on the way."

I gasped, slapping a delighted hand over my mouth. "That's great!"

I hadn't been sure if hollows and sentinels could have children, but now that seemed a silly assumption. They were *mahjo*, not sterile.

"First baby ever to be born in Etu Gahl," she said. "That'll be something."

How would Irra feel about that? Etu Gahl was a fortress of age and decay.

My house is a place of forgotten things, he had said once.

Now, it would be more.

"They'll be having a wedding once the baby's born. She hopes you'll join us."

"Absolutely," I said. "As soon as everything is settled in Ninurta."

"How many have come?" Emryn asked, bringing the conversation back to the issue at hand.

"About a hundred," Jain said. There were more than two hundred hollows in Etu Gahl, so it was heartening that nearly half had volunteered.

Emryn drew his shoulders back, his circlet glinting in the fading daylight. "That's it?"

Jain was unmoved by his affront. "One of us is worth nearly ten of you. So if it makes you feel better, think of it as a thousand instead."

"Plus gargoyles," I added.

Jain smirked. "Plus gargoyles."

Emryn looked as if he'd tasted something bitter. He wasn't used to being treated with such irreverence, but the hollows and sentinels had more reason than most to distrust Kahls. At least he didn't try speaking over her like he had at our first meeting. I had a feeling Jain would be a lot less civil in response.

Introductions aside, Emryn returned to the city while the rest of us had an early supper in the camp. We ate crusty bread that they'd brought from Rennard's kitchen. Even though the food was a couple of days old, when I broke open the crust to pick at the chewy interior, the aroma of herbs made my stomach grumble. We dipped chunks of the bread into a thick vegetable stew. It was hearty and delicious and reminded me of many meals in the mess hall.

Afterward, Jain and I gathered in her tent, the largest in the camp, to go over the plan I'd already ironed out with Emryn.

"The nest is here," I said, rotating the map I'd brought along. I pointed to a far corner of the Fields of Ishta. "Emryn's farmers have a device they use to kill the rodents that live underground and eat their crops. He thinks it'll work well enough to smoke out the chimera. The moment they emerge from their nest, your archers will pick off the ones they can." I hesitated. "Please tell me you brought bows and arrows."

Emryn had insisted arrows would be useless against the chimera with their thick, leathery hides, but the hollows' arrows were different. The armory in Etu Gahl was stocked with so many weapons that I'd wondered if maybe the fortress wasn't as securely hidden as it seemed to be, but I'd been particularly impressed with their arrows. They were longer and stronger than any I'd seen in the history texts. Certainly more lethal than the ones I'd seen here in Lanathrill.

Jain nodded. "Attacking out of range works best against giant razor-teethed lizards," she said wryly. "We've learned how to capture gargoyles. Shouldn't be too difficult with these chimera."

"They're a lot bigger," I said.

"I know. On the way here, we ran across a few attacking a wagon. We killed them."

That was good. They were now familiar with what to expect from the chimera.

"So the hollows will pick off the ones they can. Once the chimera overwhelm the Fields, we'll go in on foot. *No one* is to fight a chimera alone," I said, giving her a firm stare so she'd know I was serious. "Tell your hollows to break into pairs or groups of three."

"Understood. What about Kahl Emryn and his soldiers?"

"They'll set up a perimeter inside the tree line. They'll intercept any chimera trying to escape in the wrong direction."

"Wrong direction?"

I pointed to a spot on the map. "We want to funnel them out of the Fields, west toward the hills that drop down into the Outlands. We have to let some of them go. If they're as smart as the gargoyles, and we're pretty sure they are, then they can communicate with one another. We need them all to know that entering Lanathrill is a death sentence."

Jain looked impressed. "I'll discuss this with the camp tonight. When are we planning the attack?"

"Day after tomorrow. I know you guys recover quickly, but I want to make sure everyone's well rested."

"Sounds good."

Mason and the sentinels remained with the hollows for the night. While I wanted to do the same, it seemed more diplomatic to return to the citadel, so I rode back up the mountainside alone. Emryn met me at the entrance into the mountain and escorted me through the tunnel into the city.

The streets were nearly deserted at this time, most everyone having gone to bed for the night. It was strange not having daylight to track the hours of the day.

We traveled in comfortable silence. Once we neared the citadel's gates, Emryn suddenly asked, "Why are they called hollows?"

I shrugged. A proper explanation would mean having to tell him about their collars, which was information Emryn didn't need. Although he'd requested to see Irra's letter yesterday morning when I informed him of Dennyl's return, I'd refused and told him only about the hollows' impending arrival. The less he knew, the better.

"It's complicated," I said.

He didn't seem appeased by this, but he said nothing more. I parked my scout in its usual place across from the stables. It looked lonely there without the others.

"My soldiers have been briefed for the attack," Emryn said as he dismounted and handed the reins to a waiting servant. "We'll be ready as well."

We entered the citadel, and I waved good-bye. I had no idea where he slept, but it wasn't in the same wing that I did.

"Kai," he said as I was turning away. Something in his voice sharpened my senses. He reached out and took my hand. I stiffened. What was he doing? "I need to thank you. Not as Kahl of Lanathrill or on behalf of my people, but as a man who has lost too much."

His words caught me off guard. I'd never have believed Emryn was even capable of uttering them. "You should thank the army resting outside the city."

"I will. But they wouldn't be here without your help." He lowered his gaze, scratching at his beard and seeming uncomfortable with his display of emotion. "My father's greatest wish was to restore glory and prominence to Lanathrill. But a riding accident ended all of that." Pain flickered over his face, and then it was gone. "That's no way for a Kahl to die. I have spent my life trying to complete his work. When the chimera grew into a threat I couldn't overcome, I believed I had failed." His fingers tightened around mine. "You've given me hope again. So thank you. With all my heart, thank you."

"Lanathrill will be safe again," I said. "I just wish we'd been able to help sooner."

He dusted his lips over my knuckles and then released my hand, his brief moment of vulnerability apparently over. When he looked at me again, it was with cool green eyes and the composed face of a Kahl. He turned and disappeared into the many corridors of the citadel.

CHAPTER 25

THE NIGHT BEFORE OUR PLANNED ATTACK, NIGHTMARES KEPT startling me awake. My subconscious tended to leave me be after the first nightmare. They weren't usually so persistent.

I had hoped they'd gone away after those far more pleasant dreams, but that seemed not to be the case. Maybe it wasn't just nerves. Maybe it was anticipation to get this over with so I could go back to Reev. And Avan. I rose well before dawn and spent an hour perusing the citadel's library for a book to occupy my mind before I gave up. I tried the war room again, just on a whim, but the door was locked. Emryn must have found the broken lock on his drawer. He hadn't confronted me about it the other night, which I hoped meant he didn't suspect me.

I wished I'd gotten a better look at the papers with the foreign language. I could have jotted down a few lines if I'd had the time.

Maybe one of the hollows would have been able to identify the language of the Infinite.

I returned to my room and curled up on my armchair, watching the mist rise from the burning falls. I never thought I'd miss the ever-present sheet of yellow clouds that blanketed the sky in Ninurta. While the glimmer glass and the flowering roots that trawled the mountain walls were undeniably beautiful, there was something to be said for the open air, the wind, and the light of the sun, even if we couldn't see it.

Closing my eyes, I imagined myself back in Irra's courtyard with Avan on the first Day of Sun, watching light break from behind the clouds for the first time in a year. My hand reached out. I could almost feel Avan's fingers close around mine, the warmth of the emerging sun on my face.

I opened my eyes, and the illusion broke. I was back in my room in Vethe, and Avan was well beyond my reach. Swallowing thickly, I scrubbed my palms over my face and then went to wash up properly. It was going to be a long day.

I had breakfast alone since the others had chosen to remain in the hollows' camp. Their resting army had been quite the topic of interest yesterday. The hollows had been good-natured about the curious citizens who'd emerged from the mountain to see them. Most of the citizens, children and adults alike, had lingered around the gargoyle pen in fear and fascination. Fortunately, the gargoyles were well behaved, and aside from poking their heads out of their pen to get a look at their gawkers, they minded their own business.

When I stepped out into the courtyard, it was buzzing with activity. Servants were readying horses. Men and women were strapping on armor and sharpening swords. Their metal shields were fastened to the backs of their saddles. I hoped the shields were sturdy enough to withstand chimera claws.

Emryn had decided that only three hundred of his soldiers would participate in the attack, only half of the force currently in Vethe and less than a fourth of Lanathrill's full army. A thousand soldiers were stationed to the east, engaged in the ongoing "conflict" with Peshtigo, while the rest were spread out at guard posts along Lanathrill's considerable borders.

Three hundred would be more than enough. We didn't know how many chimera were in that nest, but I doubted there were enough to overpower a hundred hollows and a couple dozen gargoyles. Or at least I hoped. These chimera were more aggressive than the gargoyles, and more intimidating in size and build. But the hollows had experience fighting giant lizards, and if anyone could defeat the beasts, it would be them.

I hopped on my scout and searched the courtyard for Emryn. He was near the gates, already mounted and in full armor, barking orders. Amusement tugged at the corners of my mouth at the reminder of our first meeting, when I'd thought he was a pompous jerk. He was still a pompous jerk, but a much more complicated and compassionate one than I'd originally expected.

I approached him, guiding my scout around the bustle of soldiers and servants. "I'm going ahead," I said. "I'll meet you at the hollows' camp."

"We'll be down in ten minutes."

I rode past him and out the gates, urging my scout into a run as we raced through the city. We charged over the stone, the warm air blowing my hair behind me as we wove around the few carriages on the street. It was still early, but the servants who were already up and about gasped as we flew by in a blur of silver.

The soldiers standing guard at the tunnel shouted and scrambled out of the way as I burst past them, laughing like a maniac. We sprinted the entire way down to the camp.

The tents were gone and the campfires doused. My scout loped through the trees until I found the army lined up on their Grays in neat rows of four. The gargoyles obediently flanked either end of their formation. I rode ahead until I saw Jain at the front.

"About time," she shouted, grinning. "Where's everyone else?"

"On their way," I said. I headed over to where Mason and the sentinels were lined up on their scouts.

"Ready to finish this thing?" Mason asked. He looked excited, his eyes brighter than I'd seen since we arrived over a week ago. Since before we left Ninurta, actually. He must have really missed being surrounded by hollows, the people he'd come to accept as his makeshift family.

"More than ready." I had come here believing the distance might help me deal with everything happening in Ninurta: Avan, the rebel attacks, my uncertainty about Reev and where we fit into everything now that our old lives were gone. But now

I knew without a doubt that I belonged wherever Reev was. Even though I ached with missing Avan, I would accept whatever decision he'd made in my absence, and then I would take my place as Miraya's adviser and help fix the upheaval that I had wrought.

A low rumble like approaching thunder sounded through the ranks as Emryn's army descended from the mountain. Jain shouted something I couldn't make out. Then she turned, urging her Gray forward. One by one, each of the lines followed, marching down the Silver Road.

With only a third of Emryn's soldiers on horseback and the rest on foot, the Fields of Ishta took three times as long to reach. The march was a monotonous one. Because we didn't want to alert the chimera of our arrival, we slowed even more once we drew closer to the Fields.

I circled around the hollow army to signal Emryn. He gestured wordlessly to his own ranks. They divided into two lines, threading through the trees and circling the Fields on either side. The soldiers on horseback formed the first layer of the perimeter. Those on foot formed a second layer behind them. They left a single opening, the only escape route we would allow the chimera, which would lead them southwest into the Outlands.

The hollows spread across the Fields on their Grays, silent as the wind through the tall grass. Two men brought forward a bellows and a drumlike device. Leather had been stretched across the top, but instead of a solid piece of hide, holes pierced the covering. Inside, chicken feathers and coal filled the device. The men followed me, Gret, and Winnifer across the Fields toward where we'd first discovered the nest.

Sure enough, tall mounds and a series of fresh tracks indicated that the chimera were still here. Gret and Winnifer slipped into the surrounding trees to investigate, their footsteps falling soundlessly against the earth. A moment later, Winnifer's hand shot up in the air, waving wildly. She'd found the opening.

Emryn's men opened a trapdoor in the side of the device. One of them struck a flint, setting the contents on fire, before snapping the door shut. Tendrils of smoke began to leak from the holes in the leather covering. The hollows took over, carrying the bellows and the device over to Winnifer. I slipped around the nearest mound to see what they were doing. The entrance into the nest was huge and impossible to miss from the right angle. They had set the device about ten feet inside. At the back of the device was another hole, in which Gret inserted the bellows.

Everyone backed away as Gret tied a handkerchief around her nose and mouth to protect her from the fumes. Then she took hold of the bellows and pumped. Acrid white smoke began billowing from the openings in the leather, filling the entrance and seeping into the tunnel. The smoke smelled terrible and began to clog my throat. We had to retreat back into the Fields. Emryn had explained that something in the chicken feathers released a poisonous chemical when burned in large quantities.

When the device was producing enough smoke on its own, Gret tossed down the bellows and joined Winnifer and the others in the Fields.

It took only minutes longer for the smoke to penetrate the nest. My fingers tightened around the handle of my torch blade as muffled grunts and roars echoed out from the tunnel. There was the rumble of shifting earth as the chimera began to emerge.

Jain made a quick motion with her hand. The hollows strung their bows. With another silent command, they drew back their arrows.

The first few chimera burst from the nest. My stomach clenched. I was far enough to the side that I wouldn't get caught in the battle, but nerves flitted around my stomach anyway. Jain allowed the chimera to clear the entrance of the nest before cutting her hand through the air. The hollows released their arrows.

The chimera screamed as the steel tips pierced their thick hides. One of them spasmed and fell, its giant claws scuffling through the dirt in pain and confusion before another arrow struck its chest and it went still. The hollows were fast, nocking arrow after arrow and bringing the creatures down in relentless waves.

They had taken out a good dozen before the earth erupted around the mounds. The alarm of our attack must have spread through the pack. Chimera flooded out from underground to escape the suffocating smoke and to avoid being picked off from their single entrance. They swarmed into the tall grass of the Fields. They were on the offensive now, charging for the archers.

The hollows dropped their bows and unsheathed their torch blades. Those lying in wait behind them did the same, and their battle cries rent the air as they stormed the oncoming chimera.

I looked at Mason and Aylis, who'd offered to fight at my back and protect one another. We all nodded in unison and jumped into the melee. A chimera leaped at Mason. Aylis and I intercepted, slashing at its legs. It stumbled with a roar, its gaping jaws snapping in rage. Mason ducked its thrashing claws and sank his blade into the creature's chest. Its body gave a final tremor. We moved on.

Even though the fight was going as planned, my mind couldn't help seeking out the threads. For the briefest of moments, I thought I felt the brush of magic. My breath hitched, and I nearly forgot to dodge an oncoming chimera. But it didn't happen again, and I pushed away the disappointment, irritated with myself for not focusing more fully on protecting my comrades' backs.

After we brought down another chimera, I observed the battle for a second, seeing the vicious slice of torch blades, and a strange feeling settled in my chest. It wasn't a sense of victory or satisfaction for what we were accomplishing here.

The cries of the chimera echoed through the Fields of Ishta, their heavy bodies flattening the grass—grass that had grown wild from the earth with its remnants of magic and memories, now stained with the blood of these creatures as surely as it had been stained by the soldiers who had fought here once before.

Some of the chimera escaped. They hissed and snarled as Emryn's soldiers hacked at them to get them moving in the right direction. They saw their escape and ran for it, their powerful legs carrying them away from the Fields and into the rocky hills that would take them to safety.

I hadn't thought—hadn't even considered—what it would feel like to watch these creatures be slaughtered. To participate in the slaughter. The chimera had killed many innocent people, and they had to be driven from Lanathrill. But for centuries, they had existed as slaves, bound by the power of Ninu's collars. Now, having finally tasted freedom, to be hunted down and killed for simply being what they were . . .

I lowered my torch blade, gazing across the Fields and the bodies that lay scattered through the trampled grass. There must have been nearly five dozen chimera in that nest, the evidence of their numbers lying in the blood-drenched earth. Pain lanced through me as I spied the bodies of hollows and soldiers who hadn't been able to avoid the deadly claws and teeth.

The grim set of Mason's mouth and the haunted look in his eyes meant that he, too, realized the injustice of what we'd done. I looked at my stained torch blade in disgust. Blood had dripped down the blade to slide into the crevices of my clenched fingers.

Ninu's dead eyes flashed in my mind, and I dropped the weapon. I struggled to breathe as I wiped my sticky fingers frantically against my tunic.

Mason's hands grabbed mine, stilling them. I struggled, but he pulled me against his chest. His heart beat strong and steady beneath my cheek.

"It's okay," Mason murmured. His hands cupped my face. "It's okay."

With deep, calming breaths, I nodded and stepped out of his embrace.

The last of the chimera were making their escape. I watched them go. Hopefully, they wouldn't return, so that this would never have to happen again.

Emryn's soldiers didn't share my remorse. The moment the last chimera cleared the Fields, their cheers erupted from the trees. They rode out into the open, whistling and shouting as their fists punched the air, victorious. Emryn was smiling as he stabbed the point of his bloodied sword into the earth. Dirt spattered his face and hair, and he had a gash across his upper arm, but he looked otherwise unharmed. I couldn't fault him for being happy. These creatures had stolen his family and many of his people. He was glad to see them dead and gone.

I looked at Mason. "Let's get out of here," I said.

He opened his mouth and then hesitated. He tilted his head, listening. A sound had risen above the cheers of Emryn's soldiers, high and lilting. The volume grew until I realized what it was: singing.

I spun around, looking for the source. Some nameless power reached inside and gripped me. I gasped, my back arching as pain split my skull. I closed my eyes and pressed my palms against my temples. *No!* I pushed at the power grasping me, shaking it off until I felt its hold slip and fall away.

My knees gave out and I fell. But I was whole again. Opening my eyes, I looked around, standing clumsily.

All across the Fields, the hollows had fallen where they stood. Mason lay at my feet.

CHAPTER 26

I PRESSED MY EAR TO MASON'S CHEST. HIS HEART BEAT STEADILY. I could breathe again.

Brushing sandy hair from his forehead, I leaned close, searching his face for some sign of consciousness. I gripped his shoulders and shook him. "Mason!"

The singing continued, a haunting tune that prickled my skin with magic. It was everywhere and nowhere, impossible to track. Emryn's soldiers, who were curiously unaffected, had dismounted from their horses. They spread out across the Fields, surveying the unconscious hollows and sentinels. The gargoyles had begun huddling together, their frills standing at attention. They backed into a circle, hissing at the approaching men and women. Then one of them threw back its head, released a long, earsplitting cry, and leaped onto the nearest soldier. Its teeth sank into the man's neck, shredding through skin and bone with a brutal shake.

What the drek? I gathered Mason close, cradling his upper body as if I could protect him from the gargoyles' sudden change. I began to call out, to warn Emryn's soldiers away, but my voice caught when the soldiers raised their swords.

One man positioned himself above a fallen hollow. He drove his sword downward.

I opened my mouth to scream, but like in my nightmares, nothing came out. I hauled Mason closer and watched, immobile with horror, as the other soldiers followed suit. They targeted any hollow who lay helpless. Their swords sang a grisly chorus to the voice that continued to spin its magic.

A few feet away, Jain lay on her side, her legs twisted beneath her from an awkward fall. A soldier grunted as he pushed aside a chimera's tail to reach her. He raised his spear above Jain's chest.

With a cry, I launched myself at him, plowing into his legs. We landed in a tumble of limbs. I kicked away and rolled to my feet. The soldier stood as well, recovering quickly. When he looked at me, his upper lip curled back into a snarl. The veins in his forehead bulged, and the tendons in his neck were raised, taut. His eyes were bloodshot, pupils dilated, and his face contorted with fury.

Bloodlust. Savage, unleashed bloodlust. That's what I was seeing in him and in every soldier here. Their guttural sounds of hunger and their cries of satisfaction as their weapons found more hollows made my stomach heave. But I had to keep it together.

He lunged at me. I sidestepped, grabbing his arm and twisting it behind his back. He roared, but I grabbed a fistful of his hair and guided his head down to my raised knee as hard as I could. There was a crack, and then the soldier slumped to the ground, out cold.

I hurried back for Jain just as another soldier yanked his sword from her belly. Blood gushed from the wound.

"No!" I drew my blade. With a furious strike, I severed the soldier's sword hand. He went down with an agonized cry, clutching the bloody stump of his wrist. There was a noise behind me. I turned too slowly. Pain sliced through me as a sword cut through my tunic and ripped open skin.

I staggered, but there was no time to recuperate. I brought my sword up to block another blow, letting those long hours of training with Mason guide my movements. Rage fueled me as I kicked out, smashing my foot into the soldier's knee. She stumbled, and I swung the hilt of my sword, smashing it into her temple. She dropped.

I sank to Jain's side, my hands pressing hopelessly against her wound. Already her face had gone pale.

"Drek, drek, drek," I whispered, my eyes stinging, the wound in my side throbbing.

Fear and adrenaline rushed through me, but I didn't know what to do. I scanned the Fields, hoping to find some kind of help. The gargoyles—I realized they'd been unaffected by the song and had sensed the danger. But the sheer number of Emryn's army had overwhelmed the creatures, and there was no help to be found. There was only death and horror. I spotted Aylis, his chest a bloodied mess of bone and skin. My stomach tried to heave again, but I held it down. I couldn't find Gret and the others, lost as they were amid the bodies.

"I'm sorry," I said brokenly. "I'm so sorry, Jain." And then I gasped. I whipped around as I realized I'd left Mason unprotected.

A soldier stood over him, bringing his axe down on Mason's neck. My heart stopped. I was too far away. In the space of a blink, I saw Avan's back as he stepped into the path of Reev's blade.

I would never watch someone I love die again.

My entire body—every nerve, muscle, and bone in me— screamed: *Stop!*

Everything stopped.

The threads of time burst into view in a blinding flash. They shimmered around me, brighter than I'd ever seen, swaying as if greeting me after our long separation. Something inside me rose in response, eager to embrace those shining threads, but I didn't have time for a lengthy reunion.

I sucked in frantic, uneven breaths as I scrambled forward, my fingers clawing through the dirt and bloody grass. Tears blurred my vision as I collapsed beside Mason's body, the axe's blade poised inches above his neck.

The threads vibrated, warning me. Time began to stutter forward again. I took hold of Mason's shoulders and heaved with all my strength, dragging him across the dirt. I could feel my control slipping. The threads snapped free of my grip.

In an instant, time surged forward. The axe streaked downward, dirt spewing through the air as the blade struck the earth. I hovered over Mason a few feet away, the farthest I could lug him.

"Leave him alone!" I said, pointing my weapon at the soldier. The soldier wrenched his axe free of the grasping dirt. His nostrils flared, and his face flushed red. The veins in his forehead looked ready to burst.

He swung his axe.

"*Wait.*"

The soldier twitched, his axe veering wildly to the side. I turned to see who'd spoken, although I knew the voice.

Cassia and the rest of the Council rode from the trees. At the gruesome sight before her, she sucked in a sharp breath. But then her mouth flattened into a severe line, and she surveyed the Fields, assessing her losses.

She had known this would happen. They had all known.

Movement behind her caught my eye. It was Emryn, the back of his head and the gold glint of his circlet visible between the trees as he rode away.

"Emryn!" I screamed, my shrill voice echoing around us. "Emryn, you coward!"

One of the Council members—Henna—pushed his horse forward, blocking my view of Emryn. "We should kill her," Henna said, scowling down at me.

"Silence," Cassia ordered curtly. But her eyes pleaded with me to understand.

There was no forgiving this. My hands trembled, but not with fear. Fury, dark and violent, reared inside me. My fingers clenched around the torch blade. In that moment, I knew what I was capable of, and whether it had anything to do with the Infinite inside me didn't matter. I would twist my fingers into the threads of time and drive my weapon into every one of them for the lives they'd taken, for deceiving me, for making me an accomplice in luring the hollows here to be slaughtered, after they'd played their part in ridding Lanathrill of the chimera.

I was the daughter of Time, and I would make them pay.

I raised my sword arm, the movement jostling the weight in my lap. Looking down, I suddenly remembered Mason's still form, his head cradled against my legs. My fingers dug into the leather that covered his chest. I swore. And then I swore again. I couldn't leave his side. I wouldn't leave him unprotected again.

Instead, I focused the full force of my anger on Cassia. "How could you do this?"

She flinched, the barest of movements that I didn't think anyone else caught. Then she lifted her chin, looking down her nose at me. "Take her prisoner."

"Cassia," Brienne said, objecting.

Cassia silenced her with a look. That was new. I suspected they were ranked by level of power. That would explain why Cassia, the youngest of them, was the voice of the Council.

"The goddess's song didn't work on her. She's different. Didn't you feel it before? The way the world wavered and slowed." Cassia's blue eyes searched mine, as if trying to work out what I'd done. "Looks like I'm not the only one who's been keeping secrets."

The singing had grown faint, and the Fields had gone eerily still. That could mean only one thing. I had to look.

Bodies and blood everywhere. Pain dug talons into my chest, making it hard to draw a breath. Every hollow, sentinel, and gargoyle was dead—except Mason. The enormity of Cassia and Emryn's betrayal crushed me. Despair threatened to eclipse my fury.

The soldiers had gathered around. A few of them realized Mason was still alive and stepped purposefully forward. I rose to my knees, torch blade ready.

"Leave him," Cassia said. The soldiers stepped back. I wondered how much of their obedience came from the song's spell and how much was simply ingrained instinct and training. "Take them both prisoner."

I brandished my blade as they circled me and Mason. There were too many of them. The threads quivered, practically begging to be used. My fingers twitched. If I slowed time, I could escape. But not with Mason.

"Kai, you know you can't win," Cassia said reasonably. I could read the warning in her voice. She didn't want to hurt me—but she would if necessary. "You're surrounded and utterly outnumbered. Come with us peacefully, and I promise no harm will come to you or Mason."

I scoffed. "What good are your promises?"

"I haven't allowed them to kill you yet, have I?"

"As if you could," I said, sneering.

"And what about Mason? What is his life worth to you?"

She had me cornered. The only way I was going to get Mason out of here alive was to cooperate. "Give me a promise I can trust you to keep."

She pursed her lips in distaste but eventually said, "I swear on the goddess and the magic she has bestowed upon me that Mason will not be harmed."

Even though every instinct I possessed was screaming at me to snag the threads and escape, I lowered my torch blade. Hands grabbed me from behind, a soldier at either side keeping me immobile. They hefted Mason like a sack of flour and tossed him over the back of a horse.

"Be careful with him," I snapped.

"Take him to the dungeons," Cassia said. At my glare, she added, "Try not to be so rough."

A woman jumped into the saddle in front of Mason. Then she nudged the horse into motion, and the soldiers parted to allow them through.

My palms grew clammy as I watched Mason's limp form disappear from view. Once they were gone, Cassia nodded to my captors, and they began wrangling me toward a horse. Out of the corner of my eye, I glimpsed the silver panels of a scout.

"If you want answers from me," I shouted to Cassia, "you'll keep your word."

"As I said, Mason will remain unharmed."

"Good," I said. "Then I'll meet you at the citadel." Before she could question what I meant, I spun on my heel and slammed my forehead into one of my captor's faces. His nose broke with a crunch. He cried out, his hands falling away from me. My mind leaped for the threads.

Time slowed. Cassia was caught in mid-shout. Her auburn hair floated around her face, riding a still wind. I eyed my torch blade, lying a few feet away where I'd dropped it.

While she deserved it, killing her now would feel too much like what her soldiers had done to the hollows. So instead, I shoved through the wall of people while my control over the threads still held and jumped onto the scout's back. My fingers scrambled for the button on its neck before I slapped my hands over the sensors.

I released the threads, and we shot forward as time rebounded. We sprinted through the trees, leaving behind the sounds of horses and bodies crashing through the woods after us.

CHAPTER 27

THE SCOUT CARRIED ME THROUGH THE SPARSE WOODS AND INTO farmland. Its metal paws tore over cresting hills, heedless of the way we ripped through stalks of wheat, until we reached the Silver Road again. There was no sign of the soldier who'd taken Mason. I turned my scout in circles, torn. Find Mason and take him to safety before returning to the citadel? Or hope that Cassia's promise held and meet her in the citadel as I'd said?

Maybe they'd taken Mason back via a different route. I had studied the map of Lanathrill for long enough that I'd picked out half a dozen other paths from Vethe to the Fields of Ishta. The one we'd taken wasn't the most direct, just the most accommodating for a marching army.

With a curse, I urged my scout north for Vethe. I needed answers to what the drek just happened and what they were planning next before I could make a proper escape. And I wasn't leaving without Mason.

At full speed, I reached the entrance into the mountainside within ten minutes. The guards opened the doors with little more than a few puzzled questions about why I was alone. It seemed not all of Emryn's soldiers had been in on the betrayal.

Had any of them known? Had they left Vethe today, knowing that they would become murderers? Or had their goddess's song been as much a surprise to them as it had been to me and the hollows? Pain pressed around my lungs again at the reminder of so many lost lives.

I thanked whatever power was higher than the Infinite that Hina had remained in Etu Gahl.

Once I reached the citadel, I left my scout on the steps and stormed inside, ignoring the questions of the soldiers who'd been left behind. I headed straight for Emryn's war room. The door was locked. I reached for my torch blade, and then swore when I remembered I didn't have it. I lifted one foot and slammed my boot against the thick metal. The door clanged and rattled on its hinges, but didn't budge. I did it again.

"What are you doing?" Behind me, the cries of servants filled the hallway. "Stop! You must stop!"

They grabbed for me, but I shoved them away. Wincing from the wound in my side, I delivered one last furious kick to the door. It wouldn't give.

"Have you gone mad?" one of them asked, as he tried to restrain me. I knocked him aside. They murmured to one another about getting the guards as I pushed through them and headed back outside.

I sprinted across the courtyard, following the shadow glass walls of the citadel until I came to the Temple of the Council of Vethe. I had no idea where Cassia's room was, but there were only four Council members. Couldn't be that hard to find, right?

Wrong. The corridors around the gallery were lined with doors, all of them nearly identical. And there were three more corridors just like them. *Drek.*

A servant turned the corner and startled at the sight of me.

"Yara!" I rushed forward. "Can you tell me where Cassia's room is?"

"K-Kai," she stuttered, her face pale. "Why are you here?"

Disbelief and anger clamped down on me again. "You knew."

She dropped her head in shame. Her fingers brushed the tattoo on her face. "I'm Cassia's personal servant. There are things I can't help overhearing." She looked at me. "I'm so sorry, Kai. I didn't know when I left Lanathrill that the reason I was bringing you back was to . . . to . . ." Tears welled in her eyes.

I hardened myself to them. "You could have warned us. You're as guilty as they are." I stepped in close, squashing my guilt when she shrank away in fear. "Show me where Cassia's room is."

"I . . ." She glanced over her shoulder, looking for an escape. I grabbed her collar. She yelped, her fingers grappling against my hold.

"You didn't care that you watched us march to our deaths this morning," I said coldly. "As long as the goddess commanded it.

You rode into the Outlands on nothing but a promise. Of course you'd let us die as well if that's what your goddess supposedly wants."

Yara didn't reply, but the way she squeezed her eyes shut was answer enough.

"Show me her room," I demanded again.

She gave a frenetic little nod, and I eased my grip on her tunic. She led me down the corridor and up the stairs to the third floor. We stopped in front of a door with a pale blue circle painted into the wood and a gold starburst at its center.

With shaking hands, she pulled a set of keys from her dress and unlocked the door. I nudged it open with my foot, in case Yara had tricked me somehow.

The room was tidy and sparse. Books from the library were piled on a dresser along with two makeup pots and a shadow glass comb. The mirror hanging above the dresser was old and spotted, a spider web of fine cracks at one corner. A braided rug covered the floor. A few fat candles and glimmer glass lined the mantel above the fireplace along with a bowl of scented water. I recognized Cassia's robes draped over the back of a wooden chair.

I yanked Yara inside and pushed her at the bed. "Sit."

She did, wrapping her arms around herself and watching me with fearful eyes. I wasn't actually going to hurt her, even if she deserved it.

"So what's their next move?" I asked as I felt around the mantel for any hidden compartments. The fireplace was cold, as if it hadn't been lit for a while. Unsurprising, considering most of the fireplaces in the citadel remained untouched. The burning falls kept the air warm enough.

"I don't know," Yara said. I glared at her, and she shook her head. "I swear! I don't know. I only knew about what would happen today because I overheard Cassia and Brienne while I was washing Cassia's clothes."

I kicked aside the rug to make sure it wasn't hiding any trapdoors. As I knelt to peer beneath the bed, the threads shimmered and I felt a slight tug to my left. I turned, my eyes fixing on the dresser. I felt it again, a building sensation in the pit of my stomach.

My hands roamed over the makeup pots, but they weren't the source. I bent over, studying the grain in the wood as I ran my fingers along the side of the dresser. *There.* The slightest break in the wood. I curled my fingers beneath the bottom lip of the dresser and yanked. A hidden drawer popped open.

A silver box rested inside on top of some loose papers. I touched the box. Magic and darkness shot through me like an arrow. I hissed, snatching my hand back and nearly smacking Yara in the face. She had crept up behind me.

"What is it?" she whispered, trying to get a look inside the drawer. I ignored her.

Shaking out my fingers, I focused on my own magic and reached for the box again. The threads flowed around me, soothing and constant. This time, when I touched the box, whatever magic was trapped inside remained at bay. The words on the papers caught my attention. I set the box on the dresser and reached in for the pages.

I scanned the foreign words. This was the same language from the papers locked up in Emryn's war room. Since I still couldn't make sense of them, I set the papers aside and leaned over to study the silver box.

The silver looked tarnished. When I swiped my finger across the lid, a fine layer of black dust stained my skin. I removed the lid. The dread in my stomach deepened. Inside was more of that same black powder. The slight timbre of its magic tugged at me, a sense of foreboding trickling across the back of my neck, like I was standing in the Void again.

I frowned, dipped my finger into it, and then lifted the substance to my face for a closer look. It was solid black, dull, and fine like silt. I'd seen traces of black powder on Cassia's gown the night of the ball, but I'd assumed it was soot. Looking at her disused fireplace, that clearly wasn't the case.

What was this stuff?

A country of madmen. I wiped the black powder from my fingers with the hem of my tunic.

"We call it Dust."

I whirled around, my mind already hovering over the threads. Cassia stood in the doorway, several of her soldiers waiting behind her in the hall. Yara had sunk into the bed, watching Cassia with bleak apprehension.

Inches from my neck, a knife was suspended in the air. "That's original," I said.

The knife wobbled, moving another inch closer. I backed into the dresser. The contents on the top rattled. Dust from the silver box spilled onto the dresser.

Cassia's gaze fastened on the Dust. Hunger flared in her eyes. Her hands trembled as if fighting her need for it.

Her reaction reminded me of the people huddled beneath the awnings of the North District, their eyes dull and red-rimmed as they sucked down whatever latest street tonic was making its rounds. More often than not, the Watchmen found them curled up in the gutters, dead, a few days later. Reev said that's what happened when people lost hope.

Those people didn't get farewell ceremonies.

"What is the Dust, then?" I asked. "I'm guessing you think it's what gave you magic."

Maybe it had. But I couldn't rule out Irra's theory about the sepulcher, which would present a much bigger problem.

"The magic is a gift from the goddess," Cassia said, turning her focus on me with visible effort.

My lip curled. "Your drekking goddess. Can't you see what that stuff is doing to you? The reason it takes such a physical toll is because it's not natural. You're not meant to have magic anymore."

"And you are?" Her face twisted with sudden venom. "You hold time at your command. How are you able to do this and not suffer like I have?"

I'd suffered plenty. But that was between me and Kronos.

Seeing her now, where was the woman with whom I'd joked and laughed? The friend who'd convinced me to attend a party so she wouldn't be alone?

"How could you kill all those people, Cassia?" I asked. "We trusted you."

For an instant, her veil of cold arrogance fell, and the look in her eyes was anguished and raw. But it vanished as quickly as the clouds swallowing up the light on the last Day of Sun.

"I have kept my promise," she said. "Mason is unharmed. You will allow us to take you prisoner as well, or he will be left in the dungeons to rot."

I held my breath as the knife at my throat inched closer. While I was pretty confident I could grasp the threads before the blade pierced skin, I gave her a short nod to indicate I was cooperating. The knife fell to the rug with a thump as her soldiers flooded the room, grabbing me.

I let them. I still had questions, and I had a feeling the answers would come only from Emryn.

This prison cell was nowhere near as hospitable as Ninu's.

Beneath the citadel, the dungeons weren't constructed of the same gleaming shadow glass. The dreary cells had been chipped out of the mountain.

Matted straw was piled in the corner along with a tattered blanket. Stains discolored the stone floor and walls, and everything smelled like the sewers beneath Ninurta. Metal bars separated me from the corridor, where the only light was from two glimmer glass torches sitting farther down the hall. The *tap-tap-tap* of the fidgeting guard kept my thoughts company.

In the cell across from me, Mason was sitting against the wall, scowling, his eyes unfocused. Like me, he was shackled to a metal anchor in the floor. I had filled him in on everything that had happened while he was out: how Gret, Winnifer, Aylis, and Dennyl were all gone, their bodies lost in the Fields; how he was the only hollow to survive the massacre. He hadn't spoken a word since. We couldn't really talk anyway because of the guard, but I imagined he was plotting his vengeance. That's what I would be doing.

In the Fields, it had been so easy to imagine killing them all. I shuddered. I could understand now what Avan meant about having a darkness inside him. I could feel it there, that shadowy, violent anger.

Mason's chains clanked together as he shifted his position against the wall. The soldiers were afraid of him. The shackles restricted his reach, but they were still wary about getting too close to the bars. I found it both amusing and irritating that, even now, I was always the one underestimated. I supposed in this instance, it might work in my favor.

We'd been fed only once so far, but I didn't think we'd been in here long. No more than a couple of days. The cut in my side had begun to ache. I'd barely felt it when I was storming around the citadel in search of answers. Any healing tonic was beyond my reach now—likely seized along with our scouts and weapons—and I doubted any medical assistance was coming, or that they were even aware I'd been injured. Fortunately, the wound wasn't serious, but it stung when I moved too suddenly.

A door down the corridor opened with a metallic *clang*. Mason and I exchanged a look.

Emryn stepped into view, dressed in his training gear. His hair was freshly trimmed, but a bit mussed. He must have come from the courtyard. It was so *normal*. The fact he seemed able to carry on as if he hadn't ordered the deaths of a hundred hollows and my sentinel companions made that sinister fury simmering in my gut churn and boil. He looked first at Mason and then dismissed him, turning to face me instead.

Finally. I'd been waiting for this conversation since I'd glimpsed him fleeing the scene of his crimes.

"Kai," he said. His expression was unreadable, his voice deliberately flat.

I tipped my head and spread my arms in a mocking bow. "Your Eminence Kahl Emryn."

"The goddess's song didn't affect you."

"Good of you to notice."

His lips tightened. "I know you won't believe me, but I'm glad you're alive."

"You're right," I said, letting my anger bleed into my voice. "I don't believe you."

He simply nodded, accepting the futility of trying to convince me. "I have questions."

"Oh good," I said. "So do I."

"What *are* you?" It wasn't a question. It was a Kahl demanding an answer from his subject.

I *wasn't* his subject. "Wouldn't you like to know?"

"With the goddess's blessing, Lanathrill will march on Ninurta at dawn. We'll see how arrogant you are then."

"What do you want with Ninurta?"

He clasped his hands behind his back, the side of his face limned in the light of glimmer glass, accenting the slight offset of his jaw. I wondered vaguely if he'd been born that way or if it was a war injury. "An answer for an answer. What do you say?"

I leaned against the cold stone. The warmth from Hiyamun didn't reach the air down here. Scratching my nail against the flaking rust of my shackles, I pretended to consider it.

When his face grew taut with impatience, I smiled and said, "Okay. Me first. Why Ninurta?"

"Originally, I wanted only the secrets to Kahl Ninurta's power. I'd seen his sentinels patrolling the borders with their creatures of metal and magic. That sort of power might have been what Lanathrill needed to raise us back to glory."

"But the chimera stood in your way," I said.

"During his rule, my father tried to penetrate the Yellow Wastes. After his death, I, too, tried to follow the sentinels back to your city, but the chimera have always been quick to stop us."

Ninu had stationed the chimera at our borders to isolate us, as I'd initially presumed, but I couldn't have imagined that the chimera had also been meant to protect us from Lanathrill. I turned this revelation over in my mind.

"I've told you before: the chimera are intelligent. Once they learned to fear us, they'd leave us alone. And thanks to you, we have taught them fear. Before, they would have seen our army as a feast. Now, we are a horde descending on the Yellow Wastes, and they will flee before us."

My heartbeat quickened. I pressed my sweaty palms together. He was right. We had taught the chimera fear by decimating their nest and forcing them back into the Outlands. Regret sat heavily on my chest.

"My turn," Emryn said. "What are the sentinels and the hollows?"

"*Mahjo.*" At the skeptical lift of his brows, I added, "They're faster, stronger, and heal more rapidly than the rest of us because of their bloodline, but they don't have any actual physical magic."

Mason and the sentinels had kept their collars hidden behind starched tunics in order to stave off questions, but the hollows from Etu Gahl had left their collars bare. Whether Emryn had noticed the tattoos or not, he didn't mention them.

He gestured to Mason without actually looking at him. "So he's *mahjo*. Like me. Like the Council."

"Yes. My turn again. You said 'originally,' you wanted only Ninu's secrets. What do you want with Ninurta now?"

"To expand our kingdom," he said, as though I was an idiot for not seeing this.

"But that can't be all of it," I said. "You wouldn't have gone to all this trouble to deceive us just for a little more land, especially considering Ninurta isn't exactly a paradise."

His lips twitched as if fighting a smile. There was a glint of approval in his eyes. "The goddess has promised us immortality and limitless magic if I prove myself a Kahl and a conqueror worthy of her gifts. Yara was supposed to bring back Ninurta's sentinels so that when the goddess sang, we could dispose of them and cripple Ninurta's forces."

The way he spoke of "disposing" made my fingers flex, nearly reaching for the threads. I might not be armed, but time was weapon enough in my hands.

In some ways, Emryn held more capacity for cruelty than Ninu ever had. Ninu had been motivated by the obsession to reclaim his human past. He had built Ninurta to spite the laws of his kind; he had cared little for the outside world. But Emryn *was* human, with a human's range of emotion—both kindness and cruelty—and he wouldn't stop at Ninurta.

"Immortality isn't a gift," I said. Ninu had been proof of that.

"My father died before he could see Lanathrill rebuilt. I will not suffer the same injustice."

"*Injustice?* Tell that to the hollows you had killed while they were helpless to defend themselves."

"A necessary sacrifice." He spoke quietly, as if even he wasn't sure he believed this. "How is it you can control time and not suffer the effects of magic?"

"Because my magic is real, not a poor imitation of whatever remains in the Void." With luck, Irra and Kalla might have discovered by now that the sepulcher was secure and returned to Ninurta. As long as they were there, Ninurta would be safe.

Unless the Dust had nothing to do with Emryn's magic, and it was as he'd said of Peshtigo—that the Dust rotted their minds and turned them into madmen. I had no doubt, however, their "goddess" was Infinite, and that she'd directed them to consume the Dust. The black earth in Cassia's room wasn't dirt scooped out from the Void. It had been refined into a powder, its traces of magic amplified. Whether those miniscule traces were enough to restore their magic was still questionable to me. Regardless, no one but the Infinite could have taught them to do that, and I was willing to bet those pages of foreign script had held the instructions.

Then there was the song from the Fields of Ishta. That slithering, invasive kind of power was something only an Infinite would possess.

"That's why the goddess's song didn't work on you," he said. He hadn't posed it as a question, so I didn't answer. "As her servants, the Council and I were granted immunity, but we couldn't explain why you were able to resist. How can—"

"It's my turn," I pointed out. "Was anything you and Cassia told me about Peshtigo true?"

He rubbed his hand over his beard. "My people are content to view Peshtigo as an intrusion that must be expelled. I'm sure you've gathered the truth, though."

"You attacked Peshtigo first."

Emryn's cold gaze remained firm. "We have pushed them back almost to the ruins of Westlin. Soon enough, Peshtigo will be ours."

There it was, the real reason they'd kept their conflict with Peshtigo a secret. I should have listened to my instincts and known that they couldn't be trusted. If I had, Jain and the others might still be alive.

"Why does it matter to you so much?" I asked, genuinely baffled by his fervor to expand and "restore" Lanathrill's glory. The world had changed. It was time to move on. "Your great-grandmother built this amazing city to protect her people and established a working system to support them—why can't that be enough?"

His jaw tightened. He shifted on his feet, his fingers flexing. "Do you know what we do with our dead?"

"Should I?"

"We bury them in the mountains," he said. "We dig a hole into the stone, and enclose their bodies inside. Do you understand?" He leaned forward, eyes gleaming. "Vethe is a tomb. A magnificent one, perhaps, but a tomb nonetheless, and I will not see us buried alive in the mountain."

He straightened up again, eyes closing. When he opened them, his face held a note of weariness.

"Last question," he said. "Answer me truthfully. What are you?"

Remembering the way Irra had danced around an answer when I'd asked him that same question, I replied, "I'm a conundrum."

His eyes flashed a warning. "Explain."

"Not much to explain. I'm not *mahjo*, but I'm not entirely human, either. Maybe your goddess can figure it out for you."

"Do not joke with me."

"You want the truth? Tell me what you know about your goddess—who she is and how you communicate with her—and maybe I'll share the same about myself."

I'd been mulling over the identity of Lanathrill's "goddess" ever since they locked me in here. In the story Cassia had told us about the Fields of Ishta, she had said the warriors fought "as if crazed," their bloodlust driving them to turn their weapons on one another. The story was too similar to what I'd witnessed in Emryn's soldiers to be mere coincidence.

Ishta. At least I had a name, even if this Ishta was just another Infinite I had yet to meet. Kalla had told me that there were seventy of them.

Emryn studied me, his gaze searching. Predictably, he didn't push me further. He looked down and combed his fingers through his hair. "I'm sorry it had to come to this, Kai."

"No, you're not."

Without another word, he turned and disappeared back down the corridor. A moment later, I heard the metal door shutting behind him. I sighed and slumped back against the wall.

Across the corridor, Mason watched me with a slight curve of his mouth.

"That was informative," he said, his first words in two days. His voice was soft. The sound of it washed over me.

"Now we just need to get out of here so we can actually use the information. We have to warn Miraya," I said.

Ninurta was already vulnerable with the rebel sentinels. Without Irra or Kalla to stop the goddess's song, Lanathrill would easily overwhelm the city.

Unless Avan had chosen to stay in Ninurta. Hope kindled inside me. With Avan's help, Ninurta might stand a chance.

CHAPTER 28

"KAI."

My eyes opened. I was lying on my side, my back against the wall. I had curled up in my sleep, my body chilled from the stone and the cool air.

A tall figure stood in my cell.

I gasped, jolting upright. The links on my shackles clanked loudly. My gaze darted across the corridor to Mason. He was still asleep, curled into the corner of his cell.

"Who . . ." I paused. The threads were still, but I hadn't touched them. I squinted up at the man standing over me. Kronos.

"Good to see you." Light from the glimmer glass torches lit the back of his head, burnishing the liquid strands of his hair and shrouding his face.

"I wish I could say the same," I muttered. I brushed at my tousled hair where it stuck to my cheek. "You have really bad timing." The irony would have been funny had I not been shackled to the floor. "I'm not leaving yet."

"I'm not here for my heir." He sounded amused.

"Then why?"

"Can't a father check in on his daughter?"

I snorted. Kronos turned so that the glimmer glass lit his profile. His cloak swayed around his long legs, moving in an invisible current. Pale blue eyes, so much like my own, surveyed my cell.

"Humans are such undisciplined creatures." There was no disdain in his voice, as if he was merely stating a fact. "I can't imagine why you want to stay with them. Look at what they've done to you. To your friends."

"Not all humans are alike. If you spent more time with them, you'd know." Not that I wanted him around more.

"Can the same not be said for you? You believe all the Infinite are as self-serving and callous as Ninu."

I pursed my lips, annoyed by the truth in his words. "You're not exactly a brilliant example of altruism."

"I never said I was." His voice resonated. I shivered. His feet were whisper silent as he stepped closer. "If you embraced the River, you could escape these human walls in a blink. Time and space are as water to us."

That place inside me, warm from the presence of my powers, reached for the promise in his words. But I shook my head. "And leave behind everyone I care about? I'll pass."

He crouched forward in one smooth motion that had me squeezing back against the wall. "I'm not here to collect you. Only to help you help yourself."

The angles of his face were too sharp, which meant he still wasn't fully recovered from his long-ago battle with Ninu. Although I didn't want to admit it, I understood why he'd hidden me with the humans. It was the best way to protect me at the time, and keeping family safe was something we could agree on. But that didn't mean I trusted him, or that I would ever forgive him for what he'd done to Avan.

"How?" I asked.

"You've broken through the wall you erected to block your powers. I'm glad. The threads have missed you. But now you must forget whatever boundary you think exists and step into the River."

My mind brushed against the threads, and they vibrated in response, beckoning. "Tell me how."

"Close your eyes."

Frowning, I did as he said.

"Listen to the threads, not the way they connect everything around you—but how they flow *through* you. Tell me what you feel."

I imagined the threads as they felt against my hands—spider-silk thin but strong as wire, humming with magic. The threads twined through my fingers and looped around my wrists. Magic passed from the threads into me, warmth riding my veins straight to my heart where we became inseparable, one and the same. Then the magic emerged again, darting through my fingertips and back into the threads, leaving us both changed but stronger for it.

"What's happening?" I whispered.

"You were born of the River," he said, echoing Irra from months ago. "Your existence gives it strength, and it strengthens you in return. You just needed to learn how to open yourself to it. What does it feel like?"

I pressed my palm to my chest, feeling my magic there like a second heartbeat pulsing in perfect rhythm to mine. "Home." I lowered my chin, my shoulders curving over my knees, guarding that precious feeling close. *How could I have let this go? How could I have thought I'd be better off?* "It feels like coming home."

His hand touched my shoulder. "Magic isn't something to be feared, Kai. At its best, magic is life and energy and wonder. Think of what you've done with your magic."

I opened my eyes. The cold of my cell returned, sinking beneath my skin as I thought of Avan and where he'd be now if not for me.

Kronos gestured to Mason's sleeping form. "Look at the boy over there."

Mason looked uncomfortable, the chains of his shackled ankle tangled at his feet.

"Is the fact that you saved his life worth nothing when compared to your grief?"

I exhaled slowly. I wanted to remind him that my "grief" was a result of *his* meddling, but that wouldn't cancel out the fact that he was right. Terrible things had happened as a result of my being Kronos's daughter. But good things had happened as well—if not for Kronos, I wouldn't have even met Reev.

"Okay," I said. "I understand. But then how do I get out of here?"

"You've made peace with the River." He stood and held out his hand. "Just as you've welcomed it into yourself, it will welcome you into its current."

After a moment's hesitation, I placed my hand in his. Even though he wasn't at his full health, his grip was strong and sure as he helped me to my feet. The wound in my side protested the movement, and I bit down a groan. A weight lifted from my ankle. I looked down to see the iron shackle disintegrating into the stone.

"How'd you do that?"

"Decay is but the passage of time."

"You could have a contest with Irra," I said.

"We have." He stepped back, lifting our clasped hands between us.

I wasn't sure if he was kidding or not. I wanted to ask who'd won.

The threads quivered around me, drawing my attention. My cell began to fade as the threads grew brighter, each brilliant thread sharpening into perfect focus. My gaze fell on Mason's indistinct form.

"Wait!" I tried to pull away from Kronos. "I can't leave without Mason."

"Your friend cannot enter the River," he said, sounding offended by the mere notion.

The floor fell away. I gasped. My stomach lurched. I kicked my legs ineffectually. The walls of the dungeons unraveled, scattering into a trillion shining threads.

"Take me back," I demanded.

"You have a choice," Kronos said harshly. "You can remain a prisoner while your enemy marches on Ninurta, or you can use your powers to reach Ninurta first and warn them."

I scowled, flailing my arms like I was sinking, even though the threads held me suspended. "Can't you just take me back for a minute so I can free him?"

"His fate is not my concern."

I tried to rip my hand from his, but his fingers were like steel. He had the same mind-set as Irra—they would interfere only when the situation coincided with their own goals or when it upset their "balance."

"Let go of me," he said, "and I cannot promise you'll make it out of the River. You haven't yet learned to navigate its current."

My chest stung with worry for Mason. I had to decide. With Lanathrill's army marching at dawn, possibly only hours away, I doubted anyone would even notice I was gone until the guards came around to deliver our meals, and that was only if they decided to feed us. The only real threat to him was their goddess, and why would she care about a single imprisoned sentinel? The guards he could handle, even while shackled.

I gave Kronos a curt nod. I would have to trust that Mason would be okay until I had the chance to go back for him.

Kronos seemed perfectly at ease, his hair billowing over his shoulders, his robes swaying along in a sea of gossamer threads.

No, not a sea. A River.

My hair floated around my face. I brushed it back, entranced by how everything moved as if submerged in water. I relaxed my muscles and examined where Kronos had taken me.

The threads shifted between colors, each shade glimmering like sunlight through water. My finger plucked a thread. Images flashed through my mind: the smoky air of a crowded market, the cloying scent of incense, a weathered temple, the statue of a rearing horse and its fearsome, hooded rider.

"Every moment of every person in all the world has passed through this River," Kronos said. The threads brightened, as if responding to him.

His hand released mine. I spun around in time to see him swallowed by the River. My pulse jumped. "Kronos!"

"Relax," came his voice, an echo that rode the threads from one side of me to the other. "I'm here."

I sucked in air to keep myself from panicking. "You said I'd be lost in here without you," I accused.

"I said you didn't yet know how to navigate the current. Now you'll learn. Find the right threads. They'll take you where you need to go."

"Well, *that* clears it up." I kicked my legs and waved my arms, hoping the movement might push me along. "You can't just throw me in the water without teaching me how to swim."

"You can't drown," he said, sounding infuriatingly reasonable. "You were born of this, remember?"

"This is a *really* bad time for a lesson." I forced my limbs to move slowly, fighting the urge to flail as if I were actually drowning. The fear was only in my head. *Focus, Kai.* Ninurta was in danger, which meant Reev was in danger. I had to find my way out and warn Miraya.

Ninurta might not be an ideal city—far from it—but Ninurta's people needed guidance and hope and the chance to be better. They didn't need the heavy hand of another conqueror. Without the Infinite, the sentinels were Ninurta's best hope, but with the division within their ranks, who knew what would happen once Lanathrill attacked? Even if Miraya could rally the Watchmen and the sentinels in time to put up a good defense, I didn't know if Ninurta could withstand a siege. It was unprecedented. There were no protocols for an enemy attack because we'd always believed we were alone.

But none of that mattered if Lanathrill's plan of attack was to allow their "goddess" to work her magic over Ninurta. Her song would knock out the sentinels and stir that same bloodlust in the Watchmen that I'd seen in Emryn's soldiers, and the city would collapse upon itself.

"You're not focusing."

I tried to turn back the way I'd come, but I had no sense of direction here. The threads parted to allow me through as I fumbled along, but there were only more threads, iridescent, ghostly, brushing against my skin without any true physical sensation and filling my mind with images of the past. There was nowhere to go other than to follow the current and allow the threads to carry me along.

"Don't lose yourself in the current, Kai." Kronos sounded concerned, but it barely registered. Already, his voice was a muffled hum beneath the gentle ebb and swell of the River.

I closed my eyes. The threads tangled in my hair, wove through my fingers, coiled around my legs. Images flooded through me: horse-drawn carriages; acres of golden wheat; the warmth of the sun against a blue sky; processions of *mahjo* in bright robes, their hands spinning storms and summoning flames to delight a worshipful crowd; towering spires of metal and glass; a fiery torrent of magic and manpower sweeping across the cities, scorching everything in its path.

My head hurt. It was too much. I pressed my palms against my temples.

Warmth grazed my side. I turned, something familiar in the way those threads called to me. My body floated forward, other threads curving away as I passed, parting like curtains to reveal something strange: severed threads.

I skimmed my fingers along the blunt ends, and gasped as images of Avan hurtled through me. Heart in my throat, I leaned over and curled my hands around the precious, precious threads.

These were Avan's memories.

CHAPTER 29

THE THREADS OF AVAN'S PAST CARESSED MY PALMS, SWAYING like blades of kelp in the current.

I hugged them to my chest. More memories flickered through me. A young boy with a shock of dark hair hid in a cabinet, his slim back trembling as his dad stomped through their apartment, boots slamming into furniture as he bellowed Avan's name. A beautiful woman with sad eyes, cradling Avan in her arms as she told him a story in between customers at their shop. A slightly older but more inquisitive Avan sneaking his way into his first underground club. A couple of years later, his first kiss—I flinched with irrational but unavoidable jealousy—when he learned to replace the ache in his heart with another kind of ache.

I nudged those threads aside. Those were memories I didn't want to see.

My own face flitted through my mind. I startled, wondering if I'd lost his memories to the current. But no, these were still Avan's—Avan's memories of me.

I glimpsed versions of me through the years, seen through Avan's perspective, slowly growing into my skinny legs and gangly arms. There was that moment when I used my power in his store and he'd seen it; his hands brushing mine as he handed me a package of dried apple slices; the shock and then the surging fear for me when I kicked his dad; that night he found me trapped in the sewer; when he tagged along on my DMC route and teased me about whether I'd have to wear their hideous uniform; furtive glances in the halls at school when I hadn't noticed his gaze.

My fingers glided through the threads, reaching his more recent memories: his wonder and distrust when Kronos appeared to him, bargaining his safety for my own; my body pressed to his back on his scout and the pounding of his heart when he wrapped around me during our night in the Void; his indecision in Etu Gahl as we lay in his room, our fingers laced; that instant when he rushed to protect me from Reev's blade without a single thought as to what it would mean for himself.

My throat grew tight and heat swelled behind my eyes. Everything he'd been feeling in those moments remained like an imprint on each memory. I clutched his threads, livid for the time that he'd lost, for the memories he would never be able to make.

Warmth pulsed from the threads. The severed ends prodded my fingertips as if seeking out contact. My hands prickled with magic that vibrated through the waves around me like a call that wanted to be answered.

The realization seized me: I could mend his threads. I had the power. I could weave his memories back into the fabric of time. That's all the River was—one long tapestry stretching into Infinity.

I could fix Avan.

My breath quickened, my powers surging within me. I gathered each broken thread, my magic seeking just the right place to reconnect them. I had to be careful not to disrupt the other threads.

Another memory surfaced within me—this one mine.

"You could come," a beaming Avan said as he walked backward along the sidewalk so he could see me. "We're just hanging out. It's an empty building off the old train tracks."

"Can't. My brother would kill me."

"Oh, come on," he said, flashing me a gorgeous dimpled grin that made my heart skip a beat, "never sneaked out before? I've been getting past my dad since I was six."

I looked down at my feet, suddenly embarrassed. I hopped back and forth on the sidewalk to avoid stepping on cracks. "No. I don't know."

"How do you not know?" He sounded genuinely curious.

I shrugged. "Because I can't remember."

He tilted his head so he could see my averted face. I blushed at his attention. He'd grown what seemed like half a foot in the last year, and his shoulders had gotten wider, his face more angular. With all those changes, he was still beautiful.

"What do you mean you can't remember?" he asked.

"Just what it sounds like. I can't remember anything before I was eight." I felt stupid admitting it, and I wondered what Reev would say. Avan was the first person I'd ever told, but he was also one of the few people I trusted. I knew he wouldn't tell anyone about it.

Avan didn't say anything for a long time, and I began to wonder if he believed me. What if he thought I was a liar? I peeked up at him.

He was frowning. He looked past me, not really focusing on anything. Something dark passed over his face.

"Avan?"

When he looked at me again, his expression was shuttered and his eyes were dull. I wanted to reach out and take his hand, but I couldn't.

"You're lucky," he said. "I wish I couldn't remember, either."

I dropped the threads. They fanned out around me, catching the current again. I swallowed past the vise constricting my throat.

"You're *waiting for me to remember*," he'd said. "*I don't know what it is* I'm *waiting for anymore*."

A sob rose in my chest, and I choked it down. I squeezed my eyes shut for a moment to stem the tears. I couldn't do it. I wanted to. With all my heart, I wanted to.

But it wasn't my decision to make, and I couldn't rob him of that choice. Even if it meant I would never have my Avan back. Even if it meant he would leave with Irra and Kalla for the realm of the Infinite, and I would never see him again.

It wasn't up to me to "fix" him.

I watched his threads sway and ripple for a moment longer. Then I turned away.

Closing my eyes again, I envisioned what I wanted: the palace in the White Court, its milky stone walls a stunning contrast to the shadow glass of Vethe's citadel. The River shifted around me as the threads bumped against my fingers, coming to me instead of forcing me to find them. I felt Kronos's approval sing along the threads. Guess that meant he'd found me.

My feet touched the ground. The palace rose above me, its crimson banners snapping in the wind.

A presence disturbed the threads, and Kronos emerged from the River.

"If you accepted your true form as an Infinite," he said, stepping onto the flagstones, "you wouldn't need to use the threads. You could move through all of time and space with nothing but a thought. It is an ability no other Infinite possesses, not even Death."

The River began to fade back into what I was used to seeing: sheer threads connecting everything from the buildings to the stone at my feet, unobtrusive and ethereal. The threads grew clearer in my mind as I focused on them. The palace grounds hadn't yet fully solidified, and I could still feel the weightlessness of the River's current.

"You said time can only flow forward."

"We only observe the past. Interference is forbidden by the laws of the Infinite. We watch and we listen and we remember." He looked down at me, the long strands of his dark hair floating back over his shoulders. "Changing history would have unknown, far-reaching consequences. The River could unravel. I have never dared to try."

"Have you ever been tempted?"

A smile brushed his lips. "Yes. But although we have this ability, it isn't absolute power. As you witnessed with Ninu, balance must be maintained even within the Infinite. No matter how powerful one of us might be, there must always be ways to stop one another."

I nodded, reminded of the imbalance happening to the *mahjo* in Lanathrill. Their use of magic drained them and ultimately would probably cost them their lives. Although I no longer cared about the toll the magic took on them, I did care to find out *why* their magic had manifested. Whether it was the Dust or the sepulcher, I needed to know so we could prevent this from happening again.

"Have you heard anything about the sepulcher?" I asked.

Kronos went still. Those pale blue eyes sharpened on me with what I might have called alarm if he wasn't always so placid.

"I'll take that as a no."

"How do you know of the sepulcher?" he asked, the threads darkening around him.

"Irra told me. He and Kalla went to check on it. He said something might have happened to the sepulcher, which would explain why the *mahjo* in Lanathrill have magic again. But I also found out that they're eating the earth from the Void, so I'm not sure if that's the real reason for their magic or if it's just made them all crazy."

He looked away, his expression pensive. "I have not been in contact with either Irra or Kalla since Ninu's passing. I have to go."

He vanished into the threads.

"Hey!" I called out, floundering, but he was gone. I wasn't sure how to leave the River completely. Focusing on my surroundings, I felt the air shift with actual wind and the ground solidify beneath me. That sense of weightlessness dropped away. I stumbled, finding my balance—

—and collided with Avan.

His hands came down on my shoulders to steady me. He looked just as bewildered as I felt staring up at him.

"Avan," I breathed, drinking in the sight of him. His memories were still fresh in my mind, and seeing that he was here made me weak with relief. Before I could think it through, I cupped his face and guided his mouth down to mine.

Avan tensed. A breath later, his hands were tangling in my hair, smoothing down my back and circling my waist to pull me tight against him. I gasped against his mouth, and he took the invitation by sliding his tongue along my lower lip. Fire lit in my belly, the heat spreading through me like a fever.

My fingers clenched around his arms, and it took all my will-power to break the kiss.

I dragged in air as Avan curled over me, pressing his lips against the top of my shoulder, his breaths hot even through my tunic. He flattened his palms against my spine and hugged me close.

He turned his head, his mouth against the curve of my neck. "Kai," he murmured.

Despite how my stomach fluttered and my heart tripped, I suddenly remembered that I'd been trapped in a dank cell for days and I probably smelled as awful as I looked. Avan didn't seem to mind, but now the warmth in my face was from more than his touch.

I gently disentangled myself from him. "I missed you," I whispered.

He gave me his crooked smile, and I felt like I was floating all over again. "I may have missed you as well."

I allowed myself a moment to savor his words, to let them imbue me with hope for us. Then I straightened my shoulders and focused on what I was here to do.

"Kalla and Irra—have they returned?" I asked. He shook his head. It was disappointing, but not unexpected. "Then I have to talk to Miraya."

One day soon, I would tell him that he didn't have to wait anymore. I could give him back his memories if he wanted them. Imagining what his answer would be terrified me, but I would accept whatever decision he made.

For now, he had enough to worry about.

At the sudden shift in subject, the teasing faded from Avan's voice. "What's wrong? What's happened?"

"I'll explain after," I said. "Where's Miraya?"

"In a meeting with the Minister of Law and her sentinel captains."

"Perfect." I followed Avan into the palace. "Why are they in a meeting?"

"Discussing what to do with the rebel sentinels they've taken prisoner."

When I realized where Avan was leading me, I asked, "Why are they in the waiting room?"

"Miraya likes it. And it's more convenient than Kalla's tower."

We approached the door. My palm skated down my side, expecting to feel the ache of my wound, but there was no pain. I poked at my skin through my tunic, surprised to find no trace of the cut. Had Kronos healed me without my knowing or was this an effect of being in the River? I stowed my questions away for later.

Avan lifted his hand to knock at the door, but I pushed it open without pause. Miraya and three others were seated around a low table, speaking heatedly. At our interruption, Miraya looked up, scowling. When she saw me, however, she rose to her feet.

"Is it done?" she asked.

"No, I escaped so I—"

"Escaped?" Miraya asked sharply.

I told them everything. Well, almost everything: how we'd been manipulated from the start; how Emryn and his Council had orchestrated the massacre; and how they were, likely at this very moment, marching across the Outlands to lay siege to Ninurta. I decided not to mention anything about their magic until I could be alone with Miraya.

She slammed her fist against the tabletop. "Lanathrill will pay for their betrayal."

"I knew that going there to assist them was a fool's errand," said the Minister of Law, a short, portly man with a bald spot and a loud voice. He glared at me as if I was responsible for our current situation. "A proper adviser would have known to—"

"Oh, shut up," I snapped.

Before he could start up again, Miraya told him, "Inform your captains to gather every Watchman available and put them on standby for battle." She turned to her sentinel captains. "Assess the defenses at the wall. I want every sentinel armed and ready when Lanathrill arrives."

After the minister and the sentinels had left, Miraya cursed and dragged a hand through her hair. She looked wearier than when I'd seen her last, although she now possessed a self-assured authority that hadn't been present before.

"This couldn't have come at a worse time," she said. "Does Lanathrill know about what's been happening here?"

"I never told them."

"Good." She slumped into her chair. "I need a moment to breathe and think."

"How bad has it been?"

Avan took a seat across from Miraya. "There was an attack on the Tournament arena. The fire destroyed half the building and killed six cadets and two civilians."

My shoulders tensed with renewed anger. The Tournament was the final challenge for graduating cadets of the Watchmen Academy. It was their last chance to improve their ranking and placement after graduation. Kahl Ninu had selected new sentinels from among the winners of the competition.

Before discovering what the sentinels really were, I had believed that they were simply the Kahl's elite private guard—a coveted position for any cadet. But the "winners" had been determined long before the Tournament's completion because only *mahjo* were taken as sentinels, and by the time they realized their fate, it was too late.

I'd killed Ninu during the most recent Tournament. When the final round had ended, Kalla revealed to the public that their Kahl had died in a tragic accident, leaving no biological heir. For the first time in Ninurta's history, the competing *mahjo*—some of whom didn't even know what they were—had been spared the collar.

I understood why the rebel sentinels had targeted the arena, but how could they claim to be acting in Ninurta's best interests when they cared so little for the lives of its citizens?

"Avan was able to stop them," Miraya said.

I stared at Avan. He returned my look without a hint of remorse. I hated with all my being the thought of him succumbing to the Infinite, but it would have been difficult to overpower the rebels in any other way without hurting more people. It was frustrating as hell.

"The city is on lockdown at the moment," Miraya said. "The rebels—those we haven't captured—have gone into hiding, and the Watchmen are enforcing a curfew. There've been some attempts at rioting, but we've been able to placate them without violence. So far."

"Things are tenuous," Avan said. "Order must be restored within the city if Ninurta is to survive."

Miraya nodded grimly. "Ninurta's walls were built to protect us from the gargoyles. They will stand against an army of men."

"And *mahjo*?" I asked. "Did you read the letter I wrote to Irra?"

"No," Miraya said, suspicion creeping into her voice. "It was not addressed to me, although shortly after it arrived, both Kalla and Irra needed to leave on 'urgent Infinite business.'"

While I respected her honor, I was still surprised. Had I been Kahl, I would have at least demanded to know the contents, especially if they concerned the welfare of Ninurta. Avan watched our exchange without a flicker of emotion. I was fairly certain *he* had read the letter.

I explained that Emryn and the Council of Vethe had regained their magic, but I kept the possible reasons why to myself. I needed to discuss those with the Infinite first. She looked to Avan, but he only lifted one shoulder to indicate he was as clueless as the rest of us.

Miraya scratched the back of her neck where her collar was and said, "I don't think they'll be much of a threat if their powers are as damaging to themselves as you say."

"I'm not so sure about that," I said. "Their army might have the power of an Infinite on its side." The memory of Jain's blood warm between my fingers lurched through me. I pushed it firmly away.

Miraya stood. The weary stoop in her back was gone, replaced with steel. Her gaze fell on Avan. "So do we."

CHAPTER 30

AVAN GAVE NO REACTION OTHER THAN A SLIGHT NARROWING OF his eyes.

Miraya gathered up the papers on the table. "Both of you need to prepare as well. And the city needs to know we're in danger of attack. Maybe, for once, its citizens will put aside their own squabbles and join together to fight a common enemy."

I wasn't holding my breath, but who knew? Maybe they'd surprise me.

After she left, I crossed my arms and paced restlessly across the burgundy rug. "Do you think you could influence a whole army with your powers?" I asked Avan.

"I thought you didn't want me to use my powers."

I threw up my hands. "I don't! But unless Irra and Kalla come back, we're out of options. We can't fight Lanathrill's goddess.

Her magic will knock out the sentinels and have everyone else killing one another."

"So I'm your backup plan."

"Right now, I think you're our *only* plan. Everything else is just . . . blind luck." I pressed my fingers to my temples and tried to massage away the beginnings of a headache. If Miraya and her sentinel captains could come up with a plan of defense, then we might have a chance. But only if Lanathrill's goddess wasn't a factor, and I doubted we'd be that lucky.

I thought about how it had felt being suspended within the River—all that power swirling around me. If I were Infinite, there would be no need to ask Avan to sacrifice more of himself. I would be able to stop her.

I swallowed and gently set aside those dangerous thoughts.

"I don't know if I can influence a whole army," Avan said. "Kalla was helping me access my abilities, but how our powers work is an individual experience, unique to each of us. It can't be taught."

I resumed pacing. My fingers dragged along the top of the table against the wall. "Is there a way to contact her or Irra?"

"If there is, I don't know it."

There was no guarantee they'd come anyway. Irra had already made his position clear, and Kalla had done her part, leaving Ninurta in human hands.

And what about Mason? As long as Emryn and the Council weren't in Vethe, I wasn't terribly worried about his safety. I was more worried about Mason thinking I'd left him behind to die.

Avan stood. I tried to ignore him, but it was impossible. He reached for my arm so I would stop pacing. His hands fell on my shoulders, massaging the tightness there. I sagged against him, allowing him to work magic of a different kind on me.

"I have to go back for Mason." It would be a simple thing if I could figure out how to travel by the River, but one lesson hadn't made me an expert. The idea of asking Kronos for help, even if I knew how to reach him, wasn't appealing.

"Mason can take care of himself," Avan said.

His words gave me pause. Did he remember something? "Why do you say that?"

"Mason is a hollow," he said, as if it should be obvious. It was, but that wasn't the answer I'd been hoping to hear. "He's equipped to handle himself far better than most people."

I chewed on the corner of my lip, feeling foolish for hoping in the first place when I had seen the severed threads of his past myself.

"He might be okay for now. But if Ninurta falls, then what? Or if we somehow manage to fend them off—" I shook my head. "I have to go *now*." On horseback, it would take days for an army of Lanathrill's size to cross the Outlands. Maybe even a week. With luck and a scout, I could get to Vethe, rescue Mason, and return before Lanathrill even set up camp outside our walls.

Avan turned me in his arms. His fingers were gentle as he tipped my face up to look at him. "Well, I can't let you leave."

My Avan would have understood. It was an unfair thought, and I winced for thinking it. We'd agreed to take the time apart to think about what we wanted, but I knew that Avan had long since made his decision. Despite the leaf he'd given me or our kisses, there was little hope he would keep chasing after a past he couldn't remember rather than embracing a future with the Infinite.

I had wanted to see Lanathrill, but I'd also been running away from having to face his decision so that I could hold on to the illusion for a little while longer that Avan would choose me.

Now I could restore his memories, but Avan didn't know that yet. The enthusiasm in his kiss and his protectiveness—what did it mean?

"You barely know me," I pointed out, as much as it hurt to say it.

Telling him about his threads would only make the decision harder on him, especially if he'd already made up his mind to move on. I wanted him to choose his past because he truly wanted it, not because I was dangling it in front of him like bait.

His hands closed around my wrists and pressed my palms to his chest. "I know you *here*," he said fervently.

I sucked in my breath. "Does that mean you've figured out what you want?"

His hold grew slack and my hands slipped away, dropping back to my sides. Not the reaction I was expecting. We were still close enough that his body heat felt like a furnace, but he wasn't looking at me anymore.

"What I want and what I *think* I want don't quite match up."

I sighed and rested my forehead against his chest. "Listen," I said, too cowardly to look into his eyes for fear they'd undo me and I'd kiss him again. "Once this is all over, if you're still here, we need to talk, okay? I mean *really* talk. And I'll have something important to ask you."

"Why can't you ask me now?"

"Because it's too important for you to make any hasty decisions. I want you to give it time. And right now, you don't have that time."

He was silent a moment. "Okay," he said, sounding uncertain. "And what do you mean *if* I'm still here?"

I mumbled into his tunic. "I thought maybe you'd want to go where the Infinite are supposed to live."

He took my shoulders and nudged me back so he could look at me. "You belong there just as much as I do."

I slowly closed my fingers into a fist, feeling again the power of the threads surging through my veins. Avan and Reev had been hurt because of who I was, and so long as I was the daughter of Time, it could happen again. But the difference between then and now was that I knew I had the potential to become powerful enough to protect them.

I twisted away from Avan, silencing that inner voice. "I don't."

He regarded me, his expression frustratingly blank. Finally, he nodded and released me. I stepped back.

"I'm going to find Reev," I said. "I'll talk to you soon."

I left without waiting for his reply.

After some running around, I located Reev in the oasis, at our usual spot inside the gazebo. He was sitting on the stone bench, an open book in his lap. I paused on the cobblestones, next to a skinny tree with huge leaves and purple blooms that reminded me of the flowers in Vethe. I didn't recognize half the plants in Ninu's oasis, but even in his absence, the servants had continued to maintain the grounds meticulously. The gazebo was purely decorative since the clouds broke for only one week a year.

Reev hadn't noticed me yet, and I took a moment to observe him. He looked tranquil sitting there. His hair, dark brown and wavy, rustled in a slight wind, and he lifted his head, turning his face into the breeze. The motion sharpened the line of his jaw and the cleft in his chin. The longer I observed him, however, the more I realized he wasn't relaxed at all. His back was tense. He kept shifting minutely as if he wasn't comfortable. There was a line between his brows as he turned another page in his book, and his other hand picked restlessly at the bench.

I sighed. It wasn't a loud sigh, but Reev's hearing was exceptional. He looked up.

His expression brightened, all the little signs of his anxiety receding as he stood to greet me. I grinned, and practically flew into his arms, which closed around me, folding me into his warmth and strength. I pressed my face into his shoulder.

He drew back to look at me. His thumbs smoothed along my cheeks as he made a quick perusal to ensure I was all in one piece. "Have the others returned as well?"

I shook my head and pulled him back down on the bench. I told him everything that had happened in Lanathrill, not leaving out any of the details this time. Fury flashed in his eyes. I watched him, knowing what I was looking for and hating myself for it. I wanted reassurance that he believed Lanathrill's betrayal was unforgivable, that he would never do the same thing. But his carefully controlled rage was probably more about the risk to my life than the threat to Ninurta.

Part of me wanted to take Reev and Avan, and run. Let Ninurta and Lanathrill work out their drek on their own. Why should I have to risk everyone I loved for a city that had never cared about any of us?

But I couldn't. I had given my word to Miraya to help her. More than that, we had the chance to prevent people from dying. Not only would running away disappoint Reev, but I would never be able to live with myself. I wasn't going to be the cold-hearted Infinite that Kronos and the others wanted me to be. I was human. And that humanity meant I had to stay and fight.

"You understand, don't you? I have to go back for Mason."

"I do," Reev said. He looked unhappy about it. "But it's dangerous."

"Then come with me."

Reev closed his eyes with a soundless exhale. A spark of anger kindled inside me.

"Why do you look reluctant? Mason helped me rescue you when you were still trapped under Ninu's control."

"Kai, that's not it. I'm not thinking about Mason—"

"Fine, then," I said, standing. I strode back up the path. "I'll go by myself."

I brushed aside tall fronds and ducked under a branch. When I was halfway to the path that bisected the oasis, Reev gripped my wrist to stop me. I hadn't even heard him following.

"Stop," he said. "What I'm objecting to is the fact you keep insisting on putting yourself in situations where I might not be able to protect you. And it scares me."

He looked so pained that my anger melted. I rested my hands on his arms, feeling the corded muscles beneath his tunic jump at my touch. For some reason, I blushed, but I didn't shy away.

"Reev, I'm not a little girl anymore. We can't keep living with the same rules we had in the Labyrinth. *Keep silent, keep still, keep safe.* That's just not possible for us anymore. Sometimes, things are going to happen that you can't control, and you're going to have to accept that I can protect myself."

One corner of his mouth tugged up. "I already know that. You killed Ninu. But that hurt you, too, and I don't like thinking you might have to get hurt again."

His concern flattened my defenses as only he could. My sturdy, invincible brother. What would I do without him? Even though we weren't related by blood, he was more family to me than Kronos would ever be.

"You'll always be my champion," I said.

"I'm pretty sure that's the other way around now." He nodded toward the exit. "All right. Let's go save your friend."

CHAPTER 31

REEV AND I STUFFED A PACK WITH A FEW DAYS' WORTH OF WATER and food, and stole two scouts from the stable. It wasn't difficult. The sentinels normally stationed around the palace grounds were gone, likely being briefed and devising a strategy should Ninurta's outer wall be breached.

The Watchmen at the gates didn't question us when we approached. They looked a little rattled, though, which I took to mean news of an impending siege had spread through the ranks. At least the Minister of Law was doing his job.

We sped into the Outlands, dust and dirt flying in our wake. Reev motioned for me to slow down. I did, but the look on his face made my fingers tighten around my scout's sensors.

"I have something to tell you," he shouted, keeping his gaze straight ahead.

My stomach dropped. I maneuvered my scout as close as I could without our Grays colliding. I could reach out and touch him if I wanted.

"Can I ask you something first?" I was stalling. If Reev was involved with the rebels, then I wasn't ready to hear that he'd had a hand in the deaths at the arena.

"Sure," he said, but he was frowning, like he knew what I was doing.

"This situation with the rebel sentinels—what do you think about it?" I watched his face, the way he squinted against the wind, the lines around his mouth. "About who should rule, I mean."

"I don't know Miraya. She became a sentinel after Kronos pulled me out. I don't like that Kalla specifically chose her, but if she proves to be a capable Kahl, then let Ninurta have her." He shrugged. "But I won't serve her. I'll never serve anyone again."

I couldn't glean anything from his reply. Looking forward again, I steeled myself. "What do you want to tell me?"

"Has to do with the sentinels, actually. I've been trying to get in on the rebel network."

"Does . . . that mean you weren't involved in planning their attacks?" I asked.

"They don't give me that information. I only wanted to find out who their leader is."

"You were spying." A weight lifted off my chest. I tilted my head back, looking up at the blanket of yellow clouds gliding across the sky. The wind in my ears drowned out everything but the revelation of his words.

"The problem is that nobody knows much about their leader. I haven't been able to get into a meeting with the guy, and no one will answer my questions other than to stress how absolutely certain they are that he should lead them. Their loyalty is . . . intense."

That didn't sound good. "You put yourself in danger."

"Not really. After what Ninu did to us, they were ready to accept that I want the Infinite gone. I guess because I do, mostly."

"I thought . . ."

"I know what you thought. I couldn't tell you the truth because the rebels have ears and eyes all over the city. We're safe enough out here."

"Thank you for telling me." I was the worst kind of idiot. Shame burned through me.

"I know I've done things to make you question my trust. But the one thing you can always be sure of is that I will never betray you. Never again." Although he wasn't looking at me, I knew by the fierce sincerity in his voice that he meant it. "I'd rather die than do that to you again."

What happened during the Tournament wasn't his fault. Intellectually, I had always known that. Now, I could finally feel the resentment shake loose.

"I know," I whispered.

You keep insisting on putting yourself in situations where I might not be able to protect you. And it scares me.

While I'd realized my own reasons, however idiotic and unwarranted, for letting the gap between us spread, I couldn't figure out why *he* hadn't reached out sooner. Was Reev scared because he couldn't protect me or because I didn't need his protection? Had he somehow gotten it into his head that I no longer needed *him*?

"Reev," I said. "I love you."

He looked at me, dumbfounded. I almost laughed.

We'd known forever that we loved each other, but the words had never actually been said. This was the first time I'd ever thought that maybe Reev *needed* to hear them.

He faced forward again without a word, but the flush to his neck made me grin, my heart feeling lighter than it had in months.

I should have trusted that Reev had nothing to do with those attacks. The boy who had taken responsibility for a kid he'd found on the riverbank would never knowingly take part in hurting innocent people. Nothing about him had changed since that day. It had been my own fears twisting him into something he wasn't and would never be, and I wouldn't let him think he'd failed me ever again.

We leaned low over our scouts, allowing them to run at nearly full speed. Clear visors rose from the crowns of our scouts' heads to help shield us from the wind. At these speeds, we couldn't talk, but that was fine. For once, the silence wasn't laden with unspoken things.

A couple of hours later, I noticed something moving against the horizon. I motioned to Reev, who squinted in the direction I was pointing.

Whatever it was, it was approaching fast and headed straight for us. It looked too tall to be a gargoyle. Maybe a chimera? But it was alone, and what would it be doing this far south?

Reev and I slowed our scouts to a more manageable speed in case we needed to swerve. One of my hands remained on the sensor, but the other gripped the handle of my torch blade. The figure drew closer, and the metal body of a Gray horse glinted, even in the muted daylight.

Reev and I exchanged a look. He gestured for me to spread out.

I urged my scout wide so that the approaching rider would be caught between me and Reev. The rider had likely been sent ahead of Lanathrill's army to make sure their arrival would remain undetected. Well, we were going to disappoint them.

As I unsheathed my torch blade, I wondered how a soldier, even riding a Gray, could have made it this far south in so short a time. It had been less than a day since Kronos transported me from my cell into the River.

The stretch of desert dwindled between us. The rider was close enough now for me to pick out details. Judging by the broad shoulders as the rider bent low in his saddle, he was male. Sandy hair whipped wildly around his face.

Mason. My legs tightened against the scout's sides, and it surged forward. Reev shouted something at my back.

"It's Mason!" I called, but I didn't know if he heard. I sheathed my torch blade, racing faster.

At the last moment, I slammed my foot on the emergency brake. My scout skidded to a stop in a clamor of metal heels and flying dust, jostling me forward and nearly unseating me. Mason's grin was contagious, and I jumped off my scout before it had fully stopped. Mason dropped from his saddle, and I flung my arms around his neck. His arms circled my waist and picked me up off my feet.

"Kai," he said breathlessly. "You're alive."

"Of course I'm alive." I laughed. "And so are you. I knew you'd be able to escape after I did, but—"

"So you did escape." He set me back on my feet. "You were gone from your cell when I woke up, and the guards refused to answer any of my questions. I hoped that you'd escaped, but I didn't know for sure."

"I didn't mean to leave you," I said. "I would have taken you with me if I could, but—"

"It's okay." He dipped his head, looking me in the eyes so I'd see he meant it. "I'm glad you got away."

Reev rode up alongside us. He and Mason exchanged firm handshakes.

"Good to see you," Reev said.

"How *did* you escape?" I asked.

Mason smacked his palms against his tunic. Dust exploded from the creases. "Even after watching us fight the chimera, they really have no idea how to handle hollows. They decided to take me along for the journey south. The Council kept interrogating me about Ninurta's military numbers. I just waited a few days for their army to grow tired before I knocked my guards out and stole a Gray. Or stole *back* a Gray."

His expression darkened at the reminder of what Lanathrill had done to his friends and comrades.

"A few days?" I asked.

Reev gestured with his chin to the flat line of the horizon. "How far behind you are they?"

"Less than a day's ride on horseback."

"Wait, wait, wait," I said, holding up my hands. "A *day*?" I cupped my forehead, stunned. How much time had I lost in the River? "Mason, when was the last time you saw me?"

"Almost a week ago."

I staggered back. Mason reached out to steady me. *Damn Kronos and his "lesson"!* I had lost almost a whole week swimming around in the River, not knowing what the drek I was doing.

"What is it?" Mason asked.

I explained about my time in the River and how, for me, it had been less than a day since I'd been locked in the citadel's dungeons.

"I thought I had all this time to rescue you while Miraya planned our defenses." I swore and swung my leg over my scout, settling into the leather seat. "We need to get back to Ninurta."

It took us another few hours to reach the city, every minute that passed a frustrating loss of time. Kronos had known I wouldn't be able to navigate the River properly, and he'd still left me to flounder around on my own. What if I'd surfaced in the past? Would he have left me there until I accepted the Infinite inside me just to get home again?

We headed straight for Kalla's tower. Miraya lived in one of the lower levels. Avan was coming down the path, his red tunic stark against the gray buildings. We rode up beside him.

"Do you know where Miraya is?" I asked.

"I was just with her. Why? What's happened?" His eyes widened when he saw Mason.

I told him that Lanathrill's army was little more than a day away from Ninurta.

"So you left Ninurta anyway even after I asked you not to?"

I scowled. "You didn't ask. And you're missing the point here. Lanathrill is practically at our doorstep."

"You're right," Avan said, but his brooding look remained. "I'll let Miraya know."

Before he could turn away, Mason pushed his Gray forward. "Wait. I found something I need you all to look at."

He pulled a leather pouch from his pocket. Almost immediately, I felt its effects. Reev's fingers found the sleeve of my tunic as he moved closer. Avan took the pouch from Mason and loosened the drawstring. As I expected, it was filled with midnight-black powder.

"What do you make of it?" Mason asked me, noticing my reaction. "You've seen this before."

"Cassia called it Dust," I said. "Where'd you get it?"

"Filched it off of Cassia. I saw her eating from it the first night after we left Vethe. It was dark. I don't think she knew I could see her."

Reev eyed the contents of the pouch, looking ill at ease. I'd already told him about the Dust, but seeing it—feeling it—was altogether different.

"Is it magic?" Mason asked.

Sort of. "It's—"

"Yes," Avan said. He brought the pouch to his face and sniffed lightly. He wrinkled his nose. "But there's something wrong with it."

"What do you mean?" Mason leaned forward. Reev and I dismounted, gathering around as well.

"This magic is old. Very old." Avan's voice lowered, resonating like an echo in a great space. "This is earth from the Void."

Mason looked surprised by this revelation. We watched curiously as Avan dipped his finger into the pouch. When he withdrew it, his fingertip was lightly coated in the silty black substance. He touched the tip of his tongue to the Dust. He cringed, leaning over to spit it back out.

"This stuff is poison."

"I could have told you that," I said dryly.

"But why is it so strong?" Mason asked. "It's a little bag of dirt, but it feels like we're standing in the middle of the Void."

"Because the magic has been awakened." Avan closed the pouch and returned it to Mason. "But it's too old and its original source too chaotic. This was magic cast in wartime, filled with suffering and strife."

Strife? My mouth opened with a silent gasp.

Istar.

Irra had said that Istar's talent was to stir humans to war. The battle that gave the Fields of Ishta its name had taken place so long ago that it was possible her name had been somewhat different then.

Avan hurried off to let Miraya know what was happening, and I bit my tongue to keep from voicing the name of Lanathrill's "goddess."

How did Avan know so much about the Dust? He was newly Infinite. Maybe knowledge of the magic came instinctually to him. But how could he have known the Dust came from the Void?

"I'm going to hold on to this until I get a chance to talk to Irra," Mason said, tucking the pouch back into his pocket. I nodded in agreement.

Climbing onto my scout, I told myself that these thoughts about Avan were little more than the same unfounded suspicions that had driven a wedge between me and Reev. I had to stop seeing things where there was nothing.

"Kai, you should get some rest while you can," Reev said, putting his hand on my shoulder. "When's the last time you slept?"

In my cell, barely. I rubbed my eyes. I needed a proper rest to face the oncoming fight.

With Reev's promise to wake me if anything happened, I turned gratefully for the palace and my bed.

CHAPTER 32

I COULDN'T SEE THE SKY THROUGH THE BRANCHES. THE TREES were too close and the leaves too thick. My palms pressed into the moss as I rose up onto my elbows.

"Avan?" I asked.

There was no response because I was alone. I looked around the space, as if I might find him hiding behind a tall fern. Something metallic glinted from beneath a bramble of yellow flowers. I reached for it.

There was a sound like the incessant roar of the burning waterfall, filling my ears as I freed an old dagger from the grasp of weeds. The forest blurred, distorting like the surface of disturbed water. The trees and mossy carpet faded into blackness, leaving me crouched over a bit of dry earth, illuminated only by the silver blade of the dagger.

Footsteps came from my left. My head snapped up. Reev emerged from the darkness, dressed as he'd been that day in the arena: in the black leather armor of a sentinel. I could feel myself standing, could feel the intent in the dagger as it guided my hand forward, its point seeking Reev's skin.

With a cry, I wrenched back control and flung the dagger into the dirt. It shattered, almost blinding me as it exploded into hundreds of lights. I watched, transfixed, as each speck of light transformed into a wispy, shimmering thread.

I awoke with a start. It took a moment to realize that thudding sound was in fact someone pounding on my door.

I dragged my blanket off my head, my mind still fuzzy. Confusion lingered at the edges of my consciousness, but I wasn't sure why. I cracked open my bleary eyes. As beautiful as the glossy black stone and glimmer glass lights of the citadel had been, I was happy to see the white walls and elegant tapestries of my room in the palace. Instead of the stale humidity in Vethe, the air was cool, a breeze blowing in through the window.

"Kai!" It was Reev's voice. I sat up, rubbing the sleep from my eyes. "Lanathrill's army is within sight."

"Drek," I whispered as I shot out of bed. I scurried around the room, dressing as I went. I secured my hair into a braid and then put on my boots before throwing open my door.

Reev was standing in the hall. "Ready?"

I answered honestly. "No."

He pulled me into a hug. I pressed my face into the firm plane of his chest, my fingers digging into his back, letting his strength fortify me.

"We'll get through this," he said.

I nodded, but I didn't feel as confident. The sentinels might be equipped for war, but the Watchmen were different. They were well-trained and skilled fighters, but that didn't equal real world experience. The Watchmen relied on the city's laws. Nothing would prepare them for the chaos and carnage of battle.

The memory of screaming chimera and broken bodies filled my mind, and I jerked my head to dislodge the images. Now that I suspected it was Istar who stood at the helm of Lanathrill's army, maybe I could do something to stop her. She must have been hidden somewhere in the woods near the Fields of Ishta for her voice to have reached us. The Infinite's powers were far reaching, but Istar would still have to be present to be effective. Which meant she was now out there somewhere amid the army.

I recalled the brief glimpse of red curls—the girl from the crystal garden. I should have taken a closer look at her. After being manipulated by the Infinite, I'd been left to question every-thing I thought I'd known about myself and the world. I needed to learn to trust my own instincts again.

"How well do you know Istar?" I asked as we made our way out of the palace.

At my sudden question, there was a flicker of emotion in Reev's face before he said, "Not very, which is still better than I'd like. She was the one who branded me."

"*Istar* did?" My eyes strayed to the back of his neck.

"She did all the brandings for the new sentinels. Ninu would look them over after she'd finished, and any further work, like the mind blocks or cleansings, Ninu performed himself. But the initial branding was Istar's work. Why do you ask?"

I told him my suspicions about Istar being Lanathrill's goddess.

"It makes sense," he said. "But what does Istar gain out of all this?"

Neither of us had an answer. Maybe war was really all she wanted, and Ninu had stood in the way until now. But there had to be more to it that I just didn't understand.

Fortunately, her powers couldn't control me. If I could find her, maybe I could stop her before she enchanted all of Ninurta into a frenzy of bloodlust.

Reev and I took scouts through the city. Not a single civilian Gray occupied the road. The Watchmen must have ordered everyone inside and closed off the streets. It was eerie. The White Court looked deserted, its usually crowded sidewalks and bustling shops empty except for the occasional smoking grill, as if the owner had left in a hurry. In comparison, the North District looked as if it had been abandoned for years, its dusty streets and crumbling buildings the products of time and neglect. I glimpsed faces in the corners of windows and behind draperies, fearful eyes watching us as we passed.

The nearer we came to the front gates, the more that knot in my gut tightened. Where were all the Watchmen? Where were the sentinels?

I looked at Reev, whose eyes were like steel as he scanned the empty streets. "Are the Watchmen on the wall?" I asked.

Reev gave a shake of his head that wasn't quite an answer. He looked troubled, which wasn't the least bit reassuring.

We were close enough to the gates now to see that while the metal doors were shut and barred, they were unmanned. Stairs to the right of the gates led up to the battlements where the Watchmen archers should have been stationed. There didn't look to be anyone up there aside from a group of sentinels.

They must still be organizing their lines, but why hadn't they done that hours ago? The sentinels began descending the steps. They held their torch blades. Blood threaded down some of their weapons.

Reev's scout intercepted mine, forcing me to stop.

"What are you—" At the look in his eyes, I closed my mouth. Swallowing hard, I looked from him to the sentinels who had yet to notice our arrival.

"We have to get out of here," he said. "Those are rebel sentinels."

My hands tightened around my scout. We had to do *something* besides run. I was about to argue when the sound of groaning metal carried down the road. We both paused to look.

The sentinels were opening the gates. The pounding in my ears grew louder, faster. The parting gates revealed Lanathrill's army, literally at our doorstep. In the lead, Emryn sat atop a black horse. He was in full armor and draped in a black cloak emblazoned with the gold star of Lanathrill. I wasn't close enough to see his face, but the arrogant set of his bearded jaw sent a rush of anger through me.

"Kai," Reev said urgently.

I looked at Reev and made a quick decision.

He must have seen it in my face because he reached for me, his mouth forming my name again.

Reev was too slow. I grabbed the threads and held tight. Time ebbed to a crawl. I brushed aside the threads restraining my scout, and then I leaned low and switched the lever on my scout's control panel to its last setting. We veered around Reev, the scout's powerful metal legs singing against the still wind as we plunged toward the open gates.

I drew my torch blade, focusing on Emryn.

I would be the first to admit that Ninurta was a terrible city. Most of its citizens would sooner stab you in the back than help you if it meant they got something out of it. But I had hope that they could change. With time and Miraya's guidance, we could tear down the walls and learn how to take pride in being Ninurtans.

Istar would see Ninurta's streets flooded with the blood of its citizens, and Lanathrill would enslave the survivors, stamping tattoos on their faces so they could never escape. Emryn would do more harm to Ninurta than Kahl Ninu ever did.

He was right there in front of me, unprotected. My fingers flexed around my torch blade. I would cripple Lanathrill's forces before Istar could open her mouth.

I shot through the gates, holding up my torch blade.

I had felt no remorse when I killed Ninu. He'd been prepared to sacrifice Reev and Avan to gain access to the River. His death had been the only way to keep them safe.

I felt no remorse now. Perhaps I really had become as cold as the Infinite.

I swung my blade.

The threads broke free, plucked from my grasp. The shock caused me to lose control of my scout. The threads sprang forward. Emryn's sword whipped up in that instant of speeded time. The sound of metal striking metal screeched in my ears. Emryn shouted something as the force of my swing sent him twisting sideways, nearly unseating him.

My scout faltered, skidding and then toppling over. I hit the earth, pain everywhere, as I tumbled over the hard ground, dirt tearing at my skin. I rolled to a stop just short of the first line of Lanathrill's army.

For a long moment, no one did anything, too shocked to move.

Then I struggled to push myself up. Through the mess of hair that had fallen free of my braid, I could see Avan standing between the gates.

Avan had stopped me with the same power that Kahl Ninu had possessed. Avan had opened the gates for the enemy.

This couldn't be right. My ears were ringing from my fall, and I squeezed my eyes shut as if that might erase the knowledge of what had just happened. My chest suddenly felt too tight. I couldn't breathe. Avan wouldn't betray me. Even without his memories, he would never betray me.

But the evidence was there in the pain of my bruised and battered limbs, in the threads that vibrated around me from the jolt of interference, and in the form of Emryn, who was still alive and being helped down from his saddle by his soldiers.

The earth beneath me rumbled as metal paws pounded across the dirt. Avan jumped aside as Reev tore out of the gates, his scout's mouth opened in a silent roar. The soldiers behind me scuttled back in fear.

Groaning, I grabbed for my fallen torch blade and lurched to my feet. My arm reached out as Reev bent low over the side of his scout and snatched me around the waist. I gripped his shoulder as he swung me up behind him.

He swerved his scout back around. Sentinels jumped in our path. I drew Reev's blade so I held one weapon in each hand, blocking their slashes to our legs. They could do little with us on a scout. We blew past them back onto the main road and into the city.

My gaze caught Avan's for only a breath. He watched us go.

CHAPTER 33

THE SAFEST PLACE TO HIDE WAS THE LABYRINTH. NOT ONLY would its people fight to protect their own, but intruders wouldn't easily navigate the maze of stacked freight containers.

We were recognized as soon as we crossed the creaking wooden bridge. The people guarding the entrance regarded us warily, but they agreed without much fuss to allow us in. Apparently, with Ninurta under imminent attack, the only unwelcome "outsider" at the moment was Lanathrill.

We hid the scout under a pile of trash inside a caved-in freight container, and then made our way to the very top of the Labyrinth to try to see what Emryn's army was doing, and to put as many obstacles as possible between us and anyone who might have followed. We emerged onto the roof, the old metal riddled with rust spots and puddles of trapped rainwater that never quite dried. We walked carefully to avoid causing someone's roof to collapse.

While we didn't have the same vantage point as in Kalla's tower, we were still high enough to see over the outer wall. The last lines of Lanathrill's army were spread out against the dusky yellow of the Outlands. Large shapes lurked behind them, clustering at the fringes of the army. The soldiers crowded inward to put distance between themselves and those moving shapes.

They were too big to be gargoyles.

"Chimera," I whispered.

"*Those* are Ninu's chimera?" Reev blinked, as if to clear his vision. "What are they doing here?"

"They must have followed the army south." I had no idea why. Curiosity? They should have been afraid after what had happened in the Fields of Ishta.

The army had stopped advancing, but we couldn't stay up here and do nothing.

"What do you think Avan did to Miraya?" Reev asked. I had given him back his torch blade, and he rested the point against the metal roof, slowly rotating the handle.

Drek. I hadn't even considered it, but Avan had been the last person to talk to her. He wouldn't have hurt her.

The same way he'd never betray you?

Pain stabbed my heart, and I shoved away that taunting inner voice. "He's probably keeping her captive in Kalla's tower. And he must have the Watchmen confined somewhere as well." My guess was that he'd tricked them into gathering for a briefing and had locked down the location. "The only buildings in Ninurta large enough would be the palace, the barracks, the Tournament arena, and the Academy."

"We were just in the palace," Reev said. "The barracks are too spread out, and half the Tournament arena burned down."

"That leaves the Academy," I said. "Do you know where Mason is?"

"I spoke with him right before I came to wake you. He'd been asleep as well. Must be how he missed getting imprisoned with the others."

Mason would have probably made his way to the front gates, like we had, in order to scope out the army. I hoped he hadn't ridden right into the rebel sentinels.

"Find Mason and see about freeing those Watchmen. We're going to need them. See if you can find the other sentinels as well," I said.

"And what about you?" he asked.

We looked at each other, as if needing a moment to adjust to the realization that I was the one giving Reev orders now.

"I'm going to talk to Avan."

He gripped my shoulders, hard. "You're not going anywhere near him."

"I *have* to," I said as calmly as I could. I understood the fear in Reev's eyes because it mirrored mine, but I couldn't let him see how shattered I felt.

"Kai, I'm not letting—"

"It's not your decision, and the longer we stand here arguing, the more time Emryn and the Council will have to invade the city unchallenged."

Reev glared unhappily, lines of worry creasing his forehead.

"Don't you see?" I said, needing him to understand. "Avan *is* the rebel leader. He doesn't just have the power to manipulate how people feel. He can also manipulate their senses. Remember how he got those sentinels under control after they attacked Kalla's tower? He was creating illusions that only they could see. With that kind of ability, he could disguise himself right among the rebel sentinels. And not only that, but he could make them *feel* absolutely certain about their loyalty to him." I looked toward the wall. The buildings stood in the way, but the image of Avan standing inside the gates was burned into my mind. "The only thing I don't understand is why he would help Lanathrill."

Or why he'd be working with Istar.

"It's obvious," Reev said. "He's been corrupted by *them*—the Infinite. He's Conquest now. He'll manipulate his way into getting what he wants: to rule Ninurta like Kahl Ninu did."

I couldn't believe that of Avan, but I had to admit that this new Avan was a stranger to me, regardless of those fleeting moments when I glimpsed otherwise. A day ago, he had pressed my hands to his chest so that I could feel his heart beat against my palms and told me that he *knew* me. Had that been nothing but a trick so I'd let my guard down?

Maybe I should have restored his memories when I'd had the chance. But altering his threads without his consent would make me no better than the Infinite. No matter the circumstances, I had no right to play with anyone's life.

"I have to talk to him," I repeated.

We made our way down through the Labyrinth to the ground floor. I instructed Reev to enter the sewers. That had been our path into the White Court when Mason led me and Avan in to save Reev. Any barriers he might come across could be split with his torch blade. There would be no gatekeepers this time, and nobody would care about broken locks.

"Will you be okay?" I asked.

"You're asking *me* that?" He touched my face, his calloused fingertips grazing my jaw. "I can't keep making you leave marks on a post for me, can I? I have to trust that you'll be okay."

I smiled. Reev and I used to leave marks on an old wooden post in the North District. It stood alongside the road that led down to the docks. Whenever we passed it, we made a mark to let each other know that we'd been by and that we were safe. That had always been one of Reev's most stringent rules.

I hugged him. His arms crushed me to his chest. I wanted to tell him that we'd see each other again, but my mouth couldn't form the words. Instead, I closed my eyes and breathed in his scent, a mixture of soap and the fresh grass of the oasis. I counted the beats of his heart against my ear and allowed myself a moment to pretend that nothing had changed, that my world still consisted only of him and me.

"Be careful," he murmured against my hair. Then he set me roughly aside, and he was gone, disappearing into the sewer.

The scout would be too conspicuous, so I left the East Quarter on foot. The moldy planks of the bridge wobbled and bowed beneath my weight. I had crossed this bridge a thousand times, and like the Labyrinth's roof, I knew where to step to avoid the rotten boards that might dump me into the water. Crossing the river left me completely exposed, but no one noticed as I hurried across and ducked into the alleys between the pleasure houses along the riverfront.

Even this section of the city was quiet. The docks were usually peppered with men and women wasting their credits on the prostitutes who worked and lived in these garishly painted buildings. Today, everything was still. I marveled that the Watchmen had gotten the pimps to cooperate. I'd crossed paths with a few of them over the years, and they didn't seem the sort to close their businesses even for an impending assault on the city. If anything, they'd set up a sign and welcome the new customers.

I crept along to a back road where piles of garbage created a stinking wall of refuse. I covered my nose, the stench making me gag, as I followed the alley until it intersected with another one. I would bet that I knew my way around the North District better than any of Avan's sentinels, so I had the advantage if they spotted me.

Avan's betrayal remained a knife lodged beneath my ribs, and every time I thought about it, the blade drove deeper, ripping me open a little more. I had to talk to him. I had to hold on to hope.

I navigated my way through narrow streets, up and down fire escapes, and along a dozen hidden paths until I reached the sliver of a footpath near the main road. The space between two squat apartment buildings gave me a perfect view of the open gates.

Surprisingly, Lanathrill's army had yet to flood the main road. From behind a collection of overflowing trash bins, I could see a group of rebels talking to Cassia in the shadow of the metal doors. My back tensed at the sight of her. Of course she would speak on Lanathrill's behalf, being the voice of the Council. Emryn stood behind her, silent and stoic.

Avan sat off to the side, his back to me as he lounged at the bottom of the steps leading up to the battlements. He was overseeing the discussion but not actually participating. I braced myself against the rush of emotions—not just pain and frustration but also anger. I wanted to scream and rail at the unfairness of it all, that Avan should have lost so much to help me rescue Reev only to become a shell of who he'd been, the vital parts of him shorn away and discarded within the River.

I circled around the last building until I was as close to Avan and the stairs as I dared to get. I'd have to thank Mason again for teaching me how to move silently. The sentinels would have noticed me by now otherwise. I imagined myself skimming my fingers over the threads, disturbing them just enough that my magic rippled outward.

Avan's back stiffened. He glanced over his shoulder, and our eyes met. My fingers dug into the dry crust of the building as I waited to see if he would alert the sentinels.

He didn't. I retreated behind the building, pressing my back against the flaking bricks. I waited. The seconds felt like an eternity.

Avan's shadow fell across the half-collapsed fence that bordered the alley. I turned to face him as he slid neatly into the cramped space beside me.

We didn't speak. I searched his face, hoping to see . . . regret, maybe? Some sign of remorse. But there was only a steely resolve. I remembered that look from another Conquest's face.

Finally I asked, "Why?"

He looked away. It reassured me somehow. "You wouldn't understand."

"Then explain it to me. I'm Infinite somewhere inside, right? Maybe I *will* understand."

He seemed to consider that, which made me want to shake him. "Ninurta is in turmoil. The city needs a leadership that Miraya can't provide," he said.

"It needs to be *conquered*?"

"That's the only way to secure the citizens' loyalty and to restore proper order."

I clenched my teeth to keep from screaming at him. These weren't his thoughts, his beliefs. They were Conquest's.

"There are sentinels who have lived under Ninu's control nearly their entire lives," he continued. "They liked knowing that they belonged to something greater than themselves, a life unburdened with mundane, everyday decisions. Why do you think it was so easy to gather a group of rebels? They don't know how to think for themselves. And the rest of these *humans*"—he said the word like it was an obscenity—"they're just like them: scared and witless without the firm hand of a leader. They *want* to be controlled, but they're too proud to admit it."

"How can you believe that?" I asked, unable to keep silent any longer. "You've seen the other sentinels—they're *happy* to be free. Reev and his teammates were desperate enough to be free of Ninu that they risked their lives trying to kill him."

"True desperation would have led them to either success or death. It would not have accepted any other options. Humans find unity in chaos, purpose in war, honor in battle. It is their curse that they cannot flourish without conflict. So I will give them conflict," he said, his voice lowering to a thrum that sent shivers through me. "And then they will welcome control."

There was no use trying to understand this. Avan had been Infinite for a matter of months, and already they'd poisoned his mind against humanity.

Or Istar had.

"When did Istar find you?" I asked. "She's the one behind all this, isn't she?"

Avan's eyes brightened until they shone like liquid gold. "Istar has had a busy few months."

He didn't deny it. I pressed my palms against my closed eyes, trying to breathe. When I felt stable again, I grabbed his shoulders.

He stiffened. When I did nothing but hold on to him, he slowly eased.

"The Infinite are . . ." I struggled to pull my thoughts together into something coherent. "The Infinite are incarnations of . . . of notions like strife and death, trapped by the limits of those concepts and by the rules of their kind. But *humans*, Avan—humans have the ability to determine their own futures, to make their own rules. *You* wanted that once. And to . . . to jeopardize your own safety by accompanying a friend into the unknown, to stand and fight under siege—" I made a wild gesture at the army on the other side of the wall. "It's not a *curse* that humans rise to meet their challenges."

He watched me intently, as if entranced.

"Avan," I said, hating the way my voice broke. I had to stay strong. "Don't let the darkness win. If any part of you loves me at all, fight that darkness. Please." My palms slid over his shoulders as I pulled him close, encouraged by the way his expression softened. I spoke against his collarbone. "I can't lose you a *third* time."

I felt Avan relax against me muscle by muscle. His hands came up, fingers tangling in my hair. Something was getting through to him. I could feel it.

"I dreamed about you," he said, his voice surprisingly bleak. "While you were gone. I don't know why, but we were in the Tournament dorms, and I was telling you about how I wasn't used to anyone having the power to hurt me anymore."

I went still. "What?" I whispered, my own dream from more than a week ago rushing back to me.

Do you remember our first kiss?

"Kai," he whispered, his eyes shutting. He gently pushed me away.

I didn't understand what any of it meant, and I didn't have time to explain anyway. I spoke quickly. "You told me once that loyalty can't be willed. That real loyalty is a decision you have to make for yourself." My fingers pressed into his skin. His pulse fluttered against my fingertips as I pleaded, "Let the people *choose*."

Our gazes held, but as usual, his face gave nothing away. His eyes were mesmerizing, like looking into the heart of a flame. He focused on something behind me.

I wrenched away, my mind jumping for the threads a second too late. Pain burst in my temple, followed by darkness.

CHAPTER 34

SOMETHING HEAVY WEIGHED ME DOWN. WARM AIR KICKED UP around me, pelting my skin with dust and tossing my hair against my face. Light jabbed my eyes when I tried to open them. I winced, blinking rapidly and squinting until my surroundings came into focus.

My side ached from lying on hard stone. I groaned and rolled onto my back to find myself looking up at a veil of clouds. I tried to sit up. Metal chains clanked against the shackles around my wrists and ankles. I guess that explained the weight.

Avan, I thought, my heart fracturing. I pushed him from my mind. Now wasn't the time to break down. I had to figure out what was happening.

There was a slight throb in my temple, but I seemed to be in one piece. I sat up as best I could to get a better look around. I was on the battlements at the top of the wall. Parapets flanked my right, the side that overlooked the Outlands, but there was no barrier between me and a long fall on my left. Judging by what I could see of the city, I was right above the front gates. I didn't need to strain my ears to hear the restlessness of Lanathrill's army on the other side of the wall.

Nearby, Cassia sat in an embrasure, looking unconcerned about the forty-foot drop. She looked pensive instead. I hoped she was plagued with guilt. When she noticed I was awake, her back snapped straight and her face went blank.

"Where's Avan?" I asked. I blew irritably at the hair falling over my eyes. I couldn't brush the prickling strands aside because my wrist shackles were connected to my ankles. I folded my legs to give my arms more reach and knocked the stray hairs back.

Cassia watched me. "I don't know," she said. "We're waiting for word from Kahl Emryn."

"Word about what?"

"The goddess has demanded a sacrifice to honor her and herald the coming victory."

"What victory? There hasn't been a battle. The gates are open. Just let your army in."

Cassia regarded me with that haughtiness I remembered from our first encounter. "The only way a conquered city will truly submit to its new leaders is if it knows the consequences of defiance. If we simply walked in and said we were staying, do you think anyone would accept it?"

"You can't, Cassia. So many people will die. You already have the blood of the hollows on your hands, and now you want to add civilian men and women? *Children?*"

She closed her eyes tight as if trying to shut out my words. She lowered her face, her hair falling limply around her cheeks. Her lips were leeched of color, and her skin looked sunken, dark, and wrinkled. She appeared twice her age.

"I have to," she said, a dull acceptance in her voice. "The goddess has willed it, and she cannot be denied. I'm sorry, Kai."

A sacrifice. I looked again at where I was. Directly above the gates made a convenient spot for a public execution. Dozens of homes spread out before me. People simply had to look out their windows to watch. Or maybe Avan and his sentinels would force the citizens out of their homes to stand in the street like spectators at the theater.

I scanned the sidewalks, the shadowy spaces between buildings, the darkened windows. I spotted a few faces pressed to the glass but no sign of Reev or Mason. Cassia had fallen silent, and I looked to find her staring out at her army. There was a faint tremor to her hands as she gripped them tightly in her lap.

"Out of Dust?" I asked coldly.

She flinched. "I'm sorry for lying to you," she said. "But the Dust . . . It's like I've been missing something my whole life and didn't even know it until the magic showed me how it felt to be complete."

I rolled the links of my chains between my palms, annoyed that I did understand. That was how I'd felt when my powers returned.

"Without it," Cassia said, lifting her arms and glaring hatefully at her shaking hands, "I feel empty, like there's a great gaping hole inside me that can't ever be filled."

"Cassia, there's a reason nothing's grown in the Void since Rebirth. The magic there is poison. By eating it, you're taking in all that chaos and anger from the war. It's not surprising there's a cost."

Cassia looked dubious.

"Ask Emryn if you don't believe me. But you can see yourself what it's doing to you. Using magic isn't what drains you; it's the magic itself. The Dust is making you sick." Mentally as well as physically, although I didn't say so. If I called her crazy outright, she'd probably be less inclined to listen. "If you don't stop, it'll kill you."

Her fingers closed into a tight fist, but even then, she couldn't still the trembling. "I can't. The goddess taught us how to awaken the black earth, and once you've known magic . . ." She swallowed. "There's no going back."

"Her name is Istar," I muttered. I looked out over the battlements. Istar was somewhere out there. I wondered if she could see me. The fury inside me flared hot and red. "Come out and face me like your brother did instead of hiding behind these people like a coward!"

Cassia gaped. "How dare you attempt to speak to the goddess?"

"I've *met* Istar. She wasn't all that impressive."

"You're lying," Cassia said, incensed. "The goddess has never given her name, and we would never dare to ask. She has proved her presence and her power to us. You would do well not to anger her."

"Why? If you think I'm going to be a willing sacrifice, you don't know me very well."

"No," she said. "I don't. We've both kept secrets and lied to each other."

I slid across the stone so I could sit up against the parapet. I twisted my head around and could just see through the embrasure to the army beyond. The soldiers looked travel weary and they spoke under their breaths to one another, passing time while they waited for their Kahl. I looked away. It was easier to hate them when I didn't think of them as human.

From here, I could see the industrial chimneys and dirty rooftops of the North District.

"When you told me about your brother, about leaving a legacy, was that a lie, too?" I asked.

Cassia shifted uncomfortably.

"This is how you want to be remembered? As someone who brought war back into the world?"

Cassia stared at her lap. I didn't know if she was ignoring me or mulling over my words. Before I could say anything more, the sound of heavy footsteps caught our attention.

Emryn was coming up the stairs, accompanied by two of his men. He had discarded his cloak. His circlet gleamed from atop his brown hair, and he stood tall and striking in his recently polished armor. He looked windblown, but it was as if our skirmish at the gates had never happened. Either he ate less Dust than his Council or he didn't use his magic as often.

"So are you my executioner?" I pushed to my feet. Standing, the farthest I could lift my arms was waist level. I shuffled forward.

His men tried to grab me. Emryn held out his hand to stop them, and I inched my way across the stone until we stood toe to toe. If he meant to kill me, he'd better be willing to look me in the eyes and admit it.

I was a little surprised when he did.

"Yes," he said steadily. This close, I could see the regret in his eyes. It only made me angrier. No matter their personal feelings, he and Cassia would see this through because of their mindless devotion to Istar and her false promises of immortality and magic. "I take no joy in it, but the goddess has spoken. I can't refuse her."

"Of course you can," I said, putting every ounce of derision I could into my voice. When his gaze slid away from mine, the satisfaction was brief.

"You can try to use your powers, but it'll only delay matters. You won't get very far with those on." He nodded to my shackles.

I conceded the point. What good was slowing time if all I could do was hobble along a few feet?

He watched me, waiting for me to respond. I set my jaw and raised myself on the balls of my feet, testing my balance. Then I rocked back and bashed my forehead into his face.

The burst of pain was overshadowed by the crunching sound of his nose breaking.

He stumbled back with a cry as his men rushed forward. One of them caught him around the shoulders while the other dragged me back. I tripped and fell onto my side in a tangle of chains.

Emryn elbowed off the soldier trying to help him and glared down at me through his bloodstained fingers. Did they honestly think I was going to make this easy for them?

He waved the other soldier toward me. The two men grabbed me by the arms and hauled me to my knees. A fist in my hair yanked my head back, forcing me to look up at Emryn's bloody face. His beard shone wetly around his mouth.

"You have a right to be angry." His voice was muffled as he pressed a handkerchief to his nose. "But it won't change anything."

A foot planted in my back, forcing me to bend over until my forehead almost touched the floor. I struggled to break free, but the soldiers only dug their fingers deeper into my skin.

"Emryn," Cassia said. "Maybe . . . Maybe this isn't necessary."

I tried to look at her, but the soldier with my hair wrapped around his fist thrust my head back down so I could see nothing but the stone between my knees.

"Cassia?" Emryn's voice was sharp with suspicion.

"I can talk to the goddess," she suggested. "I can see if there's another way. Kai has abilities that we've never even read about from past *mahjo*. Maybe we could use—"

"You've never questioned the goddess before. Don't let her play to your sympathies simply because you were friends."

"If friendship means that little to you, then why were you so broken up about the friends you lost to the chimera?" I asked scornfully. "Would you have killed them if your goddess told you to?"

Emryn didn't reply. One of the men holding me pulled my hair off my shoulders to expose my neck. I tried to get my feet beneath me so I could thrust upward, but they held me down.

Now would've been a great time for another lesson in how to slip into the River, but of course, Kronos remained silent.

The low murmur of voices carried up from the street. People must have noticed what was happening and either stepped out of their homes or opened their windows for a better look.

"Last words?" Emryn asked.

"I suppose you think chopping my head off will make your family proud."

"Restoring Lanathrill will make my family proud."

He drew his sword.

CHAPTER 35

I SEIZED THE THREADS. TIME SLOWED.

I bent and twisted as much as I could. My bones and joints screamed and hair was ripped from my skull as I worked myself free of my captors. After long, agonizing seconds, I was able to move my neck out of the path of Emryn's sword. I raised my head and gasped, flinching back.

An arrow was caught in the threads, not a foot above where my head had been. Was someone else trying to kill me? I wrenched my arms from the men's hands, seething with frustration.

Finally free, I whipped my legs around just as time stuttered forward. I grappled for control of the threads and kicked out at Emryn's leg.

My hold slipped and the threads sprang forward. In the rush of speeded time, my foot smashed into Emryn's knee. He collapsed, his cry cut short as his cheek cracked against stone. His sword fell with a metallic *clang*, and the arrow found its mark in the chest of one of my captors. The soldier gaped, stumbling backward. His arms flailed as he toppled over the parapet, screaming.

A second arrow whizzed overhead, landing with a *thunk* into the other soldier, who dropped to the stone. Shouts rang out from below. The rumble of feet pounding over the main road was followed by the *clang* of striking weapons and the whistle of arrows. I crawled to the ledge, ignoring a dazed Emryn as I peered down on the city.

The Watchmen had been freed. And the sentinels. Lanathrill soldiers were now swarming through the gates to meet them. I scanned the chaos for Mason and Reev.

Emryn muttered curses behind me. I turned to see Cassia helping him to his feet. He grabbed his sword, using it like a cane to help him stand. With a frantic look at me, Cassia tugged Emryn toward the stairs.

They didn't make it very far. Emryn jerked backward, his sword flashing up to block a glowing torch blade.

I shuffled forward, my chains getting caught around my legs. "Reev!"

His eyes found mine. Then he turned on Emryn.

With chilling intent and single-minded strikes, Reev drove Emryn back. The memory of Reev advancing on me in the arena crowded my vision, threatening to paralyze me. I gripped my chains and let the pitted metal ground me. This wasn't the cold detachment Reev had shown me in the Tournament. This was unadulterated rage.

I'd never seen Reev's true skill with a sword. He was every bit Emryn's equal. It was all Emryn could do to block the white blur of his blade.

Mason had come up the stairs behind Reev, snagging Cassia before she could sneak past him. She watched the fight, her hands slightly outstretched as if deliberating whether to use magic to help Emryn.

I could understand Emryn's own hesitance to use his magic. I'd seen what even the smallest demonstration could do to him, and he needed his strength.

I scooted across the wall, away from the ledge and its perilous drop. Then I pushed along the side of the parapet toward Mason. He had a torch blade, which would be enough to sever my shackles.

Reev slammed the butt of his sword against Emryn's temple. Emryn fell to his knees beside me, fresh blood dripping down the side of his face. He wavered, looking ready to collapse.

I wanted to feel triumphant. Instead, I felt ill.

"I'm sorry, Kai," Emryn managed between ragged breaths. Reev pressed the tip of his blade beneath Emryn's jaw.

"Are you?" I didn't know why I asked. His answer didn't matter.

Reev rotated his sword. Red welled up around the shining blade. "An apology won't save you," Reev said.

"I'm not looking to be saved." Emryn didn't flinch as blood dripped down his neck.

"Emryn!" Cassia's desperate cry seemed to strengthen him. He looked up at Reev, waiting.

Did I want Reev to have to carry this death with him always, the way I carried Ninu's with me?

"Reev . . ." I began. A sound rose on the wind. My body went rigid. "No," I whispered.

The faint whine strengthened into a voice, clarifying into words I couldn't understand. The song filled the air, attempting to slip inside me. I raked my fingers across the rough stone, ripping the soft tissue of my fingertips, and pushed the magic away.

Reev's torch blade slipped from his hand. He took one faltering step backward and then his legs gave out. I lunged forward, half tripping on my chains. My knuckles scraped painfully on the stone, drawing blood, but my hands caught his head before it could strike the surface. I carefully rested his head on the ground. Mason lay nearby. He had fallen on Cassia, who was extracting herself from beneath his limp body, looking shaken.

"No, no," I repeated as I rose clumsily to my feet and looked out over the street.

Every sentinel, rebel or loyal, had been knocked out. Lanathrill's soldiers and the newly freed Watchmen were awake, but unnaturally still. I knew what would happen next. Even the citizens came pouring from their homes in the grips of sudden violence. They grabbed the nearest objects that could function as weapons and hurled themselves at the spellbound Watchmen while the soldiers began stabbing at anyone within reach.

Horror and helplessness seized me. I wasn't strong enough to stop them. I couldn't freeze time the way Kronos could. I dragged in lungfuls of air as I bent protectively over Reev.

I can't save them.

Emryn gripped the edge of an embrasure as he struggled to his feet. He blinked hazily. A scuffing sound drew my attention to Cassia. She had Mason's weapon in hand and was walking toward me.

"Cassia, don't!" I shielded Reev with my body as I scrambled for his torch blade. My fingers wrapped around the handle, and I raised the weapon as Cassia swung downward.

My sword met empty air, but hers landed with a loud *clang*. She had severed the chain binding my wrists to my ankles.

"Stay still," Cassia said. She had a wild look in her eyes that had nothing to do with Istar's song.

Keeping Reev's sword in hand, I stretched out my shackled wrists and ankles. She broke the chains, but the manacles couldn't be removed without the keys or a more skilled swordsman. It was good enough. At least I was free to move now.

I didn't thank her.

She threw down the torch blade and stepped past us, reaching for Emryn. She helped him up, but she couldn't shoulder his weight, and they stumbled against the parapet.

"Can you make her stop singing?" I asked, looking out over the Outlands and Lanathrill's army. With soldiers, Watchmen, and fallen sentinels choking the street and blocking the entrance into the city, the rest of Lanathrill's army remained trapped outside the walls, away from the bloodshed. The excluded soldiers waved their weapons in the air and hacked impatiently at the dry earth, shouting and working themselves into a frothing mass. Soon, they would turn their swords on one another if Istar didn't stop.

I searched the teeming bodies in case Istar had hidden herself among them. She had to be close by.

"It's impossible," Cassia said. "You should escape while you can."

"Not without my brother."

My gaze searched beyond the army, squinting at the horizon. A rocky outcropping rose against the flat landscape, past the army's left flank. A figure stood at its crest. My nails bit into the stone parapet.

She was too far away to see clearly, but the silhouette of her full petticoats and the vivid red spot of her hair was unmistakable. *Istar.*

I would never be able to reach her quickly enough without a Gray, and I couldn't leave Mason and Reev unprotected. Grinding my teeth in frustration, I turned to Cassia.

She was looking at Reev. "Your brother," she said, sounding pained. "I see."

"Your *goddess* is right there," I shouted, pointing at Istar's distant figure. "Are you really going to stand here and do nothing while they all slaughter one another?"

Pounding footsteps made me twist around. Soldiers were coming up the steps, their swords drawn. Mason was still lying at the top of the stairs.

I rushed them, raising Reev's sword. The broken manacles weighed down my wrists and ankles, but I rammed myself into the first soldier. My shoulder struck his midsection, and he went tumbling down the steps, taking another soldier with him.

The next soldier was on me in an instant. I blocked her strike, but she struck again. I ducked and dropped to my haunches before kicking out, my heel striking her shin. Something snapped in her leg, and she screamed as she fell. I brought down the hilt of my torch blade against the back of her head, and she went limp. I hoped she wasn't dead.

A burly Watchman came sprinting up the steps as I leaned over to drag Mason away. The back of Mason's head left a red smear against the stone, and I gasped. He must have hit his head on the way down.

There was no time to staunch the wound. At the sight of me, the Watchman's nostrils flared and he lifted a torch blade, which he must have taken off a fallen sentinel. I straightened, bringing up my sword to block. The Watchman's blade struck mine with jarring force, knocking the handle out of my hand. My weapon landed a few feet away. I lunged for it, and then leaped back when the Watchman's blade nearly bit through my wrist. His boot rammed into my shoulder. There was a sickening pop, and pain tore through me.

The Watchman advanced on me. I was breathless with agony as I scrambled back. I held my useless arm at my side as I looked frantically between Mason and the Watchman pursuing me. I shouted for help, but Cassia and Emryn had disappeared. They must have escaped while I was fending off the soldiers. Already, another soldier emerged at the top of the steps, his crazed eyes finding Mason.

I grappled for the threads. Time slowed. I somehow found enough breath to scream through the pain as I struggled to my feet. Ducking under the Watchman's descending blade, I hobbled back to Mason's side. With a glance backward, I realized my mistake. The Watchman was now a mere foot away from Reev.

I held on to the threads with a shaking grip, but I could already feel them growing taut with the need to spring free. *No, no, no.* I looked between Mason and Reev. Then, with a strangled cry, I lurched back toward Reev as my grip broke.

Time sped forward. The Watchman's sword smashed into the stone where I'd been, spraying chips across the wall. A beat of confusion followed before he lunged for Reev.

With a heave, I plowed into his back, sending him screaming over the ledge.

Pain racked me. I dropped, rolling onto my uninjured shoulder. My lungs refused to work. For excruciating seconds, my vision went black. I struggled to hold on to consciousness.

Please. I wasn't even sure what I was asking for. I stretched my working arm, my hand slapping against the stone until I touched Reev's tunic. I wrapped the material around my fist, Reev's body heat warming my bloodied knuckles. I needed help. I couldn't stop Istar and protect them on my own. I closed my eyes. *Please, Avan.*

If I were Infinite—

A sudden roar vibrated through the battlements. From below came a flurry of screams and inhuman snarling. The wall shook as something monstrous climbed the steps.

I forced my eyes open. The soldier hovering over Mason's torn body had turned back around to face whatever new threat had arrived. Before he could even raise his weapon, razor-like claws cut through him.

An enormous chimera climbed up onto the wall. The stone cracked and buckled beneath its weight. It stood directly above Mason. Terrified, I fumbled for the threads.

The chimera lowered its huge head and shoulders. I gaped, forgetting the threads in my astonishment.

Sitting between the bony spines of its upper back was Avan.

CHAPTER 36

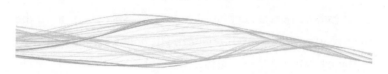

DUMBSTRUCK, I WATCHED AVAN DISMOUNT FROM THE CHIMERA'S back. The creature bent its forelegs, pressing its chest to the wall, allowing Avan to use the crook of its massive arm as a foothold.

He paused to search Mason's bloodstained neck for a pulse. The sight jolted my senses back into order long enough for me to rasp Mason's name.

"Alive," Avan said, and my breath came in a shuddering sob. But the blood beneath Mason's body continued to expand.

"Help him," I pleaded, using my good arm to try to lever myself up. "Avan, help him."

Avan flicked his hand at the chimera. With a low grunt, the creature reached down for Mason with one immense, clawed hand. I swallowed a sound of distress as it picked up Mason, with startling gentleness, and deposited his limp body between

341

the back spines of another chimera that had lumbered up the stairs. I bit the inside of my cheeks to keep from crying out at the sight of Mason's injuries. The soldier who'd attacked him had cleaved clear through Mason's shoulder, nearly taking his arm off. The weapon had caught his jaw as well.

The chimera bearing Mason turned and sped away down the main road, toward the White Court. The hollows who'd remained in the city after Irra's departure would know what to do when they saw him. Surely, Irra had left some healing tonic behind. If Mason's own healing ability kept him alive long enough for tonic to be useful . . .

I rested my head against my arm, shuddering weakly. Hands touched the back of my head, and I looked up to find Avan kneeling over me, his face tight with concern. I was too shocked by everything that had just happened to even react to his presence. There were so many questions running rampant in my head that it was impossible to settle on one.

His fingers lightly probed my shoulder. I hissed with pain, recoiling from his touch.

"It's dislocated," he said.

Even through the confusion, the sound of his voice made me want to lean into him, to ensure this wasn't a dream born of pain and delusion. I thought I'd lost him. My eyes stung, and I took deep breaths to keep from breaking down. If I let this deluge of emotions engulf me, I might never find my way back to the surface, and that was more terrifying than the chimera.

"Avan," I said, gripping his arm with my good hand. "You have to stop Istar. She's in the Outlands, past the army on some rocks—"

"Kai." Avan lowered his face so that our noses brushed. I went still, swallowing the rest of my words. "Listen."

I held my breath and listened.

The wind was silent. The singing had stopped.

I struggled to my feet. Avan helped me up, letting me lean on him as I looked out over the city.

Chimera had overtaken the main road. Citizens had been chased back into their homes while the Watchmen had retreated, likely all the way back into the White Court. Emryn's soldiers, those who'd made it into the city, had either rushed out the gate into the Outlands or slipped into the alleys to escape. The fallen sentinels were waking. Finding enormous chimera hovering over them would be a shock, but at least they were alive. My chest felt heavy at the sight of so many bodies, at the blood-stained cobblestones, at Mason's uncertain fate.

I swung around, searching past the parapet. Two chimera now lingered on those rocks where Istar had been standing.

"I found her," Avan said. "But I'm sorry. She escaped."

Nearby, Reev stirred. He rolled onto his stomach, his arms bending to raise himself off the ground. His forehead was creased with confusion. Avan leaned over to help him.

Reev's baffled look turned into a scowl. Before I could say anything, Reev struck out.

Avan ducked, narrowly dodging Reev's elbow.

"Reev, stop!" I shouted, and then gasped.

He was immediately at my side, his hands skimming over my shoulder. "What happened?"

"It wasn't Avan," I said.

Whatever else he'd been about to say was cut off when he saw the chimera. He crossed the wall to the ledge, looking down at the pack of chimera waiting docilely in the streets below. "Someone explain," he demanded, glaring at Avan.

It must have felt like the world had gone crazy while he was unconscious. I guess it had.

"Istar's song knocked out everyone with a collar, and it drove everyone else into a frenzy. I had to fight off a few soldiers. Mason . . ." My voice wavered, and I shook my head, discarding what I'd been about to say. "Avan was able to stop them." I looked at him. I didn't know what to think, but I knew how I felt. "He saved us."

"How are you controlling them?" Reev asked Avan, gesturing to the chimera. His distrust wouldn't be so easily mollified.

"When Ninu died, Kalla and Irra removed his mark from your collars. But no one removed them from the chimera. Since I am Conquest now, I learned how to call on that connection to them."

"You brought them south?" I asked.

He nodded. "I wasn't sure it would work until I saw them arrive with Lanathrill's army."

Avan's control over these creatures was every bit as unjust as Ninu's had been. But if he hadn't intervened, the city would still be ripping itself apart. The Infinite had always been mercurial, going out of their way to help me in one instant and then flinging me into danger the next. It wasn't the least bit comforting to realize Avan had become like them.

"So what now?" Reev asked, looking out at Lanathrill's fleeing army.

If Emryn and Cassia were still alive, they would probably regroup their scattered army and run back to Vethe to plot their next move. I didn't believe Istar was ready to give up.

"Lanathrill will retreat," Avan said, his eyes finding mine. "And Ninurta will be allowed to make its own choices."

"Why?" I asked, needing to hear his answer.

Avan spoke only to me. "I won't lie. I was ready to let Istar have her way. She wanted conflict and blood. Her powers are strongest in wartime because she feeds off the strife of humans. I would handle the aftermath—order and control. Part of me still thinks that humans are too irresponsible to be allowed to lead themselves. But I guess another part of me agrees with you. They should be afforded the right to choose."

"You couldn't have come to this conclusion a week ago?" Reev asked skeptically.

Avan's eyes glowed, but it was a gentle pulse of warmth, and I felt that warmth echo in my chest. "Not without Kai."

But that isn't exactly true, I wanted to say. There was goodness in Avan even without me here to remind him of that. Avan had worked to unsettle Ninurta from within as Istar plotted with outside forces, but wouldn't it have benefited him to keep the peace within the sentinel ranks? Miraya might have sent her sentinels to help Lanathrill, where they would have been killed. It would have devastated Ninurta's defenses, just as Emryn had wanted. Instead, Avan's interference had kept those sentinels here.

I wanted to believe that even then, he'd been unable to send them off to their deaths. And I doubted he'd known that Irra would send the hollows.

"And besides," Avan added, looking at me, "Istar wanted to sacrifice you. That was unacceptable."

"Reev, please help me up," I said, clutching his forearm. I rose to my feet, trying to move away from the support of the parapet.

"Kai, you shouldn't—"

"Help me or move aside," I said. I didn't mean to snap at him, but my shoulder was in agony. Reev helped me stand.

Avan understood what I wanted, because he didn't wait for me to reach him. He rushed forward, his hands replacing Reev's. His fingers trailed up my neck to cup my face as he rested his forehead against mine. I closed my eyes, focusing on his warmth and his breath.

"Does this mean you've finally figured out what you want?" I asked quietly.

He didn't answer right away, and I opened my eyes to see a flash of dimple and the barest of smiles. "Want has nothing to do with it," he said. "Want is something born of will and weakness. To want is to lack something, and I feel nothing of that with you." A line formed between his brows. "Seems so unfair . . . for him to have loved you this much, and to be repaid with—"

It took a moment for me to realize Avan was speaking of himself—his old self.

"I promise you that he never meant for things to end that way. He hadn't wanted . . . *I* didn't want to die."

I was trembling, from pain and emotion, but I managed to whisper, "I'm sorry I couldn't protect you."

"It wasn't your duty to protect me. But Kai . . . I don't know who I am now. All I know is that even when I was trying to let you go, I failed. You give me light and life." He ducked his head, his lips passing over my cheek. "You're my energy stone."

I'd been holding my breath, and I released it slowly. "I hope you know that when I heal, I'm going to punch you. Really hard."

Avan's lips curved against my skin, and he tilted my head back with a gentle finger beneath my chin. His mouth touched mine. I savored the contact, however light. But when he pulled away, his smile was tinged with sadness.

"Avan, no."

That kiss had been a good-bye.

"I have to—"

"You can't leave. Not again."

"It's only for now." His thumb rested against my bottom lip. "I have things that I need to figure out."

"Avan—"

"I am Infinite, but I want to remember what it means to be human, too." He brushed his lips along my jaw until his mouth reached my ear. "I will never betray your trust again, and I will spend a thousand lifetimes if necessary proving it to you. Someday, Kai, we'll have forever. You and me."

His words left me aching, and I could no longer decipher one pain from the other. Then he backed away, taking his warmth with him.

"Stay safe," he said, turning away.

I was so taken aback by those two simple words that, for a moment, I could only stare dumbly at his retreating back. My hand lifted, and Reev stepped in to support me, refusing to let me follow.

"Avan, I can help you," I said as he walked to his waiting chimera. "I can bring back your memories."

But he only gave me another sad smile and climbed onto his chimera's back. He didn't understand. He didn't know that I had seen the severed threads of his past, had held them in my hands and heard the call of my magic to mend them, and I was an idiot for not telling him sooner.

I shouted his name, but he was no longer listening. His chimera rose to its full height, maneuvering itself awkwardly over the wall as it turned to descend the steps.

"Reev, stop him," I demanded, but Reev only watched him go. "Wait!" I stumbled forward.

My legs gave out. Reev caught me around the waist, but that only jarred my shoulder. I screamed, and this time, I couldn't fight the lure of darkness.

CHAPTER 37

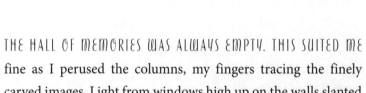

THE HALL OF MEMORIES WAS ALWAYS EMPTY. THIS SUITED ME fine as I perused the columns, my fingers tracing the finely carved images. Light from windows high up on the walls slanted across the columns, illuminating the dust motes as they drifted through the air.

I found what I was looking for in the far corner. Standing on my toes, I reached up to brush my fingertips against the meticulous details of a fauhn herd. Their stunning double horns curved high above their heads, twining into branches that sprouted tiny, delicate leaves. They were elegant animals, relics of a past when magic had been as common as bread. All that history and all those creatures . . . lost because the *mahjo* had refused to accept a rapidly changing world. In that way, I understood Emryn's desire to restore a time when Vethe had been so much more than a magnificent tomb.

But his desire had turned to madness, and whether that was the Dust or Istar's influence or his own ambitions, I didn't know. In the end, it didn't matter.

I sighed, studying the way the fauhns frolicked across the white stone.

If you accepted your true form as an Infinite, Kronos had said, *you could move through all of time and space with nothing but a thought.*

I could have the power to walk through history, to see the way these creatures and all the others now extinct had lived, to experience the world as it had been when *mahjo* were revered as Kahls. It was a temptation like no other.

But it was also a sadness I didn't know if I could bear.

The nostalgia became a knot in my chest, and I moved on. I left the Hall of Memories behind, making my way up to my bedroom.

For all the unforgivable things Lanathrill had done, I had to concede that they'd done some good, too. Fauhns had survived because of them, and that was something. It didn't mean I wanted to be cheerful neighbors with them, though. What Emryn and the Council had done would not go unanswered.

I pushed into my room, gently rolling my shoulder as I did. My arm was in a sling, and my shoulder ached. The medic had pushed it back into place a week ago, but it would be a while before the shoulder fully healed. There had been only one vial of healing tonic left, and that had been used to keep Mason alive long enough for the medic and his own healing ability to save his life.

A pile of plump sweet rolls and a saucer of cream sat on a silver tray on my dresser. I smiled and made a mental note to thank Master Hathney. He'd been sending extra meals up to my room ever since he'd heard about what almost happened to me on the wall. While I wasn't keen on being pitied, I could hardly argue with the pastries.

I sat down in the armchair to enjoy a roll, wishing Mason were here to share these. The thought of him made my brow furrow. He'd left yesterday to return to Etu Gahl, with two hollows to watch over him and keep him safe. He'd barely been able to do more than grit his teeth and cling to his scout.

For the first few days after the attack, I had watched over him as fever scorched his skin. His entire upper body and his jaw had been stitched back together and bandaged up as best as the White Court medics could do, but there was little doubt whether he would have survived had he not been *mahjo*. It had been difficult even to look at him, knowing that he'd almost died because I had chosen to protect Reev instead.

The first thing he'd said to me upon regaining consciousness was "You're not Kalla."

I had frowned, wondering if he was delirious. "No, I'm not," I'd said tentatively.

Even as pale as Death herself, he'd cracked a smile and said, "I figured if I was dead, it'd be *her* I woke up to."

Once the fever broke, he'd begun healing more quickly. It wasn't like that moment in the arena when I'd watched Avan's skin knit back together in a matter of seconds. Hollows recovered faster than regular humans, but such a devastating wound would still take time to heal. He was lucky not to have lost his arm. Even with the ready supply of healing tonic that awaited him back in Etu Gahl, Mason would carry the scars of his injury for the rest of his life. Another item to add to my vault of guilt.

I hadn't wanted him to leave yet—he'd broken a sweat just sitting up in bed—but he'd insisted on taking his chances on the journey rather than languishing in a hospital bed. Miraya had approved his departure with the added hope that the hollows in Etu Gahl would have heard something from Irra. There'd been no word from either him or Kalla.

I could only imagine how Irra would react when he learned about what happened to his hollows. If he chose to retaliate, even a mountain wouldn't be enough to protect Emryn from Irra's retribution.

There was a knock at the door, and I called for whoever it was to come in.

Reev opened the door, smiling when he saw me. "Hey. How'd the meeting go?"

I turned to face him as he sat on my bed. "Looks like war."

I'd just met with Miraya, her ministers, and the sentinel captains. For once, they'd all been in agreement: Lanathrill would pay for their treachery.

The rebels had elected a new leader, and she had been in the meeting. After holding a citywide farewell ceremony for all the lives lost, Miraya and the rebels had struck a truce. With Istar at the helm of the attack, the rebels had their proof that Miraya wasn't the Infinite's puppet, and they would unite to face their common enemy. I had left Miraya in her newly designed war room with the sentinels to discuss their campaign. A rider had been sent out to make contact with Peshtigo in the hopes that Ninurta could form a true alliance this time with a neighbor. And the hollows who'd accompanied Mason would extend an invitation to those in Etu Gahl. No doubt they would be crying for vengeance as well.

I wouldn't be joining them. After the meeting, I'd resigned as adviser. Let the ministers trip over themselves to win her favor and the position.

I hoped she wouldn't pick one of them. The ministers' loyalty still felt shaky to me, so I'd suggested to Miraya that she bring in someone new. Someone who wouldn't care about upsetting the ministers so long as the decisions made were in Ninurta's best interests.

Naturally, I'd recommended Reev. He'd spent hours cooped up in Irra's impossibly humid laboratory to help work out a solution to their technology issue, which proved his devotion to the tasks he set for himself. He'd said he would never serve another Kahl again, but an adviser wasn't a servant.

"War," Reev repeated. "Good." I lifted my eyebrow. "They were going to sacrifice you, Kai."

I ripped a roll into chunks to keep my hand busy.

"What would you have done if it was *me* they almost sacrificed?" Reev asked, snatching a roll from my plate for himself.

"I would have killed them," I said without hesitation. It scared me how easily I could say that, but it was still true. "But they didn't. Miraya will deal with them."

And I will deal with Istar. But Reev didn't need to know that.

For a couple of minutes, we ate in silence. I watched the muscles in Reev's jaw tighten and relax as he chewed. He'd seemed a bit aimless this past week, as if he was still trying to find his place in this new life. Whether it was tinkering in a lab or trying to infiltrate a rebel network, Reev thrived when he had a purpose. His purpose used to be protecting me, but things were different now. If Miraya asked him to be her adviser, I hoped he would accept. He would make a much better adviser than I had.

"What about Avan?" Reev asked.

"What about him?" I touched the leaf brooch pinned to my tunic, rubbing my finger along its smooth edges. He'd taken his chimera and headed north. I had no idea where he'd gone or when he would come back.

"It's not like you to do nothing."

My lips curved. "Are you implying I'm an instigator?"

"Not implying anything, although trouble does tend to happen around you."

"And yet you stick around."

He shrugged. "I guess I like you."

I laughed and stood. I crossed to the bed and reached for his hand. Twining our fingers together, I said, "Avan will come back when he's ready. And if he takes too long, then I suppose I'll have to go drag him back."

He grinned. I held up our linked hands, studying how smooth and unmarred his skin was next to the scars still fading from my knuckles. I remembered the way his hand would engulf mine when I was little. For the longest time, I'd looked up at him and thought how unattainable he was—my impervious big brother, more an idol than a person. It had felt reassuring back then when I'd needed his protection, when I could remember so little that he'd been the only anchor I could grip.

But now, having known a few of his secrets and having seen him at the mercy of Ninu, he felt more real. Closer somehow. More reachable. I rubbed my thumb against the center of his palm. Warmth filled my chest, rising into my cheeks, and I looked up to find his gray eyes studying my face with a strange thoughtfulness. I shied away, suddenly embarrassed and blushing for no reason.

Before either of us could say something, there was another knock at the door. I went to open it.

It was a servant. "Excuse me, but do you know where your brother is?"

I opened the door wider so she'd see him.

"Ah!" the servant said with a relieved smile. "Kahl Miraya has requested your presence in her war room," she told Reev.

I turned to him with what I hoped was an innocent shrug. He looked wary, but he left with the servant and a promise to go with me to the oasis later.

I settled back into my armchair with the rest of the sweet rolls. The city was a bit lonely without Mason, Hina, or Avan. I dipped a chunk of bread into the cream and then tensed. The threads were vibrating. I reached out hesitantly. Awareness prickled my neck, and I spun in my chair.

Kronos was standing by the doorway.

"Can't you drop in like a normal person?" I asked.

Kronos clasped his hands behind his back as he made a slow perusal of my room. His robes fluttered around his feet as he wandered over to the mantel where he paged briefly through a book about the Temple of Light that I'd borrowed from the library. Picking at the seam of my tunic, I watched him poke around my room, seemingly not in any hurry. It was extremely disconcerting. I supposed any girl would feel this way about her dad looking through her things.

Kalla had promised to keep him away, but that was before she left to deal with the sepulcher. And besides, the arrangement had been only if I remained as Miraya's adviser.

This whole situation with Lanathrill had shown me how much I not only needed my powers, but also how much I had left to learn. There was no more denying the threads. My magic was vital to me, and I couldn't reject such a huge piece of who I was.

My dreams had changed again. I still had nightmares, but now they were about what I'd seen in the Fields of Ishta. The dreams where I had to witness myself murder my loved ones had stopped.

After much reflection, I'd decided I needed to stop ignoring what Mason had said in Lanathrill, the theory I hadn't wanted to hear at the time. My nightmares—and likely the dreams of Avan, which had also stopped—had been a result of guilt: guilt over what had been done to my loved ones because of me, and guilt over taking Ninu's life, no matter that I would do it again if necessary. That guilt had been tied directly to my powers, so as I began to deny them in my waking hours, they had appealed to me in my sleeping ones. When I'd opened myself to the River, I could only assume that all the parts of me had finally accepted that I was not at fault for what had happened.

In truth, the guilt would never truly go away. But at least now, without those nightmares, I could try to leave it in the past.

"Can I ask you something?" I said as Kronos paged through my library book again. There was one aspect of my dreams that was still bothering me.

He smiled, but didn't look up at me. "You may ask me whatever you like."

"While I was in Vethe, I dreamed about Avan asking if I remembered—" I caught myself before I could admit to my father that Avan had been my first kiss. "Um, asking if I remembered something. And then Avan mentioned later on that he'd dreamed the actual memory. What do you think that means?"

He closed the book and set it back on the mantel. "Emotions are a powerful thing," he said quietly. Hadn't Mason said something similar? "Particularly yours, with your tie to the River. You never lost your powers, Kai. You only blocked yourself from them."

"Are you saying that I inadvertently restored that particular memory?"

He closed his eyes. His fingers moved through the current, threads flashing in and out of sight as he searched for something. It took only seconds before his fingers stilled.

"No," he said, returning his hand to his side. "The memory remains severed, but I imagine you must have presented the thread to him subconsciously."

"I can do that?" I traced the air above the nearest thread with my forefinger. It shivered, glinting at me in welcome.

"There are a great many things you can do. You could even heal that shoulder simply by immersing yourself in the River." He turned to face me fully. I could see in his eyes that, despite his indulgence of my questions, this wasn't a social visit. It never was.

"What is it?" I asked.

"The sepulcher is missing."

I found it suddenly difficult to breathe. "That can't be good."

"No," he murmured, taking a seat on the stool in front of my dresser. "Kalla is attempting to trace it. It's been releasing miniscule amounts of magic, which means it is, in fact, fractured."

"Wait, so it wasn't the Dust that gave magic to Emryn and his Council?"

"The magic in the Void has withered to ash and madness. It isn't nearly enough to restore a *mahjo*'s powers. However, it did weaken the humans and make them more pliable to Istar's manipulations."

"I don't get it. Why would only Lanathrill's *mahjo* be affected by the sepulcher?"

"Since I imagine Istar has the sepulcher, the magic leaking from it responded to the nearest magical source—the *mahjo*." He straightened out the long sleeves of his robes. "Istar has access to more power than any single Infinite should ever possess. And once she figures out how to invoke that power . . ."

"No more balance?"

"No more balance," he confirmed.

Istar had wanted Emryn to attack Ninurta so that she could feed off the bloodshed. It seemed she would get her way after all, with Miraya determined to go to war. But with the sepulcher, a war between countries would be nothing. Strife would rip the world apart until there was nothing left.

As I was now, there was no way I would be able to face her and live. The utter helplessness I'd felt on the wall, unable to do more than cling to the threads as Reev and Mason lay vulnerable—I would never allow myself to be cornered like that again.

If I was to become stronger, I would need to access what Kronos had locked away: the Infinite inside me.

"So now what?" I asked. He wouldn't have come just to tell me what was happening.

"Now the Infinite gather to discuss what is to be done."

"And what about me?"

"You are Infinite," he said. "Should you choose to attend the Gathering, you may."

I considered this. "But I'm not a full Infinite."

He lifted his chin. In daylight, the shadows of his face looked less severe. "Being that you are my heir, born of the River, you will be allowed entrance."

"And I won't lose myself?" Although I asked, the prospect no longer scared me. I knew what it meant to be human. I wouldn't forget.

"Hardly. I offer nothing more than a glimpse at the world in which you belong." He stood, his robes billowing around him, and extended his hand to me. "Tell me, are you ready to learn what you *could* be? The true extent of your powers?"

I stared at his hand, his long, elegant fingers. Every thread within my vision and beyond had been crafted by him. I didn't think about the enormity of the duty he wanted to place on me. I thought about the power that awaited me if I had the courage to embrace it.

If I refused him, where did that leave me? Here, in this palace, waiting: for news from Mason, for the war with Lanathrill, for Avan to return. For the next time danger found me, and my strength failed again.

A glimpse. That was what he was offering me.

I wanted more.

I placed my hand in my father's.

"I'm ready."

Acknowledgments

A SEQUEL IS A CURIOUS BEAST. COMPLETING THIS BOOK WAS PERhaps one of the most daunting things I've ever done, but I couldn't have done it without an army of people supporting me. Thanks first and foremost to my editor, Robin Benjamin. She is a constant source of insight and skill.

Thanks also belong to:

The team at Skyscape: Courtney Miller, Miriam Juskowicz, Timoney Korbar, Andrew Keyser, Melody Moss, Tony Sahara, and Megan McNinch.

My agent, Suzie Townsend, who is as intelligent and savvy as she is fabulous, and the New Leaf crew for always being ready and eager to help.

Mindee Arnett and Lauren Teffeau, without whom this book would be far less legible. Thank you for being so amazing and such inspirations.

GfA: Natalie Parker, Amy Parker, Amy Tintera, Corinne Duyvis, Michelle Krys, Gemma Cooper, Deborah Hewitt, Ruth Steven, Kim Welchons, and Stephanie Winkelhake. Publishing would be a much more formidable undertaking without them.

My fellow 2014 Skyscape debuts: Christina Farley, Jessie Humphries, and Meredith McCardle. Debuting was considerably less terrifying thanks to their support and wisdom.

The librarians, teachers, and booksellers who helped to get my book into the hands of readers.

My family, for always being over-the-top excited at every piece of news I have, however small. And to Cha, Katalina, and Oliver, who mean everything to me.

Finally, to my readers: thank you for every e-mail, every tweet, every Tumblr post. I'm grateful every day for your support and enthusiasm.

About the Author

Photo © 2012 PrettyGeeky Photography

LORI M. LEE WAS BORN IN THE MOUNTAINS OF LAOS. HER FAMILY relocated to a Thailand refugee camp for a few years and then moved permanently to the United States when she was three. She has a borderline obsessive fascination with unicorns, is fond of talking in caps lock, and loves to write about magic, manipulation, and family. She currently lives in Wisconsin with her husband, kids, and a friendly pit bull. She is the author of *Gates of Thread and Stone*. Visit her at www.lorimlee.com.